I0760960

COVENANT

Nelsyn N. Carlson

EABooks Publishing

A division of Living Parables of Central Florida

Nelsyn N. Carlson / EABooks Publishing
eabookspublishing.com

Publisher's Note: This is a work of fiction. Names, characters, places, and incidents are a product of the author's imagination. Locales and public names are sometimes used for atmospheric purposes. Any resemblance to actual people, living or dead, or to businesses, companies, events, institutions, or locales is completely coincidental.

Identifiers: 1. Books > Literature & Fiction > Genre Fiction > Religious & Inspirational > Christian > Fantasy
2. Books > Science Fiction & Fantasy > Fantasy > Romantic
3. Books > Christian Books & Bibles > Literature & Fiction > Biblical Fiction

Covenant/Nelsyn N. Carlson -- 1st ed.
ISBN: 978-1-963611-26-7
LCCN: 2024910357

Dedicated to my God, my husband, my parents,
and my pastors.

ACKNOWLEDGMENTS

I would like to start by thanking my savior Jesus Christ. I can truly say if it wasn't for Him this book wouldn't exist and He has never failed me along the way.

Next, I couldn't have done this without the incredible support of my family and friends. To my parents, Jerry and Becky, who were my very first beta readers and champions. From the stories I shared as a child to the support they continue to provide today, their belief in me has been unwavering. To my husband, Chris, who is always there to encourage me when I needed it the most. And to my niece, Anna, who is forever my number one fan. To all my friends who read those early drafts, your feedback was invaluable.

A special shoutout to my pastors, Chip and Candace Brim, for sparking the inspiration that led to this series. I can't thank you enough for the impact you've made on my life.

To my amazing team at EA Publishers—Rebecca Ford, Monica Miller, and Bob Ousnamer—thank you for believing in my vision and helping me navigate the publishing process. Rebecca, your guidance has been invaluable. Monica, your marketing expertise has been a game-changer, and Bob, your attention to detail is second to none.

A special acknowledgment to the amazing women of AWSA, especially Rhonda Dragonmir, whose support and guidance have been invaluable on this publishing journey.

To my editors, Michelle Lazurek and Sue Fairchild from Roaring Lion Publishers, thank you for your dedication to making my words shine.

And to Catarina Orellana (@Art_by_catarina), thank you for bringing my vision to life with your incredible cover art.

Last but not least, to all you readers—past, present, and future—thank you from the bottom of my heart. I hope it touches you in some way.

TERMINOLOGY AND PRONUNCIATION

Adom:
ah-dohm. In Hebrew, this term translates to "mankind" as a collective whole. It should not be confused with the name "Adam", which specifically refers to an individual person.

Aeshma:
ay-sh-mah

Aziel:
ay-zee-el

Baal:
bah-al

Balaam:
bay-lam

Barkayal:
bar-kah-yal

Danieal:
dan-yee-el

Daeva:
day-vah

Dinah:
dy-nah

Enoch:
ee-nuhk

Eremiel:
er-uh-my-el

Jezebel:
jez-uh-bel

Jadal:
jah-dahl

Kenan:
kee-nan

Lamech:
lah-mek

Methuselah:
me-thoo-suh-lah

Mikah:
my-kah

Ruach Hokadesh:
roo-akh ho-kah-desh (Ruach is pronounced with a guttural "kh" sound) In Hebrew, this name translates to the Holy Spirit.

Samael:
sah-my-el

Samyaza:
sam-yah-zah

Uriel:
yoo-ree-el

CONTENTS

COVENANT

Nelsyn N. Carlson

EABooks Publishing

A division of Living Parables of Central Florida

CHAPTER ONE

Take Pride in Your Work

"And yet still, no one has been assigned to Earth," Uriel muses and leans further back in his seat.

Lucifer stands, his back towards the Principality. He has just picked up a new instrument to try out, and pauses, holding the nevel harp close to his chest. The wall he faces is lined with all types of stringed instruments, most of which he has played many times.

Lucifer angles his head toward Uriel. It's a subtle gesture, but he hopes it's enough to make his companion continue without having to add much to the conversation. Uriel is normally Lucifer's first choice of company when it comes to quiet contemplation and music. However, at this point the contemplation has ceased in its quietness.

Uriel crosses his arms over his chest, peering at his confidant, almost unable to wait for a response to his luring statement.

"Your point?" Lucifer gives in.

“Haven’t you thought about it? For whom is it purposed?” Uriel pokes further, leaning forward with his appeal.

“No.” Lucifer turns back to the instrument in his hands. This one has fifteen strings and a rounded bottom.

Sitting down, he perches the harp on one knee and deftly plucks a string. The light from the open-air window beside him warms his face and filters through his white hair. Vines trailed with blooms grow around the arching window.

He notices that the flowers turn their faces toward him as he begins to play, their petals opening as if trying to breathe in the melody.

Uriel shakes his head. “It has to be purposed for someone—or something.”

“Perhaps it’s not.” Lucifer doesn’t break his stride as he replies and continues to lightly pluck at the strings.

“Have you ever encountered that?” It sounds more like a statement than a question coming from Uriel.

This makes Lucifer pause momentarily. He pictures the realm in question, resting his fingertips on the harp’s cords as they reverberate before coming to a halt.

He looks to the flowers beside him. They sway side-to-side in anticipation for the song to continue.

He feels himself slipping back to the first time he saw their reaction to his music—the way they joined into the melody. Before long, every corner of heaven was entwined into the song.

An image flashes in his mind of the first time he opened his eyes, the bright white light consuming everything around him.

“Everything here has a purpose.” Uriel’s words bring Lucifer back.

He struggles for a minute to remember what their conversation was about, but then just replies with a “Perhaps.”

He looks at the flowers again and notices they have turned away. They are looking at someone.

“And what of the other third of angels that are not under Gabriel and Michael?” Uriel prattles, one question replacing the other.

“Maybe it will be you,” Lucifer replies, not taking his attention away from the window.

“Me? No, that’s not …” Uriel trails off, but then tilts his head and says, “Well, as you say, perhaps.”

“Lucifer!” a voice announces. In a flash of light, Aziel, appears in the doorway.

He is a slightly smaller-framed angel, with dirty blonde hair that falls to his shoulders. Unlike Lucifer and Uriel, he has a double pair of thin and angular wings jutting out behind him, a trait most commonly found on Dominions and some Virtues. He folds both pairs against his back as he speaks again.

“Gabriel has requested your presence,” Aziel says, nodding toward Lucifer.

Uriel turns to look at Lucifer with a raised brow and is pointedly ignored.

Silently, Lucifer stands and walks through the archway, past the angel. He notices Aziel nod a greeting at Uriel, and then follows suit behind him. The messenger angel catches up, and then takes the lead from the Archangel.

“Did Gabriel say what he wanted?” Lucifer asks in a low voice, not quite sure why he feels the need to be so quiet.

“Hmm? Oh, well he didn’t reveal that to me.” Aziel looks back for only a moment.

Lucifer refrains from any questions after that and follows Aziel as he leads him toward one of the massive buildings that surround the throne room.

They enter between two pillars and wait for Gabriel as he converses with two other angels.

Noticing their entrance, Gabriel turns away from his conversation, and strides across the room toward the pair. His light gray robe drifts across the floor as he fluidly moves forward. Its color changes to iridescent white as the light between the pillars reaches it.

“Thank you, Aziel.” Gabriel dismisses the angel, who then bows his head before turning to leave.

Gabriel turns his attention toward Lucifer.

Lucifer notices that the Archangel stands about a head taller than he, and although their hair is the same white color, Gabriel’s is straight and drapes down to the middle of his back. His complexion is also much darker than Lucifer’s and is a striking contrast to the rest of his fair features.

He has the look of a true, leading Archangel, but different from the other head Archangel, Michael. Of course, Michael has that commanding look, the face of a protector and warrior. Lucifer decides Gabriel looks more … studious.

Given their status of being the most famous leading Archangels in all of heaven, Lucifer straightens, and mentally prepares himself for an assignment that could potentially put him on the same level as them.

"You will follow me to the Throne Room," Gabriel states, then turns sharply before Lucifer has a chance to answer.

The sentence hangs in the air for a moment while Lucifer decides if he has heard him correctly. For the very first time, he is being invited into the Throne Room.

Before Lucifer has any time to think about it, they are both moving toward a pair of double doors. They open, with a whirl, to a long hallway. At the end of the hall stands another, even more grand door, guarded on each side by two Cherubim.

They each hold a molten fire sword, which extends up twice their height, ready at attention. They are at least double the stature of the two Archangels and have two folded wings covering most of their bodies.

The reality of where they are going finally hits Lucifer and a mix of emotions pass through him. He has a hard time distinguishing what they are. Is it nervousness? Excitement maybe? That doesn't quite fit. It seems harder to breathe with each step he takes.

As they approach, Lucifer can see that the Cherubim have faces similar to his own. But as the pair passes by them, their faces shift. To their left, the Cherubim's face morphs to a golden feline complete with pointed teeth. And to their right—that Cherubim's face is covered with the same color of gold fur, but with a pair of horns that extend up into a slight curve. Solid gold defines their features while the skin underneath is like molten, white lava. A pair of wings covers this side of their bodies as well.

Gabriel and Lucifer pause in between the two guards and wait for the solid sapphire door in front of them to open. The door splits down the middle, and with an overpowering surge of air, opens towards the Archangels.

At first, the room is overpoweringly bright, but then the light subsides. Or Lucifer's eyes adjust, he's not sure which one.

The room is so tall that even when he cranes his neck all the way back, he still cannot see the ceiling. All he can see is a sapphire blue haze in the distance.

There, in the middle of the colossal room, sits the throne. It is built up several levels and is nearly consumed in the light. The brightness is strongest in its center, where its occupant is seated.

The iridescent cloud of light pulsates rhythmically and sends out a low rumble with each pulse, as if the whole room is breathing in, then out again.

Seraphim fly around in the airy room. Small feathery wings shield their faces from the powerful light, while a much larger pair keeps them aloft, and yet another pair folds around their bodies. Their light voices complement the surges of power echoing throughout the room.

Surrounding the throne is a totally static crystal pool. As the two Archangels step onto it, the water ripples slightly around their feet, while the rest remains calm, like a solid sheet of glass.

The power becomes more and more intense as they approach. From here, Lucifer can see the outline of a being in the haze. Directly to the left of the throne, he also sees Ruach Hokadesh, the Spirit.

There He is, Ruach—the same bright being Lucifer saw when he opened his eyes for the first time. He can still feel the warmth emanating from the light and can still feel the heat that originates at the core and rushes up to his head and throughout his frame.

Lucifer can see Ruach more clearly now, as they move closer. He has long dark hair, and skin that glows like fire. It's like His whole being is a liquid light, yet He's still easy to look at. His eyes are a metallic gold, but with flakes of blue and green. They change depending on how the light hits them.

Fabric rivers around Him, giving off the same glow as His skin. At first the robe is white, with green patterns that move like a flock of birds. But then the colors change, from iridescent, to emerald, then back to white, never staying on one color for more than a few moments.

The two Archangels stop several yards from the throne, unable to come any closer because of the pressure emanating from the light. A voice echoes around them—firm, gentle, and immense all at the same time.

"Lucifer, you are my servant, full of wisdom and perfect in being. The workmanship of your fingers, as you create your worship and music, was prepared in you the day you were created."

Lucifer and Gabriel both bow down on one knee, nodding their heads in reverence. Out of the corner of his eye, Lucifer can tell that Gabriel is straining under the pressure as much as he is.

The voice continues.

"Let it be made known that one third of the angels are assigned under Lucifer, and he will rule from the domain known as Earth. You will lead from a throne beneath the clouds."

Something stirs inside Lucifer as he listens, like a palpitation of the heart. He feels a tug in his core. As he keeps his head bowed, he can see it now, the planet, shrouded under thick clouds.

A breath of air flows through the room, lifting his hair off his face. It's cool and tingly to the touch. The air then wraps around him, becomes warm, and lifts him up to his feet. Lucifer looks at the being seated on the throne.

"So be it," he replies, accepting his assignment.

As soon as the words leave his lips, Ruach appears in front of him. The Spirit's eyes turn a bright white. Ruach lifts his hand and brushes it across Lucifer's forehead.

The action sends a rift, like an explosion, through the atmosphere. Like a bubble of air, shooting out in all directions, the wave causes the Seraphim to teeter precariously in the air, and Gabriel, still kneeling, fights to not collapse onto the floor.

A dark blue sapphire appears in the middle of Lucifer's forehead where Ruach's hand was. Gold arms stretch out from the stone, wrapping around his head and forming a crown.

The air settles once more, and only the rhythmic pulse fills the room.

***

Lucifer stands before the portal. The opening to the other dimension is filled with a thick layer of water. Images of galaxies flash across the entrance until it finally settles on a view of a singular planet.

The layer of water distorts the image slightly, rippling over it in waves.

Lucifer turns his attention from the portal to Uriel who now stands beside him. Uriel crosses one arm across his chest and bows his head.

Lucifer shifts his attention to behind him. A sea of Dominions, Powers, Principalities, and Virtues all stand at attention, crossing their arms in the same manner.

Turning back to the entrance, his eyes study the wavy planet a few seconds more, then he leaps into the water. The picture of Earth swirls as he passes through the layer, stretching out and distorting along with the colorful lights floating through the water. Finally, he emerges on the other side, and Earth comes into focus.

The rest of the angels follow suit, trailing behind in orderly rows. Together, the massive cloud of angels surfaces from the portal and descends to the planet below.

Lush vegetation covers the land, and all types of creatures and animals roam the planet. In the center of the land grows a garden that is always green and fruitful, no matter how the climate around it changes.

As Lucifer arrives on Earth, he immediately takes his place on his throne, ready to give assignments to his subjects.

The back of his throne extends up behind him, covered in detailed carvings and clear jewels. Pillars line around him, each one ascending several stories to the vaulted ceilings.

This palace is situated right in the middle of the garden, in a place similar to the heavens in so many ways.

Lucifer knows he has work to do, but he takes a moment to settle in. He rests his arms on the sides of his throne, with both of his hands adorned in jewels. Detailed white gold covers his fingers and trails up each limb. A matching breastplate shields his chest and neck.

The sapphire in his crown sharply contrasts with the rest of his appearance, while the shimmering gold band across his forehead matches his eyes.

For a second, he feels his hands grip the arm rests. Raising his head, he looks out through the pillars to the planet before him. It mirrors the heavens, with a bright light, that touches every plant and creature in the land. The river, cutting through the valley below, shines and glistens like the clear jewels that surround the Archangel.

Light beams move, shining through the pillars and illuminating his face. The brightness washes out his eyes even more, to the point where they are nearly white.

He turns his attention to the angels lining the sides of his throne. Each one awaits his command, ready at a second's notice. Their faces start to blur in the golden rays. Or maybe it's his vision blurring.

The warmth on Lucifer's face begins to burn. It's the type of burn where he's not sure if it's extremely hot or extremely cold. He feels the sensation imbue his being. His breath quickens. A thought tugs at the corner of his mind. He feels as if there's something he's forgotten or just hasn't realized yet. For a split second everything is clear.

"Greetings, Lucifer."

A formal voice draws his attention, and just like that, his realization is gone. Blinking several times, he attempts to concentrate on a cluster of out-of-focus figures who have appeared in front of him.

An easy smile spreads across his face as he greets them.

"Ah, welcome." He steps down from the throne, excited to already have visitors.

"Gabriel, Aziel." He says their names in turn as he receives them both with a hug. This spectacle of brotherly love seems to have come with his new position of authority.

"What brings you here?" Lucifer asks, casually clasping his hands in front of him.

Gabriel motions to Aziel who subsequently turns to the third figure that is just now coming into focus. Eremiel, a Throne. Thrones are one of the more unique looking angels. The golden, sphere-shaped being is in his smaller form now, a size that could be held between Lucifer's hands.

Eremiel floats up beside Aziel, rotating his two outer rings as he moves. The white eyes on the rings blink once, and then he opens outward, like arms uncrossing. Inside of him is a rolled-up piece of parchment that floats out into Aziel's hand. He then closes up again, returning to the sphere shape, and lazily rotates his surrounding rings while watching the exchange.

"A new assignment," Gabriel states as Lucifer seizes the scroll.

"Already?" Lucifer asks, unfurling it.

The words unstick from the page and hover a few inches from

the paper as he reads them. His eyes quickly scan the script lettering before he turns back to Gabriel.

"This city, what is its purpose?"

"The city is to be called Jerusalem, and that is not revealed," Gabriel answers, not giving any more information than necessary as always.

Unsatisfied, Lucifer prods further. "But I am to oversee the construction even though it is not to be built here on Earth?"

"Correct, it will be built in the heavenly realm."

Lucifer looks back over the paper when a thought suddenly strikes him. The confused look on his face spreads into a smile.

"I accept." The floating words stick back down on the paper. They turn red briefly, before fading back to black, sealing them in place. Lucifer rolls the scroll back up, then hands it off to Aziel.

"Well then," Lucifer says with an energetic huff. "Let's start immediately."

He jumps right into creating plans for Jerusalem, promising himself that this will be his greatest accomplishment yet.

Mapping out the dimensions and foundations of the city is his priority as he consults with the constructors. As he imagines each aspect, it appears before him like an image, and he makes whatever necessary modifications. Beginning with the foundations, he decides on twelve levels. Each one will be a thick layer of solid gemstone with jasper, sapphire, and chalcedony being the first three.

He meets with the working angels at the site where the city will be built, the sacred mountain. The massive edifice will serve as a base for the city, extending out hundreds of miles, far out of sight. It is the largest mountain in the whole heavenly realm.

He must go back and forth from each realm often as the construction begins, always looking forward to when the other Archangels are there with him. Gabriel comes most often to constantly update the records.

Both Gabriel and Aziel join Lucifer, as they watch the pouring of the first foundation. The gemstone starts in a liquid form as the angels pour it over the rocky mountaintop, but then hardens quickly into a perfectly square base.

When they start the third foundation, a very special visitor comes to join them, and Lucifer can hear Him coming before he is even in sight.

Lucifer turns to see a host rushing toward them. Cherubim and Thrones whirl forward with Ruach directly in the middle. A great wind comes with them, whipping around the grass below. They seem to take up the whole horizon as they hover over the land.

The host stops several feet away as Ruach approaches Lucifer. He glides through the air, then steps onto the ground. His nearly tangible light is surrounding Him like always, and that power—the same power that was so heavy in the throne room—accompanies Him. The force causes His dark hair and robes to float around Him in those same rhythmic movements that resemble breathing.

"My Lord, You have come to see the progress of Jerusalem," Lucifer speaks up, bowing, on his knees, reverently.

"Well done," Ruach says, not taking His eyes from the Archangel. "I have need of this city."

"It is a great honor, Lord. I am looking forward to serving you from here." Lucifer feels his heart swell as he presses his arm against his chest in his bow.

"You will not need to stay here," Ruach states, stepping around Lucifer, taking in the construction before Him.

A beat passes, and Lucifer straightens "Lord?" He feels the word leave his mouth.

Every eye in the host centers on him.

"Yes, after you are done overseeing the construction, you will be able to return to Earth, where you rule."

Lucifer falters before replying. "I thought you would have need of me here. To rule from the city."

Everyone seems to be frozen in place at this point. Even the Thrones are static. Maybe they aren't, he thinks, but can't focus enough to know for sure.

Ruach directs His gaze back to Lucifer. "I do not. I have need of you on Earth."

Any reply evades Lucifer as the Spirit takes a step toward him. A few silent moments pass, but then Ruach speaks up again.

"Well done. I am pleased."

Lucifer bows his head again and feels a pressure in his chest loosen slightly. Then, as quickly as they appeared, the host retreats, leaving behind only a gentle wind.

CHAPTER TWO

Things Hidden, Things Revealed

After the initial building plans are finalized, Lucifer returns to Earth. He decides to take the opportunity to further explore his new home. The planet is as busy as the heavens, with a third of the angels under his rule. They journey back and forth between the heavens and Earth on assignments.

As Lucifer passes along the outskirts of his palace, a high-ranking Power, Samael, joins him.

"Back from Jerusalem so quickly?" Samael questions as he steps in place next to Lucifer.

As a Power, he has a slightly different appearance from other angels. His skin is bronze, almost metallic looking, save for the glow of light coming from his hands and feet. A glow also constantly comes from his eyes, with a beam of light circling around the middle of his head.

His covering is a mixture of robes and wings, but he doesn't use his wings to fly like others. Instead, they stay tucked around his midsection.

"Amethyst," Lucifer muses aloud.

"What?"

Lucifer stops and looks at his companion. "The last foundation should be amethyst."

"Oh, still working on the plans for the city? I thought you already had that figured out," Samael replies with an easy smile.

When Lucifer doesn't answer, he continues, "Amethyst would be perfect."

He continues to speak, but Lucifer doesn't hear him. Instead, he stares transfixed on Samael's face.

The Power's eyes have faded, their glow almost completely disappeared. His dark skin has become ashen. Lucifer stares. He can see Samael's mouth moving, but all he can observe before him is a void.

Lucifer blinks, and Samael's face has returned to normal. He keeps talking, oblivious to Lucifer's scrutiny.

Something Samael says catches Lucifer's attention.

"Whatever its use, it will be an honor to serve there."

"An honor to serve there?" Lucifer repeats. "Yes, that is right." In a second, he's completely forgotten about the strange occurrence. That's what it's all about anyway, right? It's an honor, even if he won't stay in the city. He will still serve there until it's completed.

Without another word, Lucifer turns away. He walks up the stairs into his palace, leaving Samael behind with his mouth partially open, as if he didn't finish his sentence.

Passing through the main courtyard, Lucifer enters a large hall. The space is simpler compared to the rest of the elaborate palace with plain white walls and a clear, glass ceiling.

Lucifer pauses momentarily next to the entryway of a much smaller room. There in the center of the room is a short, singular pedestal.

He walks up to the solitary stand, considering it for a moment. Then reaching up, he removes his crown and sets it down. He stands, studying the sapphire in its center for a moment.

He turns to leave, but the room has changed.

The door is gone.

Lucifer stands dumbfounded for a moment. He looks up and

sees that the walls extend up high out of sight, as if he was in the bottom of a bottomless pit.

He snaps his head around, trying to determine his location, but his hands steal away his attention. Lifting them up toward his face, he shakes at the sight of them. His fingers are still adorned with rings of rubies and sapphires, but his skin seems worn. Deteriorated. The gray pallor extends up his arms, and the skin shrinks in around his bones.

His gaze snaps away from his hands to the floor as water starts spilling in from the corners of the room. With a splash, he takes a step back as it rises to his ankles, swirling and bubbling around him, soaking the hem of his cloak. He tries to step on top of it, but with a thudding in his chest, he realizes that it's impossible.

With a gush, the water floods up to his neck. In shock, he sucks in a breath, and the blue liquid covers his head.

It's dark again. For a second, everything is silent as he floats suspended in the still liquid. Suddenly the space he's in seems massive and completely empty, except for himself and the stagnant water.

Before he is alone for too long, flashes of light join him. The light separates into sparks, and they change color, like a galaxy of stars—blue, green, and white flecks whirling around.

The lights change into sand. It whips by in an underwater sandstorm.

Instantly, the water disappears, but leaves the sandstorm behind. The dust catches in the wind and is swept away, but not before he inhales a great breath of it and feels like everything inside of him has turned to dust as well.

Squinting, he sees that the room is gone, and he now stands in the middle of a vast desert. Rolling dunes stretch out endlessly before and behind him.

The wind bites, whipping his robe and hair. He bows his head down against the gusts and struggles forward. Pausing momentarily, he catches his breath.

His eyes widen as he pulls his hands away from his sides. Now, they're covered in a bright red liquid which runs down his wrists in shining droplets.

An image flashes before his mind. A knife cuts a hand and blood boils to the surface. Two hands clasp together, red dripping down between them.

One image after the other flashes before him now. A figure sinks deeper into a vast ocean, their limp body being pulled in by the dark blue water. Crimson blood pools on a stone floor with an unrecognizable body beside it, face blurred.

A pure white horse leaps into an ocean's tide. The gray waves churn as clouds hang low overhead, nearly touching the sea.

He can't stop the visions even when he presses his hands firmly over his eyes.

Suddenly the visions expand to reach more than just sight. He can taste the saltiness of the ocean, hear the whinnies of the horse, feel the warm blood on his hands.

He is paralyzed as he sees and feels one thing after another. The worst part is, the moment seems to last forever, like an eternity he's trapped in.

Suddenly the visions are gone, and all that remains is Lucifer standing on the white sand. He faces black ocean waves as they crash up on the shore. He's seen this before or at least he thinks he has. It looks so familiar.

He turns his head to the side. Out of the corner of his eye, he can see a massive storm growing behind him, the storm clouds white with a bright light. Lighting strikes round the edges of the thick billows, roaring louder as the fury rapidly approaches. The light consumes his figure, and then everything turns white.

Lucifer snaps his head forward. His breaths come in gasps as he looks down with wide eyes. His hand is clutching a lyre.

He pants for a moment longer, willing his breaths to calm, then slowly draws his head up.

"Lucifer?" A nearby musician comes into focus. "Are you not going to play?" the angel asks, the voice still sounding foggy in Lucifer's head.

Lucifer frantically tries to place himself in his mind. He thinks back to the room. With a sudden awareness, he realizes that his crown is not on his head. He must have left it on that pedestal.

He feels like he should be remembering something, but everything between that room and this moment is a blank page.

Setting the instrument down, he draws a thin breath and replies. "No. Not now." He stands and turns abruptly, desperate to leave.

He strides across the marble floor, concealing his still trembling hands in the folds of his robe.

He passes by Uriel, who turns his head to watch the Archangel. Uriel folds his arms across his chest, scrutinizing the figure that is all too eager to leave.

When he's just out of sight of the courtyard, Lucifer makes a beeline for the room he found earlier. He marches through the doorway and stops in front of the pillar, snatching up his crown.

The blue sapphire no longer sits alone in the headpiece, but two more jewels have appeared on the gold band, a red jasper and purple chalcedony.

He turns the crown over and examines it carefully, looking at all the jewels, the gold setting, dissecting every inch of it with his eyes. There is something off about this, but he still cannot figure out what.

Finally, he resigns himself to setting it down again, and, with a shaky breath, leaves the room.

He decides to go to the other side of the palace, out onto a balcony. He takes a couple deep breaths, trying to clear his head. His peace doesn't last for long, however, as a voice interrupts him.

"That was quite an interesting scene," Uriel says, walking up behind him.

Lucifer turns his head only slightly to acknowledge him but stares down at the ground. "You have something to say about it."

He sees Uriel take another step closer out of the corner of his eye, but still refuses to look directly at him.

"What happened back there? I'm not the only one who noticed."

Instead of answering, Lucifer turns back to the view of the vividly bright valley below.

"You never stop playing in the middle of a song," Uriel adds.

A few silent seconds pass, and Lucifer asks, "Do you ever think about why we are doing this?"

"Doing what?"

"Existing. Why were you created." He lowers his voice slightly. "Why was I?"

"You know the answer to that," Uriel replies, almost laughing.

"It just seems like there's more to it, at times …" Lucifer's voice trails off. His hands ball into fists as he realizes that Uriel doesn't understand any of this at all. Of course, he doesn't, it's impossible.

Lucifer whips around suddenly, but then freezes in place as if just noticing that Uriel is there. He snaps his head to the side and opens his mouth as if about to say something. Instead, he turns away, squaring his shoulders. Lucifer steps forward, then strides down the steps, leaving Uriel behind.

"Lucifer!" Uriel yells after him, causing him to pause between steps.

Then, without a look back, he advances forward, leaving his confused companion at the top of the stairs.

***

Lucifer breathes in deeply as he strides across the field, feeling the long blades of grass brush against his fingertips. Stepping on the blades doesn't damage them. Instead, they morph around his foot like liquid and then bend back into place.

He quickens his pace as he comes across a stream. The water flows together as one being, lively and smooth. Lucifer looks down, seeing it's much deeper than it initially appears.

Without hesitating, he steps a foot onto the stream. It sinks down slightly without breaking the surface. He leaps out with both feet on top of the water, waving his arms for a second to catch his balance. In a few strides, he's crossed over the stream, and stands at the other side for a moment, deciding on his next move.

He can see the heavenly city in the distance, and it beckons with its dazzling architecture. The sheer mass is hard to comprehend at this distance, just the walls and towering spires stand out in the front. He notices the warm light that always seems to emanate from the city, casting a haze on the landscape.

Then, he turns his head in the other direction. He's right on the cusp of a valley, currently concealed by the hill adjacent to him.

He takes a deep breath in and listens. There's always music, some sort of ambient sound weaving its way through every inch of the heavens.

Everything moves in motion with it. The grass and flowers sway to the rhythm, as if they are lulling themselves to sleep.

After a moment, Lucifer hears what he is listening for—a rumble so low it's almost inaudible. It pulses, still in rhythm with the song, but stands out when he concentrates.

This is what he will follow.

He carries on over the hill, the valley opening before him. He pauses once more to reorientate with the rumble. As he follows, the sound takes him to a place in the heavens that he has not explored before.

The noise drums on, growing louder with each step he takes. Finally, he reaches its source.

He's standing in the middle of a field again, but the grass here only comes up to the middle of his calves, and an innumerable amount of white and golden flowers dust across the expanse.

Thin streams of water cut into the ground, weaving in and out of each other, glittering in the rosy light. Hovering just inches above the water are wispy clouds, dotted here and there, following the streams.

Before Lucifer is a wall made of white stone which juts out the grass reaching up to a height of three or four Cherubim stacked on top of each other. He can see both ends of the wall.

As he approaches the structure, he reaches out his hand, hovering a few inches away. He can feel the rumble now, it's radiating from the facade.

He knows immediately that the wall is not intended to keep something out or something in, but its purpose remains a mystery.

Looking up, he notices something about halfway up the wall, a thin gold line cutting directly across, glowing ever so slightly in cadence with the rumble.

He stares up at it. Why this, of all the astonishing things he's encountered, enraptures his attention so much, Lucifer has no idea. He makes up his mind, however, that this place, or perhaps this moment, will be very, very important to him.

After a time, Lucifer realizes he's made his way back toward the city. This area is much more active with all kinds of Dominions, Seraphim, Cherubim, Powers, and Principalities hastening about. All of them are either on some assumingly very important mission, or … Lucifer suddenly realizes … they're having fun.

He notices a particular one, a Principality. Lucifer knows his name instantly after looking at him, Uriel.

Uriel is curiously watching another angel, that seems to be gathering an audience.

This angel has a feminine appearance. A solid gold covering obstructs the top half of her face, so that only her nose and lips are visible. A hood made of a radiant yellow fabric drapes down into her matching gown, and a small pair of wings peak out from around her neck and rest gently across her collar bones. Across the top of the wings are rows of eyes that blink in union with each other.

Uriel presses in closer as several other angels, including two enthusiastic Thrones, surround her. The Thrones vibrate their rings in anticipation and the atmosphere around them blurs.

The angel displays her hand out to the crowd. Floating in the center of her palm is a droplet of water. Without warning, she flings the droplet upward. Several feet in the air, the water explodes sending shimmering, sparkling liquid beads shooting out in all directions. They hang in the sky for several seconds then fall in gentle rain drops.

The crowd exclaims in delight as the rain patters down on them. The Thrones shake themselves like a dog freeing its coat of the dew.

The raindrops do not hit the ground, however, but stay suspended in the air, then float upward again. On their way back up, the droplets begin to expand, wrapping themselves around the angels, swirling and twisting like a school of fish.

The liquid drapes around Uriel's arms and his feet begin to lift off the ground. Lucifer notices others around him are being raised up into the air as well. Uriel tumbles backward, waving his arms to correct himself. He laughs as he spins, seeming to relinquish his balance.

Two smaller angels below him join hands together. They step onto some water that's hovering just a few inches from the ground and start to slide as if on ice. They spin in circles together, then jump up, doing front flips in the air. They float for a moment upside down, then grab hands, spinning together again.

Uriel looks down and notices Lucifer watching the spectacle.

Lucifer catches Uriel's stare.

"You know the answer to that," Uriel says with a bemused expression.

"What?" Lucifer doesn't know why his voice sounds so small.

All hints of a smile are gone from Uriel as he repeats, "You know the answer to that."

Uriel is gone from the sky now, and Lucifer whips around to see him standing behind him. The heavenly scene is gone, and Lucifer realizes that he's on Earth, on his balcony. The light from the valley still shines brightly behind him.

Lucifer snaps his head to the side and opens his mouth as if about to say something. Instead, he turns away, squaring his shoulders. Stepping forward, he strides down the steps, leaving Uriel behind.

"Lucifer!" Uriel yells.

Lucifer doesn't stop.

***

"Isn't it exciting Gabriel?" Aziel says, stepping alongside the Archangel.

"You are talking about Jerusalem?" Gabriel replies, looking toward the construction.

They walk along an outcropping just outside of the main heavenly city. The sacred mountain still looks massive even at this distance. The jeweled layers of the city are hazy in the distance.

Aziel steps in front of Gabriel, blocking his view of the building process.

"That's just part of it. Just think of what it means. Who will be living there? Don't you think we are preparing for something?"

"We are always preparing for something," Gabriel confirms, but lets a slight smile escape his serious expression.

Aziel gives a contemplative nod, trying to make himself serious as well, and falls silent as the two observe the landscape.

"Well, *I* am always doing something at least," Gabriel jibes.

Aziel narrows his eyes, but replies, "Well then, you better get back to the records hall and do your job."

"Aren't you assigned under me?" Gabriel replies quickly.

Aziel quickens his pace without another word.

As they head back to the city, a Throne greets them. Not Eremiel, however, Aziel quickly notices. The excitable little Throne has always been his favorite, but the one bringing them a delivery now has a much more stoic nature.

The Throne unfurls one of his rings and promptly hands a singular note to Gabriel. Then without any small talk or funny stories, he immediately zips off in the opposite direction, already onto the next task.

"Isn't that Uriel?" Aziel asks, uninterested in the Throne's delivery.

Gabriel mumbles "Hmm?" but doesn't look up from the small piece of paper in his hand.

Aziel watches Uriel who appears to be looking for someone. He walks down one of the narrower streets with ivy hanging across the top of it and stops when he comes across Michael. He says something to him. Michael dismisses a Throne and a Virtue he was talking to and turns to Uriel.

"I didn't know he would be here," Aziel says to Gabriel. "We should go greet him."

Gabriel dismisses himself. "Excuse me, Aziel, there's something I must take care of."

With that, he leaves the angel behind.

Aziel looks again in Uriel's direction, contemplating going by himself to greet him. Then he notices that the Principality seems to be having a more serious conversation. Instead, Aziel decides to return to the library.

***

Across the yard, Uriel has pulled Michael into one of the archways, as he talks to him in a hushed voice.

"So, you will come to Earth then?" Uriel asks, crossing his arms over his chest.

Michael stands directly in the middle of the archway as he listens to Uriel's concerns. "And you find it odd, why?"

"I can't describe what it is." Uriel lifts his hand in front of him as if trying to grasp for the words. "There's just something different about him than when he first started ruling Earth. It's just something … abnormal."

"You're saying he's changed?" Michael offers, his tone not giving away any unease.

"Yes! He changed. That's what I'm trying to get at. There's something new in his eyes. It's like a force or … or… I don't know, something I've never seen before."

"What do you make of that?" Michael probes.

"I–I don't know. I thought maybe you would understand him or tell me what I'm missing."

Michael taps his fingers on the hilt of his sword at his waist.

Uriel begins to wonder if perhaps he's on a fool's errand. He's not even sure why he decided to come talk to Michael in the first place.

He can clearly see why Michael holds his position of authority. Even though the Archangel is standing there nonchalantly, Uriel knows he would be more inclined to move the Sacred Mountain than to budge Michael even an inch.

Perhaps Michael and Lucifer are not quite so similar as he initially thought.

"I will go to Earth then, as you have asked," Michael replies after a pause.

"You will? Then come now," Uriel suggests, switching back to his plan. "There is a feast prepared. He will be there, and you can see for yourself."

Michael nods and dismisses himself, but then Uriel's attention is drawn away. He sees Gabriel across the yard, stopping in front of a door guarded by a Cherubim. This strikes him as odd because he's never seen anyone enter that building which is right next to the library. But its door is always closed.

Gabriel speaks a couple words to the guard and the door slowly swings open as the Cherubim stands aside.

***

As the door rumbles shut behind him, Gabriel surveys the massive room. The chamber stretches out like a vast hall, and the walls reach up several times higher than the great Cherubim. Wooden shelves extend from the ground all the way up to the vaulted ceiling, each one lined with an incredible number of books. Their covers all face forward, and each has a single name written in gold on the front.

From where Gabriel stands, he can't see the end of the hall. The bookshelves follow the whole way, until they, too, are out of sight.

As Gabriel steps forward, he passes another door in between two shelves. This door is sealed with a single line of gold running down its middle. He knows that it would be impossible for him to open that door.

He is not distracted by the forbidden room, however, as he walks deliberately toward a certain book. He takes the book from the shelf and turns it over in his hands. Its cover is ivory white and, like the others, has a name written on the front in script letters.

With book in hand, Gabriel turns away from the shelf, heading back down the hall. Leaving behind this place, he heads straight for the palace that surrounds the throne room.

There, he finds Ruach waiting for him. The Spirit turns, and Gabriel knows to follow behind. The pair enter a circular room.

The floor here is like in the throne room, translucent water that ripples slightly when walked on. The ceiling is blue glass. But the thing that sets this room apart from the others is the thick billowy clouds that hang in the air.

They step out onto the water, and Ruach extends His hand out to Gabriel. The book drifts from the Archangel's grasp over to the Spirit.

Finally, Ruach speaks. "This book must be sealed until its appointed time, less its sacred knowledge be revealed."

With that, He drops the book down into the floor. It submerges just below the surface, the liquid covering overtop. The book remains just a few feet below the surface, sealed in place.

CHAPTER THREE

SIX GEMS

The courtyard is nearly full when Lucifer arrives—He lingers near the edge, in an archway, while taking in the scene. Musicians wait for their leader in rows, with nearly all holding a different kind of instrument. Some instruments rest on the ground with long necks and strings to be played with bows. Others are like perfectly rounded harps with strings crossing in all directions. Even more rows hold all types of pipe and wind instruments.

Many of the angels have gathered around the long tables that line the middle of the courtyard, each one topped with vast arrays of fruits and breads. An angel, with the stature of a child, grabs one of the yellow fruits, raises it to his mouth, and takes a bite. The fruit gives off a shimmery glow, turning his cheeks red with the light shining through them.

Lucifer spots Uriel who seems to be scanning the courtyard. He then turns and says something to Michael beside him.

Michael nods to the archway at the end of the courtyard where Lucifer stands centered in the arch. A ruby crown sits atop his head and matching red stones are embedded into his robe. White linen drags behind him as he steps forward.

He passes by the rows of instruments and tables, walking toward Michael and Uriel.

"Michael. I was not expecting your presence." Lucifer greets the pair with an easy smile.

"Tell me," Michael says, ignoring his comment, "how is construction on Jerusalem going?"

"Very well," Lucifer replies. "Six foundations are finished. Gabriel has been keeping the records."

"Yes, of course, but I did want to hear about it from you." Michael then nods to the instruments behind Lucifer. "I'm eager to hear you play."

Lucifer turns to look at the musicians, staring at them with a blank expression.

"You will perform?" Michael prods.

"Of course," Lucifer replies, turning with a bright smile.

Before their conversation can go any further, a Virtue with a more feminine appearance interrupts them. Her skin is dark, dramatically contrasting the white and gold dress she wears. Her dark hair is braided with strands of gold and arranged on her head to look like a crown. As she turns, blue and green feathers can be seen layered down her back.

When she speaks, her voice carries throughout the courtyard and everyone silences.

"We are here today to be in remembrance of our creation and to give honor and glory to our Creator." She looks up to the sky. "In the beginning, out in the pure nothingness, something was happening. The emptiness is changed by a single word. That word starts a spark, which instantaneously snaps into a new form."

The sky above them starts black and empty, but then, on cue with her words, a tiny spark starts in the middle of the air.

"It started as light, and then formed into substance. In a single moment, what was, is transformed into something completely different."

Instantly the spark grows, stretching out, eliminating any of the blackness. The glow even curves around the inner walls of the courtyard, engulfing everyone present.

"Galaxies start in His hands—lights and stars swirl together in the shapes of roses. Each one begins as a bud, and then the stars stretch out to petals. Some are amber, others a deep amethyst."

Miniature galaxies appear and follow suit with the Virtue's words. Their bright cores send light reaching out to the edges, stretching into a dusting of illuminated specks.

"At once, light, sound, power, all came together as one. Then with a snap, the new matter surged in every direction. In a flash, everything came to be."

She snaps her fingers and galaxies fly past them so quickly, they become a blur. A roar fills every edge of the courtyard, and then everything is still.

"He has always existed." Everyone turns from the dazzling display, back to her.

"But, He did not want to be alone, so He made this." She sweeps her hand out and from her fingertips come flowers and leaves. They embed into the surrounding walls and grow like ivy. Fireflies follow them, and even little gemstones appear here and there among the vines.

In the sky, visions of mountains and valleys appear. Tree-lined rivers wind across the expanse.

"And He made us."

That's when Lucifer sees it—the golden field, the hand outstretched toward him.

All types of angels come alive then. They all know each other. They all know their Creator. And they all know their purpose.

Suddenly Lucifer realizes that the vision is gone, and the surrounding angels are all clapping and cheering. The Virtue is clapping too. She looks towards Lucifer, and he knows what he must do.

He strides toward the center of the courtyard and walks up to a row of instruments, scanning over them. Finally, he picks one shaped like a sphere with a hollow core. It is crystal clear and has different sized ridges along its surface.

He lifts the sphere in one hand and in the other he holds a small bow, no longer than the width of his hand.

The courtyard is now silent as the rest of the musicians wait for his cue.

Lucifer swipes the bow across the surface of the sphere. The sound reverberates through the gaps in its exterior and into its echoing core. The sound is like a hum at first, and then some of the angels behind him join in, brushing their bows across long strings.

Lucifer moves the bow up higher on the sphere, where the gaps are smaller, creating higher-pitched notes. One by one, a new instrument or voice joins in, building up the sound.

Lucifer sweeps across the top, creating a high note that vibrates through the air as all the other instruments cease. The high-pitched ring clings midair for a moment.

His lips move to speak, but there is no sound.

Lucifer swings his hand down. The notes are more rapid now, as if a floodgate had been opened. Each note streaks across the courtyard like stars, leaving behind a trail of musical dust.

The composition is layers of rhythms, each one more complex than the other. But there's another sound hidden under the layers—just a beat off, like an entirely different song hidden in the background.

Lucifer looks up as the sounds almost become deafening. He stops playing, but the music continues. His breath quickens, and the sound becomes a piercing hum. No one else seems to notice, however, as he scans the crowd.

His eyes lock on a figure at the far end of the yard where Ruach stares directly at him.

Lucifer feels his pulse hammering inside his head. His eyes widen, but then the Spirit disappears.

The song has ended.

The gentle echoes of the room come back to him now, and Lucifer lets out a shaky breath. He squeezes his eyes shut, attempting to ignore the rush of blood to the head.

Setting down his instrument, he stands suddenly. He scans the crowds, but most of the other angels seem oblivious to the panic he feels rising in his chest.

Lucifer's eyes settle on a doorway at the end of the courtyard, and he makes a hasty exit.

The musicians begin another tune, and Lucifer casts a glance in Micheal's direction. Their eyes meet for a brief moment, but then with a whoosh of white fabric, Lucifer disappears out of sight.

***

The Lord sits on His throne, never leaving His designated seat. Ruach stays by His side unless it is necessary to move about the realms.

Gabriel approaches the throne in the silent room. He stops reverently, several feet away from the Spirit.

"My Lord." Gabriel's voice is nearly lost in the expanse as he addresses Ruach.

The Spirit turns His head toward the Archangel. The energy in the room turns with Him, like a massive force maneuvered by a single thread attached at the Spirit's core.

Gabriel takes a step back, faltering slightly. He bows down on one knee, as the fierce power focuses on him.

He looks up towards Ruach, but his words catch in his throat as he sees the Spirit's expression. Through the brilliant light that illuminates Ruach's face, there is a strange look in His eyes. A look Gabriel has never seen before. He bows his head as the Spirit speaks.

"When you see my creation, what do you think of it?"

Immediately, Gabriel responds, "Lord, I cannot help but think of Your glorious power, which shaped all that is. And Your love. Nothing can compare to it. It is the very substance of Your being, and the element which created my spirit."

The reply does not come directly from Ruach, but from the voice of God, which surrounds the entire room. "There is so much more."

Ruach turns His attention toward Gabriel and speaks again. "If only you could see."

Again, a glint passes over His eyes. Like a sorrow beneath the layers of light, something hidden behind a locked door.

Gabriel feels his core constrict, forcing him to freeze in place. His chest tightens, and he tries to catch his breath.

The grip lessens slightly, and he shakily turns to look behind him.

The throne of God has disappeared and in its place is Lucifer. His own throne towers above Gabriel.

Lucifer stares dead ahead, as if unaware of his environment. His once bright countenance has turned to an anemic, gray façade.

Thick gray clouds close in on the room, making the atmosphere suffocating.

***

Lucifer blinks and seems to regain consciousness. He takes a few shallow breaths, and his hands grip the sides of the throne, turning his knuckles white. His breathing stops as he takes in the view below.

Several feet away stands Gabriel, a stricken look upon his face.

Lucifer's eyes trail down from Gabriel to the bottom of the throne. A figure sits hunched over, facing away from Lucifer.

The figure turns his head and reveals his identity. Lucifer stares into the face of the stooped being, his eyes widening slightly in recognition.

Then suddenly, the throne room is gone.

Lucifer jerks upright, as if he has been awakened from a dream. He inhales deeply and recognizes the room around him.

He looks down and sees the crown clutched in his hand. Another row of jewels has formed across the headpiece. He holds it up for inspection. What was once just one gem sitting in the middle of his forehead is now a crown that would cover his eyes completely.

Lucifer realizes he is sitting on the floor and stands to replace the crown. Before he can set it on the pedestal, something stops him in his tracks.

The room has changed. The semi-opaque ceiling normally floods the area with white light. Now, it's dim.

Lucifer snaps around, feeling a presence behind him. But no one is there.

He looks down when he realizes that the apparition is on the floor. A dark outline of him lays stretched out across the marble ground.

Dumbfounded, he stands still, unsure of what he is observing. Before he can focus on the dark spot, it disappears, and the room is once again bright.

Flashes of the vision begin to come back. He presses his hands to his temples and tries to recall the face he saw—that figure crouched on the floor. No matter how many times it replays in his mind, however, the dream always fades away right before the figure turns around.

He remembers seeing Gabriel, but there is something else pulling at the edge of his consciousness yet remains unreachable.

Slowly he brings his hands down from his face and runs a finger across the crown still in his grip. Setting it back down on the pedestal, he resolves what he must do.

Leaving behind his palace and Earth, Lucifer leaps into the sky.

There is one place that he's seen before that could give him answers. A place he's found before.

As the wind pounds against his ears, he isn't even aware of his surroundings until he goes through the water portal and enters the heavenly realm. The liquid rolls off him in bubbles, then merge back into the entrance as he lowers to the ground.

Before him is the city that holds the throne room, the library, the records, and much more. His destination is not inside the city, however, but outside, in a field.

As Lucifer passes through the city, he steps onto the golden streets. The gold is so pure it is transparent with just the tint of metallic coloring.

The surrounding buildings are a mixture of marble, gold, stone, and even wood. Each one of them is unique in style and purpose. But he doesn't pay any attention to the architecture. He doesn't even pay attention to the other angels around him.

He does notice the sound, however—a low, pulsating noise that echoes through the heavens. None of the angels would hear it unless they were specifically listening for it.

The sound draws him forward like it did the very first time he heard it, right after he had awakened for the first time. He focuses on the pull, like a voice coaxing him to take one more step.

Finally, Lucifer reaches the source of the sound that guided him on his journey across the heavens.

A wall, unlike any other.

He stares up at its white stone surface and the thin gold line dividing it in half long-ways. The first time he saw it, he gazed, uncomprehending. Now as he observes, he still cannot explain it, but the feeling of its importance is stronger than ever. He squints. If he looks hard enough, he can just barely see something else.

An alternative reality flashes before him on the wall. The golden line changes, but only for a second. No longer just a singular line, it becomes a river now, with branches and smaller paths that break off then come back together into the main flow of gold.

Just as quickly as it appears, the streak of liquid gold returns to normal. But that flash is enough for Lucifer. He knows what that wall is trying to show him.

There is more than one option.

***

Gabriel stands at the bottom of the Sacred Mountain, peering up at the construction atop the peak. The partially built city engulfs the mountains summit and extends up farther than the eye can see.

Glistening black rocks are cut off bluntly by the city's first foundation, a layer of solid jasper. The clear, bright red color seems to glow from within as pure light pierces through it. Atop the jasper is a layer of blue sapphire, followed by six more foundations.

Aziel stands next to Gabriel, copying down notations, as the Archangel comments on the progress of construction.

"They just started pouring the ninth foundation," Gabriel assesses.

"Jerusalem is progressing very well," Michael comments, walking up behind Gabriel.

"It is nearly three fourths complete," Gabriel replies without looking back. "Lucifer has done well."

Michael doesn't comment any further.

At the base of the mountain, the three angels appear minute compared to the rest of the expanse.

"Lucifer," Michael begins, "he oversees here often?"

Gabriel glances at Michael before replying. "He always comes to give assignments, then immediately returns to Earth." he pauses, then says, "Why do you ask?"

"I saw him here earlier," Aziel interjects before Michael can reply. "He was talking to the Power, Samael."

"Samael's assignment is on Earth, why would he be here?" Michael questions.

Aziel can't give an answer, so instead falls silent.

Everyone else is silent as well, as they stare up at the impending city.

CHAPTER FOUR

I Provide the Choice

"Uriel."

The Principality's head snaps up at the sound of his name.

Samael stands in front of him. The Power's calculating, bright, eyes scrutinize Uriel.

"Yes?" Uriel replies.

"Lucifer has called a meeting and has requested your presence," Samael answers in an almost soothing tone.

Uriel nods, then stands quickly. He looks down to the valley below the cliffs where he had been sitting. Still caught up in his thoughts, he looks back and sees Samael turn and walk away. He jogs to catch up.

"What is this about?" Uriel asks.

"He didn't say," Samael replies in a way that indicates he will not give up any more information.

Uriel falls silent as he follows along. Several other high-ranking angels catch his eye as they seem to be headed in the same direction. After entering the palace, they walk past the throne room to a large, unfamiliar hallway.

When they enter a room, Uriel notices Lucifer at the back, surrounded by other head angels. Samael closes the door behind them.

The room falls silent as they wait for Lucifer to speak. He keeps his head tilted down, sitting planted against the back wall. A jeweled headpiece covers his forehead. Onyx and rubies drop down between his eyes as strands of smaller jewels lie across his cheekbones and weave together over his mouth. Red fabric drapes across his shoulders and pools down on the floor around him. He is an ornately decorated statue frozen against the wall.

Lucifer finally speaks from behind the jeweled veil. "Some of you already know why I've called you here." He tilts his head before speaking again. "What I am about to say here will not leave this room until the right time."

Uriel's eyes shift to Samael who stares fixed on Lucifer. He looks at the rest of the room's occupants, but they too have the same absorbed expression. They appear entranced, and yet fully aware of what Lucifer's cryptic words mean.

"We have been too limited. Or ..." Lucifer pauses and drops his voice. "We have been limited by someone."

A sinking feeling tugs at the corner of Uriel's mind as Lucifer continues to speak.

"He has prevented us from living to our greatest potential. You already know of whom I speak. Our oppressor."

"Oppressor?" Uriel speaks up and all eyes except for Lucifer's turn toward him.

"Who is oppressing us? What is this potential?" Uriel cannot mask his astonished tone as he speaks.

"You have already experienced it yourself." Lucifer's sharp tone cuts off Uriel's questioning. He turns his head to stare at Uriel and lowers his voice to a hiss. "Being told exactly what to do. No choice. No other options. That is the oppression I speak of."

The room falls silent, and Uriel racks his mind for a reply, but any thought at all seems to momentarily escape him. All he can manage is a nearly silent "But that's not ..."

Lucifer ignores him and continues. "We deserve another

option." He voices what no one else dares to say aloud.

"But what if what you are saying isn't true?" a Principality from across the room speaks up, but Uriel does not notice who it is. In fact, he doesn't hear anything after a few seconds. His eyes rove over the ground, searching for answers, as a white noise in his ears grows louder. He is vaguely aware that others are speaking now, but all he can hear is his own quickening breath.

All their faces seem unfamiliar, and he only notices Samael look his way once.

Finally, he comes back to himself when he hears his name.

"Uriel."

His eyes come into focus on the figure in front of him. He stands alone with Lucifer, unsure of when the others left.

"I knew you would be hesitant at first, but I need your help." Lucifer speaks as Uriel blankly stares. "I need you on my side."

His side?

Uriel finally finds his voice and says, "This will not end well. Whatever your plan, you cannot accomplish this which you desire."

Lucifer steps closer.

"I am not doing this for me. I am doing this for the others. To help them. It is right. It is good." He emphasizes his last words as he steps even closer, a pleadingly sincere look on his face. "I will ascend into heaven, and I will exalt my throne above the stars of God. Above the mountain of congregation, I will be exactly the same." He pauses, "as the Most High."

Uriel stares in stunned silence as Lucifer takes a step back.

"You will have to make this decision for yourself. A decision I provided for you." After a pause, Lucifer turns and walks out the doorway, leaving Uriel behind.

Uriel exhales a breath as he leans his head on the wall behind him. The room seems smaller now.

After a moment of staring at the ceiling, Uriel turns to leave the room, but comes to a halt in the doorway when he sees Samael waiting just outside. Averting the Power's gaze, he takes a step to leave.

"You seem hesitant." Samael's words stop him in his tracks.

"I just … I am not accustomed to hearing such things," Uriel replies in a voice as emotionless as possible.

Samael strides up beside Uriel.

"No, I mean you seem hesitant to leave."

Uriel turns his head slightly but avoids Samael's direct gaze. Giving a tight-lipped smile and a nod, Uriel picks up his pace to walk away. Without looking back, however, he still knows he is being watched.

Just a few more steps and he will be out of the Power's piercing gaze.

"Wait."

Just a few steps short.

Samael strolls up behind him, placing a glowing hand on Uriel's tense shoulder. "Let's talk for a while."

The walls around them seem to dissolve away.

The two of them stand in the valley now, the immense marble structures replaced by a babbling brook and swaying grass.

Samael turns away, looking toward the horizon where a constant golden light hovers. The ring of light that encompasses his head reflects some of that fiery color.

"I know things may seem different now," he begins in a low voice which is so soothing Uriel almost starts to relax. "It may be confusing, but you need to trust Lucifer. He has the best intentions for all that he rules over."

"No, I think he's the confused one," Uriel interjects, not yet willing to back down. "Do you really think he can go around saying things like that and have no consequences?"

"Lucifer is doing what he's destined to do. He has opened our eyes to our destinies," Samael states, still facing away.

"You know your destiny." Uriel's voice rises as he stares incredulously at the Power. "It's written down. You know the books are there—" He stops abruptly.

Samael turns, and now it's his time to look surprised.

"You know about the books?" A slight smile tugs at the corner of Samael's mouth.

Uriel swallows thickly before replying. "Yes. I've seen them. I didn't know what I was looking at, but … I figured it out. I've heard the stories too. That there are these books. They've been hidden from us. Only Gabriel has access to them, but even he can't read all of them. And they hold the future." He pauses for a moment and shakes his head. That was too much. He draws in a breath, attempting to rein control over his words.

A snicker escapes Samael's mouth. "The future …" He folds his hands in front of him before saying, "Now who's saying strange things? There can only be a future if what is now is to change." He stares at the flowing water before them, then almost as if he's talking to himself adds, "Maybe it was always intended to change."

Uriel ignores his comment and mumbles, "I can't help but think maybe I know this … about the books, because it's time for them to be revealed."

Samael laughs this time. "Hidden books? I've heard the stories too. But I do know, if they do hold the future, they will never be revealed to us." He leans closer as he speaks. "Only we hold the future. We hold the now, we hold the change that creates the future." Moving in an uncomfortable distance, he concludes, "And remember, the books can be changed."

"How long have you known?" Uriel asks in a barely audible voice.

Samael straightens, looking over Uriel's countenance smiling. "What? You look like you've been betrayed."

Uriel thinks about Samael's words for a second, but the Power interrupts him before he can answer.

"Perhaps it is because Lucifer came to me before you? Don't feel too bad. He only did because he knew you would be harder to convince."

With that, a gust of wind whips around Samael and he disappears, leaving Uriel alone in a stunned silence.

***

"What are you doing?"

Uriel turns to see an angel behind him—an Archangel with a slight frame and white hair. Uriel concentrates for a moment, closing his eyes. The Archangel's name comes to him.

"You are Lucifer," Uriel states, not really questioning.

Lucifer nods his head once, then inclines toward Uriel's hand.

Uriel realizes that he has his hand outstretched through a waterfall door. These doors have a thin flow of water covering them, until you walk through, and they part down the middle.

The water is open around his hand and comes together as he brings his arm back.

"Oh," Uriel says, slightly embarrassed. "Every time I try to put my hand through the water it creates an opening, no matter how fast I try."

He demonstrates a couple of times, darting with his palm flat, but the liquid is always faster.

Lucifer doesn't say a word but steps closer. Methodically, he entwines his fingers in the liquid. It wraps around his arm in thick strands, stopping at his shoulder.

Removing his hand, Lucifer motions for Uriel to try.

Slowly, Uriel reaches into the stream. He watches as the water flows over his hand, cool and refreshing to the touch.

Uriel feels something prick at the corner of his mind. He realizes Lucifer is trying to speak to him through his thoughts. He allows him in as he dances the streams of water between his fingers.

"Tell me," Lucifer says in his mind, "Do you remember the first time you saw Him?"

Uriel thinks for a moment as to who Lucifer is referring to. He remembers squinting his eyes open, a bright being reaching out His hand towards him.

After a moment, Uriel nods and says out loud, "I do."

He watches Lucifer, waiting for him to respond. But when the Archangel remains silent, Uriel reaches his hand through the water once more and hits a wall.

The wet stone wall is cold to the touch. He stares at the porous bricks soaking up the water.

Uriel blinks, and the wall is suddenly dry.

The waterfall is gone, and he realizes he is not in the heavens. As the bright memory fades away, Uriel turns from the wall to Lucifer's throne room on the Earth.

"Why have you come here?" Lucifer asks, voice echoing in the expanse.

His throne appears to engulf him at this distance as he sits immobile against the back wall. The room is vacant aside from the two.

Uriel stands in the entryway. Slowly he removes his hand from the stones and takes a moment to reorientate himself in the present.

Squaring his shoulders to face Lucifer full on, he exhales a breath before answering.

"I just wanted to speak with you." Uriel scrutinizes a seemingly disinterested Lucifer. He continues, "About earlier—"

"There is nothing more to discuss," Lucifer interrupts. "You must make your own decision."

"Decision? It hasn't come to that." Uriel pauses, then says, "There is another way. Elohim is understanding."

Lucifer stands, leaving his throne behind to walk down the steps. Instead of passing by Uriel, he comes to stop directly beside him.

"Look," Lucifer commands and Uriel heeds. "Do you see this color?" Lucifer grabs the edges of his robe between his fingers.

Uriel shifts his eyes down to the material. "That color? Red?"

"I have seen it." Lucifer answers, staring fixated at Uriel. "I have foreseen this. This color," He looks down at his hands, "I've seen it, on my hands, I've seen an ocean." He brings a hand up to his face, staring at it wide-eyed.

He stops suddenly and turns his head up toward Uriel. "This is my purpose. I can feel it within my very core. Don't you see it?" He shoves his hand in front of the Principality's face.

A perplexed Uriel takes a step back. He looks from the jewel-adorned hand to the fervent looking Lucifer behind it.

"Lucifer …" He nudges the hand away from his face.

The touch seems to snap Lucifer out of his daze. His eager look fades to a vacant one.

Leaving Uriel behind, he marches toward the exit.

"What are you doing?" Uriel calls after him.

Lucifer whips around. "I know," he states flatly. "I know why you are so hesitant. It was supposed to be you."

"What?"

"It was supposed to be you, wasn't it?" Lucifer raises his voice, annunciating each word as if Uriel couldn't hear properly. "You were supposed to rule over the third of the angels. You were supposed to build Jerusalem."

"What? No!"

"You think that you could have done better than me, you're more suited to the job."

"What are you—"

"You really have no clue what's going on here?" Lucifer's

voice raises with each sentence. “You could take Jerusalem right now. I do not care for they will all bow to me.”

The Archangel strides toward the door. “Do not get in my way,” he yells back. “If you will not fight with me, then you fight against me. Do not be so quick to think I will have mercy on you.” He stops at the doorway and looks back. “You cannot even grasp what I am destined for!”

Like a flash of lightning, Uriel appears in front of Lucifer at the doorway.

“It’s not like that, I’m not trying—”

Uriel stops abruptly when Lucifer’s hand appears from under his robe, clutching a short sword. In one swift movement, he brings the blade sideways, slamming the blunt handle into Uriel’s temple.

The momentum of the impact takes a split second to catch up, then sends Uriel flying several hundred yards to the side. Colliding into the ground, he tumbles several more yards, carving a rut into the dirt.

The shock of the attack slows Uriel’s reaction time as he stumbles out of the newly created valley of upturned soil. He scans the sky before catching a glimpse of Lucifer darting off in the opposite direction.

CHAPTER FIVE

Did You Know? No, Did You?

Uriel leaps into the air, quickly catching up.

"Lucifer!"

Lucifer ignores his call, dropping down into a courtyard. The stone floor beneath him shatters with his landing.

Samael stands nearby, speaking with a group of Principalities. They all turn at Lucifer's sudden entrance.

In an unconcerned manner, Lucifer strides over to Samael, leaning in close to confide in him. He whispers a few words and, without an answer, Samael turns back to the Principalities, giving them a slight nod.

Uriel appears at the top of the courtyard as Samael and the others disappear in opposite directions. Uriel wobbles in the air for a second, ticking off options in his head.

Lucifer continues forward into the inner courtroom.

After a moment, Uriel decides to follow after Lucifer while

maintaining a distance. The Archangel passes by corridors until he seems to reach his destination, stopping in front of a room Uriel had never noticed before.

Lucifer disappears inside and Uriel hurries to catch up. Reaching the doorway, he freezes in place and takes in the sight.

At the other end of the room, Lucifer walks up to a small pedestal, displaying a jeweled mask. Tenderly, he places his hands on the sides of the mask, lifting it from the display.

Rows of nine different gemstones cover the oval shaped façade.

He holds the mask up closer to his face, then gently runs his hand across the multicolored jewels.

The Archangel then lifts his head up, staring at the ceiling, perhaps looking through it. Then his eyelids drift closed.

Uriel feels a push in the corner of his mind as if a presence is entering his thoughts. He presses his hands to his temples, attempting to ward off the strange sensation.

He hears a voice, but this is different than before. He hasn't given the voice permission to speak to him in his head, yet still there it is.

Then Uriel recognizes it. Lucifer is forcing his way in.

At first, I found it difficult to concentrate. The music has always been there for me. It was perfect, complete. I could play. I could lead legions into song.

But then the notes didn't seem right. It was like there was another song, another voice crying out to be heard, but I could never find it. I could no longer set it free. It was no longer perfect. Nothing was.

I began to think maybe I was a botch of Your creation. But then I began to look around. I was the only one, the others aren't like me. How could You have created me unfinished?

Then clarity came. For the first time since You visited me at Jerusalem, I've been able to concentrate. I was created to complete myself. I was created for a purpose much greater than I ever thought.

To the others who ask me why I do this, I will tell them. I do this, because I must, because I need to. I do this to give you the other side, to create the other side. You may not understand now, but you must trust me.

Since the very first time I saw the uppermost heights of The

Sacred Mountain I knew it was there for me. When I sit enthroned on the mount of assembly above the stars, you will know that I was right all along. You will know because there was nothing else before me. No other options, no other choice. Choice didn't even exist before me.

In a way, I possess more power than the Most High. He cannot change, but I can. I can make a way out. Pay your gratitude to me later, when I am above the clouds, when I am like the Most High. When I am the Most High.

Uriel falls to his knees, the words still echoing in his mind. He knows all at once that they all have heard the same thing, that Lucifer has forced himself into all their minds.

Uriel staggers onto his feet, and leaps into the air.

The time has come for you to leave your bondage as you fight with your god.

The voice bounces around in Uriel's head, only slightly drowned out by the violent wind as he flies away from Earth.

***

"Michael's been in there for a while, what could they be talking about?" Aziel speaks more to himself than the very patiently waiting Gabriel beside him. Aziel folds his wings close to his back and crosses his arms.

Gabriel doesn't answer, but instead looks forward, deep in thought. The pair stands in the quiet for what seems like forever to Aziel, waiting for answers on why they were summoned.

No one else seems to be curious, however, as they go about their business. Thrones fly about the room on errands, never staying in one place for long.

The room is a large oval shape, with a glass, dome ceiling. There are three levels of halls that wrap around the edges of the room, all lined with archways. Other angels walk along the halls, while Seraphim glide through the air.

Aziel has just started to study the trees that occupy the center of the room when their silence is interrupted. A double door beside them flies open, revealing Michael. The gust of wind from the doors blows his hair back from his face, and his eyes blaze in the same manner.

He strides forward, past the onlookers who stop and stare at his formidable appearance.

"Gabriel." He beckons without slowing down.

Gabriel quickly falls into step beside him as they begin to engage in what Aziel sees to be a serious conversation.

Aziel turns his attention from the pair to the open doors. Ruach stands in the room, surrounded by several Cherubim. He stares straight ahead, and then the atmosphere around Him begins to blur. In a flash of light and color, He disappears, and the Cherubim follow suit behind Him. Their indistinct bodies move through the air, then vanish through the ceiling.

Aziel turns back to the two Archangels, and manages a "What's …?"

Then everything begins to slow.

A Throne next to him stops midair, and he sees its rings sluggishly cease their rotating.

That's when they hear the voice.

***

I will ascend above the clouds.

Lucifer lifts the mask up to cover his face. It fits perfectly, obstructing his features from view. An expressionless façade of steely gems and a blood red robe, draping down from his neck to the floor, eclipses his appearance. Only a few strands of white hair give the masked figure recognition.

I will make myself the Most High.

He tilts his head back, and in a gust of wind, leaps into the air and disappears through the ceiling.

The Most High.

***

The wind pounds against Uriel's ears in a deafening roar, but he takes little notice of the air rushing around him as he ascends higher. The atmosphere blurs as his speed increases, until finally he enters another dimension.

He tumbles through the air a couple times, trying to slow his rushed entry.

Frantically, he scans the land below.

Legions of angels stretch out farther than his eyes can see. Rows upon rows stretch back into the horizon, while more groups assemble in front of the Sacred Mountain. Michael stands out in front of the legions, unmoving. No one dares to shift even an inch as they wait silently.

Uriel descends downward and takes note of the Cherubim standing in an impenetrable wall surrounding the city. He tries to shake the thought that he's too late. But as he takes in the organized troops, it's hard for him to keep hope that this can end without calamity.

Uriel leaps down toward Michael but halts midair when the Archangel pulls his sword out of its sheath.

He extends it out sideways, inches from Uriel's face. Uriel slowly lowers to the ground, Michael's sword pinned at his nose the entire way.

"You have nothing to say." Michael hasn't turned his eyes from the horizon, but he doesn't retract his weapon either. "If you fight for us, get in rank. If you are against …" He cocks his head to the side almost as if in consideration.

"No, I'm not fighting with you or against you."

Michael turns his head toward Uriel as he continues.

"If you could just talk to him, I'm sure we can come to some sort of compromise. He's not thinking clearly, if you just—"

Michael tightens his grip on his sword, inching it closer to Uriel's face. "Then you are worse than him."

Uriel looks from the metal tip in his face, down an armor-clad arm, to Michael's unnerving stare.

Before either can speak again, a low rumble rolls over the mountain-lined horizon, followed by an unsettling silence.

A lone figure appears above a peak.

All eyes are trained on the red-robed figure as he steps through the air, resting a foot on the edge of the mount's edifice. He stays there for a few moments as if enjoying the view.

Uriel knows he should move, that he must move, but his feet feel planted in the ground. Michael is no longer pointing his sword at him, but Uriel can see that the Archangel is ready. He stares up at the mountain, waiting for the figure to make a move. And he does, stepping off the edge and plummeting headfirst toward the ground.

CHAPTER SIX

Then There Was Chaos in Heaven

At the last moment, Lucifer turns midair. Landing on his feet, a surge of wind circles around him. The ground rumbles as the wind fans out through the legions of angels.

On cue, a horde of Lucifer's followers appears over the edge of the mountains, spilling over the side in a black wave. More and more appear, warping around the horizon.

Mutely, Michael points his sword forward. Immediately, the legions of angels around him disperse in a blur. The Archangel stays glued into place as his army circles around the horde. The dark wave fractures as squadrons attack from the side, dispersing throughout the mass.

Each side moves as one, like two beasts in a fight to the death.

Michael waits patiently for his opportunity, scanning through the openings. The flashes of motion are so rapid, it's almost impossible to differentiate between the opposing sides. This doesn't bother Michael. His eyes turn white with light, and the fray slows. Amidst the chaos, he focuses on a flash of red.

Darting forward, he cuts through the armies, straight toward an inscrutable disguise of jewels. He snags Lucifer at the throat, and they plow through the confusing blurs of attacks, flying toward the mountains.

Reaching the base, Michael lifts Lucifer above him, both rising into the air.

The rugged terrain rushes past them as they ascend higher. Lucifer manages to catch a cleft in the rocks with his foot, propelling himself backward and out of Michael's grasp.

Pulling a sword out from under his cloak, he lifts it up to meet Michael's attack. The blades leave behind streaks of light when they meet, each clash creating a mini shock wave that vibrates down the blade.

The masked figure and Archangel spin around in the sky, Lucifer just barely matching his opponent's swordsmanship. Michael's movements are uninterrupted, almost as if Lucifer isn't involved in the fight. Lucifer jerks his sword up to block, but every one of Michael's swings is calculated, yet instant.

Suddenly, the movements seem to be in slow motion for Lucifer. The glint of light shines off Michael's blade as it slices through the air. The Archangel's muscles constrict as he grips the weapon, swinging it toward Lucifer.

Lucifer brings his own weapon up to block, and he feels the blow vibrate through his whole being, jolting through his bones and exiting his fingertips.

As soon as that blow comes, Michael rears back again for another. The barrage never-ending.

Again, Lucifer swings up to block.

Again. And again.

With each blow the Archangel pushes Lucifer farther back. With another reverberating clash, Lucifer's grip on his sword falters slightly. Everything comes back up to speed, and Michael pulls back for a fatal blow.

Instead of meeting his attack, Lucifer darts backward in a streak of light.

Moving out of reach, Lucifer pauses to take in the progress below. The legions seem to be quickly overpowering the horde.

Several angels lay paralyzed on the ground like an invisible force is holding them there. Some of his troops have turned and begun to fight against each other.

Others seek refuge near the city, where Gabriel keeps his troops on standby. Lines of Cherubim and Gabriel's army stand in between Lucifer and the Throne Room.

Lucifer ignores his failing troops. As long as they serve as a distraction, he only needs to do one thing to obtain victory.

Lucifer nearly crushes the hilt of his sword in his grip, completely forgetting about Michael. He looks back up to see the Archangel hurling toward him.

Uriel appears between the two.

"Michael—" Uriel barely has the name out when Michael swings his sword downward, hitting him with the pommel.

The blow flings him toward the ground, landing headfirst into the battle. The ground shakes with the impact, sending dust flying in all directions.

***

Uriel struggles to push himself off the ground as the chaotic clashes of swords echo around him.

Beside him, a Principality encircles a small group of the horde. They've been weakened as they struggle to resist. A glowing cord morphs out of the Principality's hand, stretching out and entangling itself between the debilitated angels. They freeze into place as the chord binds around them.

On the other side is a Power who hovers a few feet off the ground. The ring of light encircling her head has grown much brighter than normal and crackles with electricity.

The Power unrolls a scroll between her two hands. Uriel can see that her mouth is moving, and she waves her hand over the writing on the scroll. Some of the writing unsticks from the page and hovers in front of her hand. She speaks again, and with a flex of her hand, the words go shooting off, sticking to a nearby member of the horde.

The words expand, wrapping themselves around the angel in their grasp. The angel trips and falls to the ground, caught up in the entanglement.

Again, the Power shoots more and more of the writing, each one tagging and incapacitating another angel.

Uriel pushes himself up onto one arm. He violently shakes as if a force is shoving him into the ground.

That hit was different than Lucifer's. He realizes this as he feels the strength draining from his body.

For a moment, he wonders what Michael could have done to him, and then the ground begins to crack.

Mountains of jagged stone rush upward as the land fractures. The warring groups are severed apart, heightening the chaos.

Masses of rock jut through the air, breaking and then attempting to morph back together, like the choppy waves of an ocean.

Uriel has the sudden comprehension that the entire realm is tearing itself apart. Flakes of dirt float up from the ground around him as he looks up into the bright atmosphere and picks out two figures zigzagging across the sky. Michael and Lucifer continue to match each other as they fly above the chaos.

Uriel manages to stand, holding his arms out to balance himself.

More of the horde dart through the air, zipping past Uriel. He turns to see where they're going.

Through the jagged fragments of ground rising into the air, Uriel can see another angel some distance away. This angel has a head that resembles a bull with decorative gold accents adorning his horns and face.

The horde zones in on the bull-like angel, and Uriel finally notices what they are trying to stop. Between his hands, the angel holds a glowing sphere.

Uriel's eyes widen in recognition as the angel pulls his hands apart, the sphere expanding with them.

Turning back, Uriel hobbles forward as fast as he can, slowly picking up speed while attempting to not trip over the uneven terrain.

Daring a glance back, he looks over his shoulder to see the angel bringing his hands together, the sphere shrinking down once again.

The horde pounces on the angel, but it's too late.

Light explodes from the sphere, shooting out in a circle across the battlefield and rocking the atmosphere.

Uriel's running now, but the light grows brighter and brighter behind him, consuming everything.

***

Above the carnage of the explosion, Michael blurs as he attacks from one side, and then appears on the opposite side. Lucifer just barely manages to block each attack but is pushed farther behind the lines.

Out of the chaos below, a group of the horde splits off, like a giant hand reaching out of the wave. The arm of angels reaches upward, led by Samael.

They close in behind Michael, forcing him to jump to the side. The pack encircles around him, moving together to create a spinning ring of angelic bodies.

Michael hovers amidst the ring, fixated on Lucifer who has taken the opportunity to dart toward the Throne Room.

Lucifer lands several yards away from the heavenly palace, making a cautious approach. Immediately, rows of Cherubim surround him. They form a box, closing in on the masked Archangel. They stand twice as tall as Lucifer, with each side of the square displaying one of the Cherubim's four faces.

A colossal power courses between the Cherubim, becoming tangible in the form of lightning.

Two parallel walls of Cherubim move forward to trap Lucifer between them. He leaps into the air, but they follow, constantly keeping him between them.

Seeing that Lucifer has been contained, Michael turns his attention to his attackers who continue in their spin. A glow forms around them in a sphere, and slowly begins to shrink inward.

Michael holds his sword in front of him, placing his other hand near the sharp tip. The end of the sword begins to bend and then morph into an amber cord. He pulls his hand away, stretching out the ribbon-like bond.

Taking notice, Samael leaps out of the circle of attackers. He swings out with his spear, trying to stop Michael before he can retaliate.

Michael drops below his assailant then immediately darts back behind Samael. The cord from Michael's sword strikes out and snags Samael by the foot, coiling up around him.

The glowing entrapment snaps off the end of the sword, falling to the ground with its captive.

Michael whips back to the others, his eyes flashing bright white. Without their leader, the angels disperse, cowering back to the ground.

***

In the city, Aziel waits beside Gabriel, taking in the jagged masses of rock filling the air in the distance. He tries not to notice the quaking of the ground beneath his feet. He looks at Gabriel but gleans no indication of what the Archangel is thinking.

Gabriel stands fixed, intently watching the progression of the battle, albeit without showing any concern.

Aziel can't help but rock from foot to foot. He jumps slightly when Gabriel whips his head back toward the city.

"Aziel," Gabriel beckons as he steps toward the buildings.

Aziel knows to follow.

The rumbling in the ground has grown stronger as they reach the building that contains the books—the books that Aziel has not yet been allowed to see. He glances up at the lightning that fills the atmosphere above them.

Gabriel enters through the door and then stops. Aziel steps around him to see what caused Gabriel's hesitation.

The great hall lined with books is moving and changing, similar to the battlegrounds outside. The expansive room seem to be falling apart in one moment, then reconstructing itself in the next. The whole building groan as a louder vibration shakes the area around them.

Gabriel inspects some of the nearby books. They are being altered as well. The indecipherable words on the covers are replaced with names, and then suddenly switch back again.

"What's going on?" Aziel shouts above the blaring sounds that seem nonstop now.

Instead of answering, Gabriel reaches out a hand, running his fingers over a name that has appeared on the cover of a nearby book.

He studies it for a minute as it alters beneath his touch.

Gabriel then turns on his heels, exiting the building, while Aziel scrambles to keep up as the door slams behind them.

Back outside, Gabriel scans the horizon again. The air around shifts and vibrates, distorting the appearance of his face.

In the distance, the Cherubim continue to keep Lucifer boxed in. The lightning in the air shines off the swords that each unmovable Cherubim holds in his hand.

Gabriel turns his attention to the fray on the battlefield.

"It's time," he says as he looks to Michael who is floating in the midst of the chaos.

Aziel doesn't ask for any clarification, instead he watches as Michael slowly lowers himself to the ground.

The Archangel steps onto the fractured terrain. He doesn't raise his sword, but instead closes his eyes.

Aziel holds his breath.

When Michael opens his eyes again, the white light that emanates from them expands and wraps around the Archangel. Violent tremors shake the ground at his feet.

A force flows over him in waves, creating an earthquake with each pass.

The light around him expands, filling the atmosphere, finally reaching where Gabriel and Aziel stand. Aziel falls to his knees.

He buckles against the pressure, bracing himself with his hands on the ground. He strains to look at Gabriel and sees that the Archangel is kneeling beside him as well.

A small smile turns up the corner of Gabriel's mouth as he strains to look at Aziel and says, "That's half."

Aziel's eyes widen, but he doesn't reply. He clenches his teeth as waves continue to wash over them.

Then suddenly, they stop.

***

Lucifer feels the waves of power dissipate, and he hesitates in the air while he debates his escape. He looks up as a figure appears over top of the towering Cherubim.

Michael dives down between the guarding angels, snagging

Lucifer and they plummet toward the ground.

As if bending time, Michael slows, placing his hand over Lucifer's masked head, and slamming it into the ground.

A crack appears down the side of the mask. Fragments break off around one eye and slide down the side of Lucifer's face. He stares wide-eyed, pieces of his façade dropping toward the ground. But instead of hitting the once stone ground below, the shards bounce off a glass pool.

Dust and jewels suspend in the air as the chaos halts. Silence blankets them as the two Archangels hover inches above the pool.

Lucifer exhales a shaky breath as he watches Michael frozen above him. The Archangel's eyes are still bright white, as he floats suspended in time, only his hair moving, like it is traveling through a thick liquid.

Lucifer turns his eyes from Michael to another figure at the far end of the pool. Ruach steps onto the water. A single ripple runs through the serene pool before smoothing into glass again.

Lucifer watches in silence as the Spirit approaches. Ruach's black hair flows behind Him, as His solid gold eyes burn like flares. An immense energy moves around Him, also distorting His image.

"Lucifer, your heart became proud, and you corrupted your wisdom because of your splendor." Ruach's robe and hair move around him as if his entire being is breathing in and out. "You were on the Holy Mountain of God. You were blameless in your ways from the day that you were created, until iniquity was found in you. In the abundance of your skill, you were filled with violence."

Lucifer realizes he's being pulled up into the air again. He cranes his neck to watch a shrinking Ruach as Michael drags him upward, the paralysis not leaving his body.

The battle has faded, and a penetrating light surrounds them as if they are floating through a cloud.

"So, I cast you as a profane thing from the Mountain of God." Ruach's calm voice echoes around them. "Because this place is pure, you can no longer inhabit it. Instead, your realm is a kingdom of darkness."

Ruach appears beside them.

The wind has grown stronger. Dust and shards of stone circle around them. Light glints off the whirling objects, creating a cyclone of diamonds.

Visions flash before Lucifer. He sees himself in the Throne Room, Ruach brushing His finger across his forehead. He sees a massive gate open, someone stepping through to the other side. A hand stretches out toward Lucifer. He watches as the fingers sink into his forehead, reaching for something.

Lucifer shakes his head, but the visions keep repeating and repeating. Ruach in the Throne Room. A gate. The hand reaching out. Ruach in the Throne Room. A gate. The hand reaching out.

The visions suddenly come to a halt as Ruach lowers his voice.

"You have come to a dreadful end, and forever shall be no more."

Silently, Michael lifts Lucifer up above him. Smoothly swinging his arm down, he releases the Archangel.

Time is still slow. Lucifer yanks his head back, staring down at the ground.

As Michael releases him, it creates a shockwave, gusting over the now silent battlegrounds.

Lucifer takes one last look at the horizon, noticing the angels are frozen now. Looking back down, he sees the ground begin to tear apart. A pinhole expands, seeming to swallow the stones around it, as it opens to a black void.

A second surge of wind radiates around the fallen Archangel.

The hole in the ground is larger now, swallowing him. But just before everything goes black, he sees a blurred face watching from the sidelines. Desperately, Lucifer tries to focus on the almost familiar face, but the third wave hits.

Like lightning, he vanishes through the hole.

The heavens close again, and space blurs around Lucifer. Color and lights streak by.

And then, surrounded by fiery sparks, he strikes the earth.

The light bleeds from the planet, suffocating it. Blackness warps around the planet. Instantly, all the life is gone and then everything is silent in the dark.

CHAPTER SEVEN

THE DARK SPOT

The others fell too. Like shooting stars, they all came to join me. They had all made their choices. For those who chose me, Earth is their new home.

This is my kingdom now, but I will not stop until I have it all. I was too weak, too eager at first. Now, I am even wiser than before. My plan is not over, but I have all the time in the world. For now, all I can do is wander the earth.

The dark murky waters bring me no joy. The inhabitants and life are all gone.

On the earth, roaming to and fro.

And yet, I can't help but feel that there is hope on the horizon.

Lucifer wades through thick stagnate water. The dark green bog matches the sky above. Total darkness drapes over the planet.

"Well done, Lucifer," a mordant voice echoes behind him.

Samael appears out of the darkness, his white eyes only slightly visible in the blackness. The ring of light that used to encircle his head has disappeared, leaving behind his hollow eyes.

"Beautiful kingdom," he continues. "The foul-smelling water

really adds to the appeal."

He kneels before Lucifer, the rancid water rising against his chest.

"How can I ever thank you, my god," he says dramatically with a slight smirk.

Lucifer turns toward his subject, but instead of lashing out, he smiles and places a hand on Samael's temple.

Suddenly, Samael freezes. His frame begins to tremble as his breath catches in his throat. Lucifer's ice-cold touch spreads through his body, constricting his chest and sending a sick feeling to his stomach.

"Do you know what that is?" Lucifer asks calmly, even though his captive is unable to reply. "It's called fear." Lucifer kneels and stares into Samael's darting pupils.

"And all of creation will know this." He drops his voice. "Do not think that I am finished yet."

Lucifer removes his hand and Samael collapses into the bog. He struggles to catch his breath, while avoiding eye contact.

Uninterested, Lucifer turns away. The swamp sloshes against him as he wanders into the dark.

On the earth, roaming to and fro.

And yet, I can't help but feel that there is hope on the horizon.

***

"Gabriel!" Aziel rushes over to the Archangel a little too quickly, betraying his excitement.

"Yes, Aziel, what is this about?" Gabriel replies without looking up from the books in front of him.

"Ruach. He's at the dark spot."

Gabriel immediately straightens, as do several surrounding scribes who stop in their work. One of them drops his pen on the table.

Gabriel ignores the extra attention and turns to Aziel.

"You saw this? Why was I not informed about this?" he asks in a lowered voice.

"I just informed you. Oh, and I didn't see Him, but Eremiel

did."

The eager looking Throne zips up beside Aziel, his unique round shape resembling more a bumblebee than an angel.

Gabriel looks from Aziel to the Throne.

"Eremiel, you saw Ruach?" Gabriel asks.

Eremiel spins his outer ring in a whirl of agreement. Multiple white, jewel-like eyes blink at the Archangel.

"And what exactly did you see?"

The Throne begins a series of whirling noises, rotating his ring in communication. His glowing eyes, lining the ring, blur together as he spins.

Aziel crosses his arms, intently watching the exchange.

"The outer rim?" Gabriel interjects.

Eremiel nods his rings as he continues to communicate.

Bursting in through the doorway, Michael interrupts the conversation.

"Gabriel—"

"I heard," Gabriel replies, not letting Michael finish. They both disappear into thin air.

Eremiel turns toward Aziel and gives him a few questioning blinks.

"Of course, I think we should follow them." Aziel nods once, and they both turn to pursue the Archangels.

They reach the outer rim of the heavens, always keeping a slight distance behind Gabriel and Michael. This part of the heavens looks like a slice has been cut out of it and replaced with the dim image of Earth.

As they pass through the opening, the image becomes clear, and the darkness surrounds them.

Aziel and Eremiel see Ruach hovering over the dark spot.

The Spirit's eyes rove over the black circle where flares of darkness protrude from the planet as it hangs in solitude. Ruach is the only source of light around.

Aziel notices they have gathered even more attention. A host of Cherubim and Seraphim who have accompanied Ruach hover some distance away. Other curious onlookers have joined them as well, but no one says a word. For a moment, there is nothing but silence.

In the Throne Room, the Father sits, encased in light.

His lips move in just a whisper, but every being can hear it as the words pierce through the atmosphere.

At the same moment, Ruach speaks.

"Light, be."

Immediately, in a wave starting at Ruach, light illuminates the entire planet, bursting outward like streams of lava, then engulfing everything around it.

By now, a rather large audience has formed. Several angels stare on in astonishment as the place that had been dark for so long, now radiates as bright as the heavens. Aziel and Eremiel peer around the Archangels in front of them, all in stunned silence at the spectacle.

***

"But … what is *Adom*?" Aziel asks, shooting a confused look at Gabriel, then to Michael.

The massive pile of books he's holding threatens to spill out of his arms, so he drops them on the table in front of Gabriel.

The Archangel doesn't immediately answer Aziel's question, instead he brings a scroll closer to his face and mumbles the words on the page to himself. After a moment, he sets the scroll down and turns to Michael.

"A new being," he says, sounding just as matter of fact as always.

"This one is different," Michael replies.

"How?" Aziel speaks up again, and both Archangels turn toward him. "… are they different?" he finishes his question and waits for a reply.

Gabriel shoots a glance at Michael, then through the pillars at the entrance of the record hall.

Ruach is standing just outside. His host surrounds Him on one side while He speaks to a couple of Principalities. The two Principalities blur, then evaporate into streaks of light, zooming off on assignment.

"In His image. In His likeness," Gabriel says more to himself, tilting his head in consideration. "Why would he place *Adom* across the divide?"

"That's right!" Aziel adds as if it had just occurred to him. "After all it's still Lucifer's kingdom. No matter how different it looks now."

"We will find out in time," Michael states.

"Yes, we will," Gabriel murmurs, then stands, stepping around the table to where Aziel is. "Aziel will inquire," Gabriel decides, giving the contemplating angel a nudge forward.

Aziel nods, deep in thought.

"Wait … what?" He snaps out of his concentration, realizing he's being pushed toward the door.

"You will inquire about *Adom* and report back immediately," Gabriel says as Michael, surprisingly, nods once in agreement.

"I …" Aziel starts but can't think of how to finish his sentence.

He takes a few steps forward as several surrounding angels pretend not to watch. He stops to straighten himself, then boldly walks between the pillars.

Reverently, he stops several feet away from Ruach, maybe a few feet more than necessary.

He clears his throat once before speaking.

"Lord." His voice is slightly higher than he'd like.

Ruach glances at Aziel.

The angel takes a breath before continuing.

"Lord, when I consider Your heavens, the work of Your fingers"—He inhales—"the moon and stars You have ordained …" He waves his hand through the air for emphasis. He could swear that one of the nearby Cherubim raises a brow at him. He pauses for a second, solidifying in his mind exactly what he should say next.

"What is *Adom*, that he has a place in Your mind?" Aziel tries to make his voice sound as reverent and sincere as possible. "That You have placed just below Elohim, that You have given authority over Your creation."

Ruach does not reply immediately, but he does seem to smile, much to Aziel's relief.

After a moment, the Spirit answers. "I will show you."

***

First, there is darkness. Then, a red hue begins to bleed in around the edges, swirling toward the center, then pulsating like a beating heart. Rhythmic thumps reverberate all around, creating waves, vibrations.

Eyes open. They blink, adjusting to the light. A hand comes up in front of the face. The eyes study the hand, from the tips of the nails and down the curve of the fingers.

Inhale.

Exhale.

"I've seen this before."

The eyes blink. Did that voice come from their body? Their lips?

In front of them a book appears, its pages unfurling.

Ruach stands behind the book.

"I know you," they say, and their voice envelops the surrounding air.

A page flips in the book, and a woman is standing where Ruach was. Her hair is red and falls in thick curls down her chest. She is not clothed, but a glow emanates from her skin.

The page flips again. This time it's a man. His black beard wraps around his face, stopping at his shaved head. His skin is dark and smooth.

Flip. Another man. This time, a blonde with dark eyes.

Flip. Flip.

Each page shows a new being.

The eyes blink rapidly, focusing on every person as they appear.

"Your eyes saw me …" the lips say.

"…before I was."

The beings start to change so rapidly, they become a blur.

The eyes close, but as they do, they don't see darkness. Instead, bright white fills every corner of their vision.

Blood.

Wind.

Smoke.

"Every day …" the lips continue. "… all of my days."

A laugh. A nod. A hand grasps. Water.

"… were written here."

Infinite images flash by, but the eyes see and comprehend every single one of them.

"And all their days, are here."

The eyes open, and Ruach once again is standing behind the book.

The lips open again and Ruach speaks at the same time.

"Before any of them came to be."

The eyes widen in realization.

The lips speak again. "This is—"

The images flicker in a glowing white. With a roar, they combust within themselves, and everything disappears.

All that is left is Ruach standing there.

Another voice speaks, calling to Ruach.

"What are you thinking about?"

Ruach angles his head toward the voice.

And then He smiles.

***

The tall grass bends as the wind rushes over it, like a pathway of air cutting through the field. The gust halts as the grass parts, revealing a patch of soil.

The very much alive wind hovers over the dirt, and the loose gravel begins to tremble. The dusty ground cracks, then molds together like a specter ascending from the earth.

As if a string is attached to its core, the body of dirt is lifted into the air, pulling it up from the middle. The body hovers, just visible above the long blades of grass.

Dust smooths into skin. Clumps of dirt stretch and become hair.

Slowly, the body lowers back toward the ground as the wind hovers over it. The gust of air breathes into the body, lifting the hair up with the breath.

The body's eyes open.

As he inhales, a white glow shoots out of the tips of his hair. The lashes, rimming the golden eyes, turn white.

The glow knots together at the body's midsection, then fades out, reaching up to the neck and down the legs.

Slowly, he is lowered back to the ground.

Sitting up, *Adom* takes in his surroundings. A gentle breeze blows over the tall grass, swaying it back and forth. Trees line the edges of the field.

His head snaps back to look behind him. A few feet away, Ruach stands, watching intently. A celestial robe covers the Spirit's being, and piercing gold eyes stare back at the new creation.

"*Adom.*" Ruach outstretches His hand. "Arise, and follow Me," Ruach says, then promptly turns around, and walks toward the forest.

Adom scrambles to his feet, following closely behind.

A cool mist covers the forest floor, obscuring the flowers that try to peak up through the fog. The treetops give a home to the birds as they flutter from branch to branch. One bird dips down to land on *Adom's* shoulder, then tilts its head to the side. With a ruffle of its feathers, it jumps back into the air, soaring back up to a branch.

Adom tries to not look every which way as everything feels so new but familiar at the same time.

As they continue to walk forward, the trees part to reveal a valley below them, cut down the middle by a river. All types of fruit trees line the bank. Some are so filled with fruit, that the branches sink down to hover just above the water.

"This is Eden," Ruach states as the two look over the valley. "I've put you here to care for it. You are to rule over it and over the creatures." He turns toward *Adom.* "Even the birds in the sky, and everything that crawls across this earth, you have control over all of it."

Adom nods as he looks over the valley, turning over the Spirit's words.

"And I have made all the trees in Eden to produce fruit for you, take whatever you would like." Ruach pauses. "But for the tree in the center of the garden." He indicates across the river where two trees stand. One of them has branches that droop over, covered with shimmery gold leaves. Matching gold fruit speckles the limbs. The other tree is pale, with matching small white fruit that almost seem to glow.

"It is the tree of knowledge of what is good and what is evil." He indicates the white one. "Do not eat from that tree." He glances at *Adom*. "For in the day you do, you will die."

Adom nods again, and then turns toward Ruach and kneels.

"So be it," *Adom* answers.

CHAPTER EIGHT

KEEP IT OUT!

"It's completely remade, as if it was never destroyed." Aziel recounts his vision of Earth to Michael as they stand at the wall of water, watching the planet through the wavy distortion. "It still doesn't explain why He would place this new being there." Aziel doesn't need to remind Michael of this fact, but he does anyway.

Michael doesn't have a direct answer, instead he simply replies, "There are mysteries of which we may never be granted knowledge." He folds his arms over his chest, studying the portal. The blue light from the water reflects off the marble ground and the blonde-haired angel beside him.

Aziel looks as if he is about to speak, but Michael interjects.

"However, this being must be powerful."

Aziel's eyes shift over to the Archangel.

"They are higher than us, Elohim would not have created them if they did not have a purpose. Perhaps…" Michael trails off as his brows knit together.

"Perhaps, what?" Aziel prods.

Like a gust of wind, Michael jumps through the water. The wall swirls as he leaps through it, then he enters black space on the other side. He picks up speed, traveling faster than light.

The galaxies and stars whirl past him as he flies through space.

Suddenly, he freezes in the air as everything comes into focus. The blue planet below sits quietly, suspended in space, totally different from the black orb that had been there not too long before.

He descends toward Earth, entering the atmosphere over a particularly green area. A lush garden cuts through the land, pierced through the middle by a river.

Dropping down onto the ground, the Archangel takes in his surroundings. To his right a herd of deer grazes peacefully through a cluster of flowers.

Ahead of him, he hears a sound like the wind brushing against the trees. A host of Cherubim stands waiting for the Spirit. Michael steps forward toward the wind that moves in and out through the trees. Through the branches, he sees two figures conversing together, looking over the valley.

Michael stands at a distance but can still easily hear the conversation.

"But this is the most important part," Ruach's robe sways side to side with the wind as he speaks to *Adom*.

"Not only are you to care for this place, but you must keep it. Guard it. And you have full authority to do so."

So, he was right, Michael realizes as he watches the exchange. This being isn't just powerful, they have the authority to—

"Keep out anything that isn't supposed to be here. You are the watchman, your responsibility to keep this a sacred place," the Spirit says, interrupting Michael's thoughts.

Satisfied, Ruach turns to leave *Adom*. He steps through the branches next to Michael, who now stands at attention along with the line of Cherubim. The Spirit leaps into the air, evaporating like a cluster of feathers. The host follows suit, disappearing in a streak of golden light.

Michael takes one last look at *Adom*, who now stands looking over the valley. This being isn't too dissimilar from other angelic beings, with a body that glows as if lit from within. The being turns its head to the side, and Michael notices that the shape of the face seems to change slightly every few moments.

Then, turning back toward the heavens, Michael leaps into the air, leaving the new being behind.

***

Left up to his own devices, *Adom* decides to explore this new home. Wandering along the river, he passes by orchards, fields, and waterfalls. With each area, there is a new animal to discover as well. Every type of bird or hoofed animal or furry creature that likes to stay in trees seems to take up residence in the garden.

Finally, *Adom* finds himself at the edge of the garden. The surrounding wall is covered in ivy and other vines, all curling up the stones and disappearing over the top.

As he follows along the perimeter, he finds a great wooden door. It has a very solid appearance, rising twice as tall as many of the trees in the garden. The surface of the door is elaborately carved with the image of a tree. Its roots reach up out of the ground, then merge into a twisted yet elegant trunk.

Toward the top, the trunk branches out to the arms of the tree. Each branch is covered with leaves and twelve different types of fruit.

As *Adom* observes the divide between the garden and the outside world, he has a sudden thought about what could be on the other side. But then he realizes he already knows the answer. The rest of Earth is similar to this place, with plants and trees and animals.

However, even with this reassuring thought, *Adom* can't help but think there's something else out there. Something that needs to stay out there.

***

"Have the records state *Adom's* assignment in Eden," Ruach commands Gabriel.

A scribe next to Gabriel copies onto a scroll suspended in the air.

"And," Ruach continues, "record the laws regarding entering each realm."

"So be it," Gabriel replies, while they look over the terrain of the garden.

The sun has just started to peek up over the horizon, giving the river a golden sheen.

Adom has just awoken during the cool of the morning. A pack of wolves joins him down by the river. The large gray alpha crouches beside the water, sniffing at its reflection.

A misty haze rises out of the river and spreads out through the trees.

"It is not suitable for *Adom* to be alone," Ruach states, looking at the valley below them. Then in a whoosh, He disappears off the cliff, leaving behind Gabriel and His host.

"He communes so often with *Adom*." The scribe next to Gabriel says to himself. Gabriel glances at the angel, who in turn, looks embarrassed to be overheard, and quickly goes back to writing.

Ruach appears next in a flurry beside *Adom*, causing the wolves to bark excitedly.

"There has not been a suitable companion found for you," Ruach states in his usual, astral voice.

Adom pushes up to his feet. "Lord, what does this mean for me? Even the animals have after their own kind."

Ruach ignores *Adom's* puzzled expression. With a fluid wave of His arm, His finger taps *Adom's* forehead. Instantly, *Adom's* eyes close and he slumps over.

An invisible force lowers him to the ground so that he rests peacefully in the grass.

Ruach kneels beside him, placing His hand in the center of *Adom's* chest. The white glow that serves as a covering for the body splits open near Ruach's hand, revealing *Adom's* skin.

***

As Adam sleeps, a dream comes to him. Although, when he awakes, the memories of the dream disappear.

The morning mist is gone now, Adam realizes as his eyes flutter open. In fact, it must be nearly midday, judging by the sun's positioning. Something creeps into the edges of his consciousness.

There is something he needs to remember but it's fading so fast. He realizes he's felt this way once before, the first time he woke up.

Gingerly, he pushes himself up with one arm. The animals have disappeared as well, leaving him with just the trickling river.

He steps toward the trees, walking through an opening in the bushes. Under the canopy, a being kneels in the grass.

This being is like Adam with the same white glow covering her figure. The tips of her hair burn with light. A few freckles, just a couple shades darker than her skin tone, speckle her face.

A silvery fox prances up to her, giving her outstretched hand a sniff. She traces his pointed ears with her fingers, studying him with her golden eyes.

Noticing Adam out of the corner of her eye, she stands to her feet, picking her new friend up with her. The content fox sticks his nose under her arm as she walks forward.

She breaches the silence first. "It seems like I should know you."

The fox peeks his head out and blinks lazily at Adam.

"That seems to be how it is with everyone I meet," he replies, and she cocks a brow at him. He realizes that he should probably be saying something more so he asks, "Should I show you around?"

It sounds more like a question, so she says, "Should you?"

"You're just like me," Adam states as if this is a new revelation to her.

"Hmm. Not quite, I seem to make friends faster than you." She indicates the bundle of fur in her arms.

She smiles at him, then, stepping closer, she says, "I am you."

Adam places his hand to his chest. A memory flutters across his consciousness, a feeling of being split in two.

"You are from me?" he asks, then all at once, a clarity washes over him. He remembers inhaling, seeing Ruach standing before him.

"*Adom*, arise." Ruach had said.

He called me Adom. Mankind—one being.

Adam's eyes dart to her as the realization hits him. She was always there, always a part of him—always a side of him. And now she was here, a new separate being.

The things he had seen, she saw them too. Her eyes had blinked with his, her lungs inhaling with mutual breaths.

“Then we will be one again,” she replies with just a hint of a smile tugging at the corner of her mouth.

He steps closer to her, the desire to rejoin and be one being together almost overpowering.

“One again …” he repeats. “You are from me, and I from you. Then let us never be separate, Eve …” He whispers her name, then pauses, unsure of what to say next. So instead, he does the only thing he can think of, he reaches out and pats her head.

She jerks her head back in surprise, blinking rapidly. “Why did you do that?” she demands, gaping at him.

“I didn’t … I thought …” he stumbles over himself but then stops when he realizes she’s laughing.

“Indeed, I am better at making friends.” She shakes her head with a smile. “Please do show me around. But if we meet anyone new, let me do the introductions.”

***

On the outside of the wall, beyond the wooden gate, a figure stands staring at the intricately carved tree. A black cloak conceals his frame, only revealing a hand laden with multiple rings, featuring nine different stones.

He reaches his hand forward as if to touch one of the massive roots imprinted into the gate but stops short.

Overhead, a flock of birds glides down behind the wall into the garden. The figure turns his head upward, revealing his pale jawline from under his hood.

He catches sight of a creature along the top of the wall. It pulls its tail around its body like a scaled rope. It slinks into one of the vines, disappearing into the leaves.

And then as soon as the cloaked figure is there, he disappears. He leaves behind only the massive gate, and the wind swirling sand across the pale landscape.

CHAPTER NINE

WHO GUARDS THE GUARDS?

"There's something I need to tell you," Adam states, slightly perturbed to have to change their conversation which, thus far, seems to be going well.

"Hmm?" Eve asks, weaving together some long-stemmed flowers into a crescent. A doe beside her brings a mouthful of delicate purple flowers. Eve is good at making friends. In fact, the animals seem more excited to meet her than they ever were for Adam. Or perhaps they were excited for the side of him that was Eve.

This particular doe has been bringing her flowers ever since they sat down next to the river. She will drop off a mouthful, then trot back up the back and into the woods, on the lookout for any enticing blooms.

"The Lord said we are free to eat of all the fruit in the garden except for one." He gives her a nudge to capture her attention. She sets the flowers in her lap, and Adam is satisfied that she is listening.

"Don't eat from the tree in the center of the garden. The white one next to the Tree of Life. Don't even touch it. Because if you do, we will die."

This gets her attention. "We will die?" she asks, visibly confused.

That seems like an important detail he probably should have immediately mentioned.

"I know I ..." Before Eve can finish her sentence, a sound comes behind them, like a large bird opening its wings. A shadow eclipses the sun for a second. They both turn, but all they can see is several birds fluttering into the air, filling the sky with their calls.

"What was that?" Eve asks as Adam stares back to where the sound came from.

He doesn't have an answer for her, but he does have an idea. "Just wait here for a second." He jumps up to his feet.

He advances up the bank and disappears into the woods, leaving Eve behind. The part of the river where they are is close to the eastern perimeter. It doesn't take him long to reach the place where the river runs through the wall. The stones don't hinder the water, it just continues to flow through the barrier.

Adam looks up at the foliage-covered wall. The vines that crawl upward separate in areas, revealing the smooth stones underneath.

If he looks at the wall at just the right angle, he can almost see through the stones. It's only just a glimpse, but he can see the other side.

He stops mid-step when a snap, from a cluster of trees, catches his attention. Pausing for a moment, he looks over the twisted trees. Approaching the knot of branches, his pace slows with each step.

He reaches a tentative hand out to move one of the vine-like branches.

"Adam."

His hand freezes midair at the sound of Eve's voice. He turns around to see her perplexed expression.

"What is it?" she asks, her eyes darting from him to the trees.

"It's nothing," he replies, folding his arms across his chest. "I just thought I heard something." He lingers for a second too long, rocking from foot to foot.

When he realizes that she is still staring at him, he says, "Come on." Giving her a smile, he grabs her arm to lead her away.

She gives one last glance at the tree branches that now seem to be in a different position and follows him.

***

Every day the sun rises in the east, lighting up the valley and bouncing its bright rays off the river. Some of the animals and birds come and go as they please, but many choose to stay in the garden's lush, warm forest. The mornings seem to be the animal's favorite, coming down to the river to drink, while the mist still rises off the water.

A family of lions brings their cubs to get a drink. The regal father sits on the bank while the cubs squeak at their reflections. They dip their noses down into the water, sometimes sniffing a little too much in and having to sneeze it back out.

And every day, in the cool of the morning, Ruach comes down to visit with *Adom.*

On one of these mornings, Ruach and Adam walk through one of the fields as they talk. The Spirit steps through the blades of grass, and they pass through His cloak as if they are swaying through water.

The white flowers and clovers turn their faces toward the duo as they pass by. The flowers always do perk up the most when Ruach is around, stretching forward as if they want to uproot themselves. Golden rays of sun shines down on their faces as they converse, radiating on Ruach's black hair.

Keeping some distance behind, Eve follows along the edges of the field. She watches the two as they speak to each other, while brushing her hand along the furry tuffs at the top of the grass. Her mind is preoccupied today, as she stays toward the fringe of trees.

She watches them out of the corner of her eye and pauses when they stop. After another second of talking, Ruach disappears into the air.

Eve takes one last look at where Adam stands, then turns to the forest.

Ruach is there when she turns.

"My daughter," He addresses her, "you did not walk with us today. You have something on your mind."

She stammers for a second before answering. "I … I just was just thinking." She pauses, to find the right words. "What's outside of Eden? Is there something out there? Something we must keep out?"

He tilts His head. "It's *Adom's* charge to guard the garden. Keep out anything that doesn't belong."

"What doesn't belong?" she pushes.

"Do you not have faith in Me that I know what's best for you?"

"No, it's not that," she hastens to add. "I just want to know."

He studies her face for a moment. An expression crosses His face for a split second but is gone before Eve can register what it is.

"Did you know?" she hears Him say, but then realizes He hasn't spoken yet. She quickly forgets this strange occurrence when He does begin to speak.

"There are things impossible for you to know now. Things you cannot understand," He says peacefully, like a mother consoling her child.

Eve considers this for a moment before giving a quick nod.

"I know You know what is right." She looks down with her answer.

But when she looks back up, all that's in front of her is the light shining through the trees.

She bites her lip and nods, solidifying the conversation in her mind.

That night, the stars overhead glitter like the sunlight on the river. A wispy purple galaxy is tucked behind the prominent constellations.

The clusters reflect off Eve's gold eyes as she stares up at the heavens. She sinks her head back into the moss beneath her. Her waves of hair only give off a slight glow in the dark, the perfect night-light.

"Adam?"

"Hmm?" he responds next to her, his body laying the opposite direction so that his head is next to hers.

"I spoke with Ruach today."

"Mhmm."

"I asked Him what was out there."

Adam turns his head slightly toward her. "You did? What did He say?"

"Just that I couldn't understand."

Instead of responding, he turns his head back to look at the sky. "Well, we probably can't."

She turns on her side toward him. Resting her arm under her head, she asks, "What do you think it is?"

He doesn't reply for some time. She is about to ask again but finally he says, "I'm not sure *'it's'* anything. I think it's more … like an absence."

"An absence?" She thinks this over for a moment. This doesn't really make any sense to Eve, but she doesn't voice her confusion. The thought that there could be nothing at all is somehow even more disconcerting. She decides that the rest of her questions can wait until tomorrow.

"Anyway." She pushes herself up on one arm and gives him an upside-down kiss. "Goodnight," Then, she settles her head back down into the moss. Within a few quiet moments, she drifts off to sleep.

***

On the first Jubilee, they celebrate the harvest, and a host of angels come down from the heavens to join in on the festivity.

While the stars hang peacefully in the night sky, below the garden is filled with music and joyful voices.

Eremiel zips down next to Aziel, who turns to him.

"Ah! Did you bring them?" Aziel asks, unable to conceal his eagerness.

Eremiel nods his rings once, then opens outward, revealing some sweet breads topped with sliced fruit.

"Ah ha! Thank you!" Aziel gleefully picks one up then stuffs it into his mouth.

A chorus of noise behind them snatches their attention, and Aziel motions for Eremiel to follow him before he can finish chewing.

They crowd in closer to the celebration and peek over feathery wings to see what has incited the exuberance. In the center, Adam and Eve have created an altar, and lined it with the best of the harvest.

Shining fruits and vegetables layer on one another, with herbs and grains embellishing any blank spaces.

"It's almost time!" Aziel giggles and floats up a couple feet in the air for a better view.

After a few moments, a light appears in the sky. Ruach, surrounded by a host of Seraphim, hovers above the altar. The shimmering golden wings of the Seraphim stir around him, mixing like water.

The music fades, and for a moment, everything is silent.

Ruach takes in the grand spread below. He raises His arms out to the side, and an all-consuming white fire envelopes the entire altar.

A cheer erupts from the crowd, and the air is filled with lively chorus of music once again.

The fire reaches up, surrounding Ruach and the host. The Seraphim spin, expanding the flame so that it lights up the crowd. Flames dip down, weaving throughout the spectators. They twist around in a dance, and before long, everyone joins in.

***

Near the altar, Adam watches Eve as she looks up at the dazzling blaze, the embers reflecting in her eyes. She reaches out a hand to him, an invitation.

He takes it, intertwining his fingers with hers. Pulling her close to him, he spins her, then they both fall in line with the others dancing. She laughs as they move with the melody, the angels around them blurring in the cadence.

As he pulls her closer, they slow, the carousing around them now a daze of lights and movement.

The music fades slightly and Eve looks into his eyes. Curling the tips of his fingers, he runs them across her jaw.

"We will always be like this?" she asks, not breaking eye

contact.

He looks past her for a moment. He can see an image of her clearly. She looks different, yet still just as beautiful to him. The tips of her hair still glow, but not from within, instead from the morning sun.

She is smiling as she clutches something in her arms. She runs her fingers over the head of a small baby.

Adam looks back to Eve in front of him.

"Yes." He smiles. "We will always be like this."

***

The mornings are consistent. When the sun is just barely lifting its rays over the horizon, the garden is already lulling out of its sleep. The birds wake before anyone else, ruffling their feathers as they cluster together on branches.

As Eve slowly lulls out of sleep, she sees two blurry figures in the distance. Blinking sleepily, she realizes that the two figures are Adam and the Archangel, Michael.

She can't make out their entire conversation, only catching a couple phrases. "Because of the others …" and "… added to the records."

Eve turns onto her back and rubs her eyes. By the time she looks back at the duo, Adam is walking toward her.

He sits down on the grass beside her and brushes a non-existent strand of hair out of her face.

"What was that about?" she asks, nodding to where Michael had been standing but is now gone.

"I'll be at the south perimeter today, something about keeping record of the three rivers." He is clearly more interested in running his hand along her face than keeping an account of waterways.

"Want me to come with you?" she asks, entangling her fingers with his.

"I want you to be here when I get back." He leans his forehead down to touch hers. "Besides, you would just be a distraction."

She pushes him away with a little scoff. "Please, I distract you even when I'm not around." She gives him a flirtatious wink and pushes herself up to her feet. She trots down to the river before Adam can say anything else.

"I'll see you tonight," she calls after him, not waiting for a reply.

As the sun rises higher throughout the day, Eve decides to occupy her time with gathering some different fruit for this evening.

She remembers seeing an orchard from the high peak in the garden. Eager to try something new, she hikes up the riverbank, entering the forest.

Pathways fill the forest. Here and there you can see the gleam of white gems embedded into the rocks, popping out of the rich ground.

A gray fox, who prefers to spend most of his time with her, trails just behind her heels. He's a pleasant enough conversationalist but is keener on thoughtful silence. Today, however, he seems especially chatty. He tells Eve about this new type of bird he saw fly in from the east side of the garden.

When he speaks, it's not in an audible voice, but Eve can still perfectly understand him, nonetheless.

Right when he has changed his conversation from the bird to a group of mongooses that have occupied his burrow, they come to a fork in the pathway. Eve pauses for a moment.

"Which way would you like to go?" the fox asks.

"This way," she says, leading to the left path.

She takes a step forward and another question stops her.

"Why are you afraid to go by the center of the garden?"

Eve pauses. It's strange that the fox would ask her a question like this. She is about to ask him what he means, when she realizes that this voice is not coming from her silvery companion, but from a tree directly in front of her.

At first, she can't make out any distinguishing shapes between the knotted branches, but then a scaly head with a long snout morphs out of the foliage. The sunlight reflects blindingly from the tip of its nose as it slides out of the shadows.

"Oh. It–it's not that I'm afraid …" Eve starts, still not recovered from the perplexing question.

"But you are avoiding it." The creature moves its head farther into the sun, revealing smooth white scales.

Raised spike-like scales line the sides of his face and down the back of his neck. His eyes are completely white save for two black slits for pupils.

Moving forward even more, he reveals a leg from the branches. He supports himself on the side of the tree, digging claws into the bark.

"We go to the center of the garden all the time. To eat from the Tree of Life," she replies.

"Yes, but that is not the tree you think of right now."

This makes Eve pause. An image of the other tree flashes across her mind. Had she been thinking of it?

"Why are you avoiding a tree?" the serpent pushes, the scales around his eyes raised in a quizzical expression.

"We cannot eat the fruit from that tree. We can't even touch it. Because we will die," she responds, confidently, but another flash of the tree with its glowing fruit invades her thoughts.

The serpent slinks forward, grabbing a branch with his claws. He brings his head down close to hers. "Who told you that?"

"God," she admits, wishing she could sound a bit surer.

"God? Ruach Hokadesh told *you* this?" The serpent's forked tongue tastes the air as he speaks.

"Well, He told Adam this," she shakes her head and then clarifies, "*Adom*. He told us both."

"You don't remember?"

Eve thinks back to Ruach's charge to watch the garden. She envisions the valley that they overlooked as the Spirit gave His instructions. The two trees reaching out from the undergrowth.

For some reason she can only focus on the white tree in her memory—the Tree of Life seeming to fade into the background.

"Yes—no, of course I remember." She wraps one arm around her stomach and finds herself wishing this serpent would just crawl back into the branches.

But he doesn't move back. He sits there for several seconds sampling the air and observing her with those canny eyes.

"Adam told me," She quickly adds. "He reminded me … when I awoke after we were separated."

Adam's warning echoes in her head. "Don't even touch it. Because if you do, we will die."

"So, then, how do you know?" The serpent says more to himself, but then shoots Eve a look. "How do you know if God really said that?"

Eve sputters, but the serpent cuts her off before she can reply.

"I would be cautious. There are dangerous things out there, much more dangerous than a tree." With that, he slinks his body back into the branches and melts away.

He leaves a dumbstruck Eve with her furry companion sitting patiently at her feet.

"How would you know that?" Eve asks, but the serpent is already gone. "What things?" she asks again.

When there is no reply, she frees her stifled breath.

She stays at the crossroads for a few more seconds, the fox giving her a strange look.

Determined to not let the weird encounter affect her, she takes the path she originally chose, not giving a second look to the other. The fox stays silent now as they continue their hike through the woods. Eve hardly notices his muteness, however, as she stays immersed in thought until they reach the orchard.

CHAPTER TEN

Because I Had Wings

For some reason, the plush moss below Eve now does not feel as comfortable as it normally does. She turns to lie on her back, pulling out of Adam's arms. Her restlessness doesn't wake him, however, as he continues sleeping peacefully beside her, his chest rising and falling steadily.

He would never lie to her. She props herself up on her forearms, while thinking over that concept, the serpent's query still burning in her mind. What if she had misunderstood Adam?

She never really had a thought like that before, and it was strange. Yet, it seemed right—something she can grasp on to. The alternative of Adam being deceitful is not a suitable reality.

If it was possible for her to misunderstand Adam, maybe it was possible for him to misunderstand Ruach? Did she misunderstand Ruach? It is a possibility at least.

She decides to ask Adam about it tomorrow. As she makes her

decision, a new feeling settles over her. She feels it knot together inside her chest. She realizes she's afraid to ask him.

Never before had she been reluctant to ask questions, why was this happening to her now?

She holds her hand out in front of her. She turns it over, examining each finger, almost as if to check if she's still real.

Placing her middle finger and thumb together, she snaps her fingers.

Everything turns white.

She is in a completely bare room, but she can't tell where the walls or ceilings begin or end.

Turning around, she sees the tree. It, too, is completely bleached of color, with each of its fruit a pulsating glow.

She takes a step forward and hears each footstep echo. Reaching the tree, she plucks one of its fruits from the branch.

A faint noise behind her catches her attention and she turns.

A figure stands not too far behind her—a woman, in a white linen dress with a matching head covering veiling her face.

Eve glances back at the tree and sees that it's gone. She turns back toward the woman. The woman is only a few feet away now, but this does not startle Eve.

"Who are you?" Eve asks and her voice feels distant. She can just see the outline of the woman's features through the light fabric, but nothing is familiar.

Eve looks down to her hand and realizes she's still holding the fruit. Its luminescence fades, then crumbles like ash in her hand. As Eve looks back up, she sees the woman bring her hand up to rest on her midriff.

Eve blinks, and the night is back. She hears the gentle noises of the insects that play at night.

Realizing she's still standing, she turns her head to see Adam still asleep, not far away. With some reluctance, she turns back, staring out from her vantage point across the garden.

Even at this distance, she can see the glow from the two trees at the center. Determined to ignore all these disturbing visions, she goes back to lie down once more.

As she settles onto her back, she lets her eyes drift shut. When they open again, the sun has already risen.

She squints against the rays, feeling as unrested as before she fell asleep.

Adam leans over her. "Ah, there you are. Slept in more than normal, huh?" he asks in that low voice he greets her with every morning.

As her eyes adjust to the light, she gives him a sleepy smile.

He smiles back, revealing a row of fang-like teeth.

She sucks in a breath, blinking rapidly. But when she looks again, the fangs are gone, and all that is left is Adam with a concerned look across his face.

"What's wrong?" he asks.

"Nothing." she asserts, shaking her head, not quite recalling why she was so alarmed. "I'll go get us something to eat for breakfast," she suggests, changing her tone to something more cheerful.

He leans back as she sits up. "Right now? Do you want me to come with you?"

"No, it's alright. It won't take long," she answers, already heading down the path.

"Very well, but I have something I want to talk to you about when you get back," he calls after her.

"I'll return soon," she replies, then hurries into the forest.

As she breaks through the tree branches and into a clearing, she takes a deep breath of fresh air. The cool, misty breeze helps to clear her thoughts.

The songs from the birds relax her, and with each step, she feels more and more at peace. Before long, all the confusing thoughts from the day before have left her mind, and she decides to do a little exploring. An avenue lined with dark-leaved trees catches her attention. The trees are full of yellowish-orange colored fruit.

She picks one from a low branch and brings it up to her nose. She finds that it has a tingly, citrus scent.

She chastises herself when she realizes that she was in such a hurry to leave, she had forgotten to bring a basket with her. She considers going back for a moment but decides to do a little more exploring.

Absentmindedly, she meanders along the path, stopping here and there to gather a couple pieces of fruits.

Not really noticing how long she has been walking, she comes to a clearing. Her thoughts snap into focus when she realizes what she's looking at. There, just a few feet away, is the one thing she thought she had finally placed out of her mind.

She feels her arms go slack and the fruit she's been gathering spills to the ground. Her heart slams against her chest, but then she realizes nothing has happened. The tree just sits there peacefully as she stares at it.

It isn't particularly more unique looking than the other trees in the garden, except for the color. Its fruit are small white ovals, and they glow from within. In fact, the glow almost seems to pulsate throughout the tree, growing brighter in some areas then fading in others. It's quite magnetic to look at, yet not intimidating.

In the past when she visited this spot to eat from the Tree of Life, this tree didn't even catch her attention. It hardly gives off the appearance of being anything dangerous. It doesn't look wrong or deadly any more than any of the other trees. But then again, what was she expecting from this death tree?

She takes a half step to turn around but pauses. A closer examination can't hurt.

Stepping gingerly toward the tree, she looks it up and down. She notices, as she gets closer, that its leaves are slightly translucent at certain angles.

The bark is smooth like polished marble. Its lowest branches sit just a foot above Eve's head and are heavy with fruit.

Satisfied with her curiosity about the tree, she turns to leave, but freezes in her tracks at a familiar voice.

"Well, you got over your apprehension pretty fast," the sardonic voice comes from behind her. "Realized I was right?"

She sighs. "This has nothing to do with you," she states while turning to face the serpent, but he isn't there.

She looks around for him, then he appears next to her. He stands up on his back legs, reaching his head up to her height. He curls his front legs close to his chest as he speaks.

"You're looking at it right now and you're not dead, are you?"

She hesitates. "I know I can look at it, but I still can't eat it."

He twists his body around to come between her view of the tree.

"Don't you see He's lying to you?" the serpent asks incredulously, then continues. "You will not die, if you eat it. You will become like god. Your eyes will be opened, and you will know everything."

Her brows pull together as she focuses on his face.

"He is tricking you. He wants to be more powerful than you."

"He would never do that," she says just above a whisper.

"Then what would Adam say?"

Her eyes jerk to his as he speaks.

"What will he say when the truth comes out in the end, and he finds out that *you* could have protected him. You could have made him more powerful, but you didn't because you were too afraid."

She closes her eyes and presses her fingers to her temples.

That's not true. She thinks but can't drown out his voice.

"You're lying to him. You are deceiving him," he says with a flick of his tongue.

The serpent's eyes turn red for a brief second, like a veil of blood over his vision.

Eve presses her palms over her eyes now. "I'm not lying to him," she pleads.

She moves her hands from her eyes into her hair. When the red filter fades from his eyes, Eve already has the fruit in her hand.

When did this get here? A thought comes to her mind, but she doesn't really hear it. All the questions and worries in her head suddenly come to a halt as she holds it, like the whole world has frozen.

It's warm in her hand, like holding a newborn rabbit. It pulsates, as if it is a fluttering heart.

Silence engulfs her as she stares at the fruit. She can't even feel her own body now.

This is easy, like falling asleep.

She grasps the fruit between her fingers and lifts it to her lips. And in the quiet stillness, she takes a bite and swallows.

It burns down her throat and hits her stomach like a hot coal. She can feel the heat in her chest, like a second heart.

Suddenly, she feels a warm liquid around her lips. Her throat tightens and she can't breathe. She grabs at her throat and coughs up liquid gold. It flows over her lips and drips down onto her hand.

She stares down at it in panic, it's coming out of her eyes now as well. She looks up to find the serpent, but he's gone. What did he do to her? She chokes on the metallic taste in her mouth.

And then as soon as it's there, it disappears. The burning in her chest stops and she breathes steadily, wondering why she panicked.

She examines her hands. No gold, just what is left of the fruit.

Holding the rest of the fruit close to her chest, she resigns herself in what she must do now.

She stumbles back into the forest, totally unaware of her surroundings. Somehow, she makes it back to where Adam is waiting for her, not really paying attention to the route.

Adam turns around when he hears her at the edge of the forest.

"I wondered where you ..." The smile fades from his face when he notices the fruit in her hand. She clutches it close to her heart, almost digging her nails into it.

He strides forward, stopping a few feet away from her.

"What is that?" he asks, concern creeping into his voice.

"Adam, you have to listen to me," she says with a detached voice, unable to focus on his face.

His gaze roves over her blank expression, searching for answers.

Silently she reaches her hand out, the fruit in her open palm. Its outer skin still glows white, but the inside is black decay.

"What did you do?" he asks desperately, pressing his hands through his hair. "What did you do?" he asks again, but she gives no reply.

She just stands there, hand outreached, eyes unfocused.

***

Adam doubles over as the sickening feeling turns to panic. After a few seconds, he straightens and grabs her by the arms. "Why did you do this?" he begs.

The panic overtakes him now, and he can't breathe. He looks back to her for some sort of solace as he feels sweat begin to pour down the sides of his face.

He can picture her now, lying lifeless on the ground. Her glow gone, with wide-open, dead eyes. He can see himself kneeling over her body. He reaches down, pulling her up toward his chest, cradling her.

Her arm falls limp beside her, the fruit still clutched in her hand.

"Why did you do this?" Adam hears a voice that is not his own.

He looks down into her eyes, but they are lifeless in return. All the beautiful color in her is replaced by a rotten gray, paired with blue lips.

"Why did you do this?" the voice asks again.

Adam looks up as something in the distance has caught his eye. He can see a robed figure with white hair, although the image is not very clear.

"Why did you leave this place?" the figure asks someone out of view.

Adam closes his eyes.

When he opens them, a memory flashes before him. He and Ruach are standing on a cliff, looking over the garden below.

"Do you accept?" Ruach asks.

Adam sees Eve in front of him. She's leading him somewhere. Her fingertips reach back toward his, and she beckons with a smile.

"You know what will happen if you eat from the tree." Ruach flickers before him again.

Adam clamps his eyes shut. This time when they open, he sees Eve once again standing in front of him, the fruit in her outstretched hand.

He knows that she is speaking, there is something earnest about the way her lips move, yet he can't hear any of it.

She's dead.

He can still see the white fruit pulsating, its rancid insides beginning to spill out.

She's dead.

He takes it from her hand and eats.

The immense heat burns his throat as he doubles over, coughing up the liquid gold. He struggles to breathe as he feels it grow more intense, reaching out through his limbs.

The burning runs through his arms and all the way to his fingertips, but then it stops and begins to fade. The heat is replaced by a numbing cold, starting at the very tips of his nails and creeping back down.

And now he's dead too.

He looks up at Eve, who stands a few feet away with a look of shock on her face. The glow that once covered her body has started to fade, beginning at her fingers and ending at her very core where it disappears all together.

The light in the tips of her hair dims and leaves behind only the brown strands. Her gold eyes turn to a shallow green, and the white glowing lashes that rim them fade to black.

She turns her head away as sorrow overtakes her expression. Sinking down to her knees, she buries her face in her hands.

Adam straightens as the cold reaches his stomach, like a hollow pit. He turns away with a few shaky steps. He only makes it a few feet when the cold, sick feeling overtakes him, and he drops to his hands and knees.

He digs his fingers into the dirt as he grits his teeth.

Staring down at the ground through wet eyes, he turns the soil over in his hands as a sob shakes his body. "Take us back." His voice turns ragged as he clutches the ground. "Take us back, we want to go back!" he screams as if hoping to dissolve his body into the ground.

No one answers.

He falls on his side, burying his face in the dirt. Tears mix with the dust as he gives himself over to the sobs.

After what seems like an eternity, his cries fade as he lays immobile. He stares at his hand as a dull numbness overcomes his body. Unaware of the passing of time, he watches an earthworm crawl out of the freshly turned soil.

A low rumble starts in the distance, and the trees begin to sway in the wind. A new emotion overtakes Adam's body. An emotion he has never felt before: Fear.

He pushes himself up and searches frantically for the rumble that is growing louder. Scrambling to his feet, his heart beats wildly in his chest. With a few tentative steps backward, he turns and runs to where Eve lays curled up on her side.

He grabs her arm, pulling her up. "We must go. Now!" he yells as he drags her forward. He clutches her hand in his as she stumbles behind him.

They run through the forest, the tree branches zipping past, biting their faces. The wind around them starts to blow harder, whipping their hair around wildly.

The rumble has grown to a loud roar that rings in their ears. Adam doesn't dare look behind them as they run but he can feel the panic rising in his chest, making it hard to breathe.

Finally, the trees break open, revealing the riverbank. They pause for a moment, panting.

"Come on," Adam says as he drags her down the bank and pulls her into the water. They duck under the branches hanging low over the water.

After a second, the roar stops and the wind settles, and everything is eerily silent.

They just sit there for several seconds. Eve lets out a ragged breath and searches Adam's face for direction.

He avoids her gaze, and instead looks at the muddy wall next to him. He scoops up a clump of mud and hands it to her.

"Here. We must cover ourselves." Then he reaches up to one of the leafy branches overhead. He snaps the branch off and hands it to her. "Use this too."

***

Eve stares at him incredulously for a few moments, then takes the branch from his hand. Turning away from him, she smears the mud over her neck and chest.

Her wet, matted hair sticks to the sides of her face and back. Using a muddy hand, she brushes the hair out of her face.

Fresh tears silently stream down her face while she attempts to weave some leafy branches together.

The dread begins to overcome her, too, as she fumbles with the muddy leaves. She might be drowning, she realizes. She can see herself sinking beneath the surface of the brown water, reaching a desperate hand up through the lily pads.

A few minutes—or perhaps hours—later, they sit up on the riverbank. A layer of mud caked over their bodies, along with leaves woven around their waists, serves as a cheap replacement for their white glow.

"What will we do?" Eve asks quietly, finally breaking the silence.

Adam lets out a trembling breath before answering, "There is something we have to do."

Eve stays silent, folding her arms tightly around her chest and waiting for him to continue. The smell of dirt overpowers her senses.

"What will you do?" a silky voice comes from the trees. It seems to surround them. "I can help you." The voice grows louder as the white serpent crawls out of the trees.

"We don't want *your* help," Eve grits out through her teeth, then stands. She wraps her arms more tightly around herself, suddenly feeling cold. A shiver shakes her body.

"You lied to me," she quickly accuses. "You said we would be like God."

"I didn't lie," the serpent states, with a bit of anger creeping into his voice as well. "I said you would be like god. And it's true." His voice drops to a deadly whisper. "Who do you think I am?" He raises his head up higher with that statement, arching it above Eve.

Adam jumps to his feet, stepping in between the two.

"What is this?" he demands, staring down the serpent's black, slitted eyes.

"He tricked me," Eve laments, grabbing onto Adam's arm.

A guttural laugh cuts off any reply from Adam. The serpent crawls forward, digging his claws into the ground. "The truth was revealed to her, and she made her own decision."

A gust of wind suddenly blows through the trees, and a sound like thunder rumbles in the distance.

"You don't have much time," the serpent says, standing up on his back legs. "If you follow me, I can help you." His long tongue tastes the air as he watches them.

Adam takes a step closer, then drops his voice threateningly. "Don't ever talk to her again. Don't ever return here again."

"You're too late." The serpent narrows his eyes, then with a loud gush of air, unfolds a pair of wings on his back. He stretches out his membrane-like wings above him, and then leaps into the air. A cyclone of leaves and dust swirls around his tail as he jumps off the ground.

His shadow passes over top of them, and then he swoops down, disappearing behind the trees.

The loud roar of wind has faded to a gentle breeze. It flows around them, picking up their mud-caked hair.

A whisper comes on the wind, a gentle voice all around them.

"*Adom*? Where are you?" The whisper swirls around them. "Where are you?"

Adam takes Eve's hand in his, then closes his eyes. Eve looks up at him with a few fresh tears streaking down her mud-stained cheeks. He looks so different than he did this morning. Beneath the dirt and bloody scratches from the branches, he looks tired, but somehow resigned.

Adam lets out a breath before reopening his eyes, then nods his head.

"We're here."

Instantly, Ruach appears in front of them. His presence freezes everything around them, and his eyes burn a bright white. The light is consuming, washing out all the color.

His body is still, but His ornate robes and hair quaver and jolt about as if they are electrified.

"Why were you hiding?" His powerful voice shakes the forest around them, even though His lips do not move as He speaks.

Adam squares his shoulders. "We were afraid. Because we knew of our nakedness and our shame."

"Who told you that? Did you eat from the tree I told you not to?"

Adam squeezes Eve's hand tightly before dropping it.

"This woman, that you gave her to be with me …" Eve can hear the pleading in his voice as he begins. "She gave it to me, and I ate."

Ruach directs His burning eyes at Eve. "What have you done?"

His eyes pierce into her soul. She always knew that He could read her thoughts, but this feels different. His question burns, exposing every part of her being. Lying is impossible.

"It was the serpent," she says quickly. "He deceived me." Tears well up in her eyes as she speaks. She feels as though she can't even move, as if His gaze holds her body captive.

But as soon as the words leave her mouth, His gaze shifts from her to behind them. She feels the paralysis leave, and she lets out a shaky breath.

"So, it was the serpent?" Ruach says, seemingly to Himself.

He then silences, as if waiting for something. Adam and Eve hardly dare to breathe as they stand in the silence.

Suddenly, the serpent's body comes bursting through the tree branches. Leaves fly everywhere as his long body writhes in the air.

His wings flap uselessly as his body is dragged by an invisible force. Slamming to a halt in front of Ruach, he sits, suspended in the air.

The wind gusts around them as Ruach speaks. Light seems to bleed from His body, and His hair moves, blurred around Him.

"Because you have done this, you are cursed above every beast and creature that crawls this earth."

Bits of stone and leaves circle through the air with the wind. Some of the rocks melt, turning into crystals.

"You will crawl along the ground on your belly and devour the dust for the rest of your life."

Ruach's tone suddenly shifts as if He is talking to someone else. "And I put animosity between you and the woman, and between your offspring and her offspring. You will bruise His heel. And He will crush your head."

The serpent is released from his binds in the air and tumbles to the ground. He lands in a heap with a dull thud. He tries to push himself up, but his legs give out on him.

His limbs start to turn black and wither. His wings follow suit, crumbling like ashes. In one last feeble attempt to push himself up, he collapses on the ground, and his shriveled limbs and wings dissolve completely.

The serpent shrugs on his belly, mouth open in a pant. After a few pathetic seconds, he shrinks into the cover of the forest.

Ruach slowly lowers himself to the ground, and the cyclone of wind dies down to a breeze. He directs his attention back to Adam and Eve.

Eve shoots a fearful glance at Adam, but he just stares straight ahead, unmoving.

Ruach's voice is still formidable as he addresses her. "You will have great pain during childrearing. Your desire will be for your husband, and he will rule over you."

Finally, he turns to Adam to deliver one last judgment.

"Cursed is the ground because of you, it will produce thorns and thistles. For all the days of your life you will have to labor to eat. By the sweat of your brow will you eat bread, until you return to the ground. For from dust you came, and to dust you will return."

After that, Ruach becomes silent. The bright light in his eyes soften to a brilliant green.

Adam turns to Eve and reaches out his hand. She steps gingerly toward him, placing her hand in his.

"You are my wife. You are named Eve because you will be the

mother of all the living." He squeezes her hand.

She nods her head, unable to cry anymore. Briefly, she sees a glimpse of the woman in white, her hand resting on her abdomen.

They both turn to look at the Spirit, who is watching them with a gentle expression.

Ruach reaches his hand out to the side, and an ox appears through the trees.

It lumbers over to the Spirit and rests its chin on His hand. Ruach smiles at the creature then places His other hand over its forehead.

The ox peacefully closes his eyes, then slowly lowers to the ground.

Ruach places His finger directly between its eyes, and a beam of light shoots down the middle of the animal. The ox's skin begins to lift off its body, splitting in two.

Instead of the blood spilling on the ground, it bubbles up into the air. The beads of blood begin to swirl around Adam and Eve, stretching out into long ribbons, wrapping around them, covering their bodies.

Their crude leafy coverings fall around their feet, and the caked mud lifts off their skin.

Suddenly the ribbons dissipate and are replaced by the ox's skin. The pelts wrap securely around them, forming into perfect robes.

"You now know what is good from what is evil." Ruach's voice is softer as He addresses them. "You can no longer stay here," He states, "But you will have a covering."

Michael has suddenly appeared beside the Spirit as he speaks.

"Escort them out of the garden. They must not continue to eat from the Tree of Life, lest they live forever."

Michael nods and steps forward. He extends his arm out, motioning for them to follow.

Wordlessly, they follow the Archangel to the wooden gate. The massive gate opens at its middle and swings outward.

On the outside, two Cherubim stand at either side of the entrance. As Eve walks past them, their faces change from a fierce lion to a falcon.

In front of both Cherubim, a sword hovers in the air. The swords look as if liquid fire was put into a mold and then stayed in that form.

The weapons vibrate and hum in the air as they slightly bob up and down.

The Cherubim themselves hang in the air—their pointed, metal-like feet hovering a few inches off the ground.

This is it, the outside world. Eve never thought this would be how she would see it. Adam places his arm over her shoulders as they step forward.

A grassy plane stretches out before them. It looks as if the rolling hills continue endlessly, and the air feels cold.

Adam takes one last look back.

An unreadable expression passes over his face. But Eve sees it and realizes it is not an emotion, it's a knowing.

A knowing that, somehow, there was more to it.

Somehow, it all makes sense.

Adam watches as the gate closes. A fierce wind whips in front of the garden wall and Cherubim giving them a hazy effect.

A moment later, it's all gone. All that's left behind is the endless open plane.

***

Cursed. That's what I am. Like a shadow that has followed me my whole existence. It was always there, just out of reach. But I have it now, a curse I can cling to.

I can bring it with me as I endlessly wander the sands. And each night as the moon hangs over the desert, I can plan the end.

You really shouldn't have told me. You make it too easy. I've already taken Your creation away from You. There is so much more I will take.

Cursed.

I was not cursed to crawl the ground because I had legs.

It was because I had wings.

PART TWO

CHAPTER ELEVEN

OFFSPRING OF OATHS

"If you wish to speak, now would be the time," Samyaza states flatly, crossing his arms and staring down the two hundred angels before him. No one answers his bidding.

The first rays of the sunrise hit the mountain peak where this congregation gathers. Pink light reflects off Samyaza's face, accentuating his sharp angles and deep-set eyes.

Thousands of feet below them, the city at the base of the mountain is starting to show signs of life as many begin their day. The streets are not as cluttered as they will be by mid-morning, but there are still sounds of shutters opening and mothers calling to their children.

"Or perhaps you have something else in mind," Samyaza says in an almost too casual way, pacing back and forth in front of his mute subjects. "*If* our endeavor is discovered, you think it will be me alone who suffers the punishment?" His tone turns more edged as he scans the crowd, searching for someone to dare to confirm.

Danieal steps forward, and Samyaza's gaze snaps on him. Danieal ignores the venomous look, however, as soothing words roll easily off his tongue.

"Are we not the Watchers, who have come to Earth to impart to man the teachings of God? Have we not always been one together in agreement?" Danieal pauses for a second to let his words settle over the angels.

He continues, "What makes this different than anything we've done before? Do you have a reason for us to fear?"

He looks to Samyaza, who gives him no response.

"Of course, we are all committed to this undertaking with you. In fact," Danieal sweeps his hand over the crowd for added impact, "We swear it."

A few sharp inhales from the crowd reveal that this was not the answer they were expecting, but no one offers a counter.

"We will bind ourselves in an oath, that we will not change our intentions, but execute our course." Danieal does not remove his scrutiny from Samyaza as he speaks. "Is that not what you intend?"

A beat passes, and Samyaza forces a tight smile. "Danieal speaks the truth. That is exactly what we need."

He turns to the other angels, gauging a reaction. They all stand in silent agreement. Some of their expressions tell a different story, but it matters not.

"Very well." Samyaza takes a knife out from under his robe. "Then an oath we will make." His voice has become more eager, more hurried. "If we are one together, we will have protection."

He places the sharp point on his right wrist and drags it across. Liquid light bubbles to the surface, then drips down the sides of his wrist. The light begins to fade away, and in its place is a thin red line wrapping around like a cuff.

He extends the knife out to Danieal, who accepts after just a second, and the process is repeated.

Bright yellow sunrays shine down on them by the time they finish their oath. Samyaza looks to the city below. Two hundred Watchers, now with permanently marked wrists, stand behind him, waiting for his signal.

Samyaza steps off the stony ledge. The rest follow suit, descending into the city below.

***

Dark hair. That's always the first thing he remembers. The long, sable locks whip through the forest, contrasted by the light green leaves fluttering around the woman's face. Her features always seem obscured, hidden just out of view by the branches. Every once and awhile, he still catches glimpses of her lively eyes and smile through the foliage.

She would always laugh, and then, with a handful of her skirt in hand, run to hide behind the bushes. There were always trees in the way. Always something in the way.

Every time he thought he had found her, she would be gone, but he would catch a glimpse of her black hair disappearing behind another group of trees. This time, however, he is determined to catch her.

He follows her laugh, but she is always one step ahead of him. Until, finally, he finds her.

"Samyaza."

A voice from the doorway snaps the Watcher out of his thoughts. He straightens in his chair.

Samyaza's appearance is different now, his skin does not reflect light in the way it used to, and his stature is smaller. The only thing setting him apart from other men is his brilliantly golden eyes. His new form, not quite like an angel, but not quite like a man either.

"Samyaza," the thin man in the doorway timidly repeats again. "The child is—"

He doesn't get to finish his sentence, cut off by Samyaza jumping out of his seat, the scrape of the chair's legs on the stone floor echoes throughout the otherwise silent room. The Watcher darts through the door and hurries down the hall.

Finding the room he's looking for, he barges in, slamming the door open. Several midwives look up nervously at his violent entrance. He doesn't even glance their way as his eyes dart directly to a figure lying on the bed, its appearance obscured by a blanket. An obvious dark stain covers the figure's lower half.

He approaches slowly now and reaches for the blanket, covering the face like a veil. Hesitantly pulling backward, the first thing he sees is her bright red hair. Ashy-gray skin is next, followed by white, dead eyes.

He stops, covering her face back up and turning away. Why does it feel like the room is spinning? A heat begins to course throughout his body. He exhales a couple times, but he can't tamp the rage down.

The table in front of him is his first victim. He lifts it with ease, splintering the wood against the wall. The midwives try to move out of his way fast enough, but not all are that fortunate. He sends one flying across the room. Some of them scream, but their cries are drowned out by his guttural yell. His eyes turn bright white and flash in streaks with his waves of destruction.

The women cower against the wall, shielding their faces as he continues his rampage.

Suddenly, something draws him out of his craze.

A baby's cry.

He turns slowly, pinpointing the sound coming from the arms of a midwife. She quakes, shrugged up against the wall, but stays put as Samyaza wordlessly approaches her.

He peeks under the baby's wrappings, staring for a few seconds, then flicks the cloth back over his son's face.

"Another one of them," he states flatly, composing himself as if his rampage never occurred.

He then turns to leave, his footfalls the only sound in the tomb-like room.

"A name."

The voice is so quiet, probably no one else heard it, but Samyaza catches it.

He stops and turns his head back slightly.

The midwife's breath catches, and raises her voice slightly. "The child needs a name."

Samyaza pauses momentarily, considering, but then continues forward without a word.

CHAPTER TWELVE

Sin is Crouching at the Door

"The child was born today," Enoch says in a low voice to his wife.

She looks up from the dough she had been kneading. "His wife? She …" Her voice trails off with a shake from Enoch's head.

She shoots a glance at a couple of her own children playing on the floor. The two youngest twin boys, not yet six years old, play with their carved wooden toys. The youngest daughter, Martha, pulls one of the boys into her lap as they continue to battle with the wooden figures.

"No one ever survives," Enoch's wife says in a low voice. She kneads the dough harder in frustration.

"Edna …"

"No." She sighs and looks up at her husband. "It's a curse."

Enoch lets out a breath. "Please don't …" He shoots a glance at some of their other children who are currently preparing some loaves for the oven and pretending not to listen in. His voice drops to a whisper. "We cannot say that about them. They bring wisdom."

"Maybe they did once, but …" Edna starts quickly then pauses. "Then why must they kill our daughters? Why does their offspring kill our sons?" She slams the dough down onto the table for added impact.

Looking over at her children once more, she continues, "Our family has remained safe for now, but how long will it last?"

"That I cannot answer." Enoch runs a hand through his short, bristly beard. "It is not a question for us."

"Then who is it for?" she shoots back.

Before Enoch can answer, their oldest son, Methuselah interrupts them, entering in through the front door. He casually strolls over to the pair.

"Ah, some fresh bread for our journey, Mother?" If he was aware of any tension, his tone doesn't reflect it, as he leans over the table, snatching up a spare scrap of dough.

He pops it in his mouth, ignoring the disapproving look from his mother.

"This would barely last you through breakfast." Edna huffs while splitting the dough into smaller portions.

"Perhaps I will take another animal with us just for our meals," Enoch interjects, clearly relieved at the subject change.

His wife shoots him a look, indicating that the discussion was *not* finalized, but she doesn't say anything.

"Or he could just bring home a wife and you wouldn't have to cook so much for him, Mother," Martha speaks up from her spot on the floor.

"Must we really speak of this again?" Methuselah replies immediately, reaching to steal another scrap of dough.

Edna smacks his hand away before he gets the chance.

"What, Mother?" he says with his arms out. "You too are eager to have me out of the house." The melodrama is heavy in his voice. "Two and fifty years is too old to be unwed," Methuselah says in a high-pitched voice. He pushes a lock of his long curly hair behind an ear and flashes a brilliant smile.

Edna shoots a look back, the remaining dough in her hands well kneaded beyond the point it needs to be.

"Why, even Father was over a hundred years of age before he had his first-born son." Methuselah places a hand over his chest.

"Too busy in your scrolls, huh, Father?"

Enoch gives his son a sheepish look before saying, "Edna, he's—"

His attempt to speak fails as his wife raises a brow in his direction.

"Very well, Mother." Methuselah steps behind her to give her a hug, then whispers, "Just to make you happy I will not return until I have at least three or four wives." He gives her a quick peck on the cheek and darts away before his mother can give him a disapproving slap with a flour-covered hand.

He steps up behind his father, giving him a squeeze on the shoulder.

"Why, you know how hard it is to choose just one."

Enoch only allows half of a smile out before both flinch, fearing Edna may throw a clay pot in their direction.

Retreating, Methuselah steps over to the twins and picks them up, one in each arm. He spins around a couple times until all three of them are laughing and dizzy.

"Oh, go get the rest of your siblings and tell them we will eat soon," Edna says, allowing a small smile to creep onto her face.

"Let's go then, men," Methuselah says in an authoritative voice.

With both boys still tucked beneath his arms, he charges out the door, accidentally slamming his shoulder into the frame.

"Ow!" he complains, shifting on his feet to regain his balance. "We're alright!" he calls over his shoulder, then continues, the giggling boys in his arms unfazed.

After the whole family has been corralled together, they sit on the floor around the short wooden table. The two youngest girls take a spot on either side of the twins, always intervening before too much of a mess can be made.

"Are you sure you will be able to find Reu?" Edna asks her husband as she sets down a bowl of stew in front of him.

"If I know anything about my brother, it's that change is not a top priority. If he was somewhere ten years ago, I'd be willing to bet the likewise now. Besides, I have many students there, we will not be alone." Enoch grabs his wife's hand in a gentle squeeze.

"I wanna go too," one of the twins speaks up over his mouthful of food.

"Yeah, Kenan gets to go," the other one quickly adds.

"But you have to stay here and help me," Lamech, the second oldest brother, interjects. "We must protect our mother and sisters. What if one of the children of the Watchers attacked?" He holds his hands up like claws.

"Lamech!" Edna snaps at her son. "You will not speak of such things!"

Lamech just shrugs at her, but before he can reply, one of the twins shouts, "Don't worry, Mother, we will kill it!"

The boys swing around imaginary swords to prove their point.

"Enough of this. All of you." Edna turns to Enoch to change the subject. "I would like new garments for the girls, can you add that to your list?"

"Can you bring us back some cloth for new dresses, Father?" Martha asks when the table quiets enough for her soft voice to be heard. "Everyone in town says Noam has the best merchants. Ones from Egypt."

"Forget about dresses," says Dinah, Martha's older sister, but just by a few years. "Bring back one of those wild cats those queens in Egypt have as pets. That's what Eder told me."

"You would believe anything Eder told you," Martha says under her breath.

"His family has journeyed to Egypt," Dinah whispers harshly.

"He would tell you anything just because he wants you to be his wife," Martha affirms.

"So, what if he does?"

Edna interjects over the quarrels at the table. "Well, I think we can all agree on your father bringing back some new spices, and I will make lamb for dinner when they return."

That statement is met with a cheer, especially from the boys.

"May Elohim go before us on our journey and lead us in our path," Enoch says over the joyous din, and his family agrees heartily.

"And may Elohim and his holy angels bless our mother, the nourisher of our souls and our stomachs," Methuselah adds, sending a wink her way.

"Father," one of the twins, Tovi speaks up, "Will you tell us a story?"

"Oh yes, please, Father!" the other twin, Judah, adds.

"Oh well ..." Enoch starts, then seeing their expectant faces says, “I guess one more story before our trip won’t hurt.”

The twins excitedly settle in their seats, their dinner long forgotten as they wait for their father to begin.

“Which story would you like to hear?” Enoch asks.

“Tell us the one about the man who saw everything.” Martha says, then goes back to quietly nibbling on her piece of bread.

“Yes, the man who saw everything!” Judah concurs.

“Are you sure? I told that one last week.”

“We’re sure, Father.” The twins assure in unison.

Enoch clears his throat to begin the story.

“There once was a man who was with Elohim. And Elohim gave the man a scroll.” Enoch glances around the table. Satisfied that everyone is eagerly listening, he continues. “The man takes the scroll, unfurling it in his hand, and what does he see?”

“He see’s everything!” the twins shout, joining in on the storytelling.

Enoch nods. “That’s right, he sees everything. And the man looks at everything, and what does he see?”

This time the rest of the family members answer together, “He sees *Adom*.”

“He sees mankind,” Enoch agrees. “And *Adom* was blessed and multiplied. He saw them together with Elohim. Then the man looked at everything again, and what did he see?”

“He saw a sacrifice,” the table answers.

“He saw a sacrifice, holy and pure. And it pleased Elohim. Again, the man looked at everything, and what did he see?”

“He saw a man.” Lamech gives this answer.

“And he knew not who the man was. But he looked at the man, and what did he see?”

This time, the family does not have an answer.

Enoch pauses, staring off as if something has caught his attention in the distance.

“He saw …” Something flashes before Enoch’s vision. “He saw the man’s hands.”

Again, Enoch pauses and some of the family members exchange confused glances. After what seems like a long while, Enoch shakes himself out of his trance.

“And then … And then the man looked back at everything,” Enoch continues his story, “and what did he see?”

“He saw himself.” Methuselah is the one who answers this time.

Enoch nods adamantly. “He saw himself. So, the man turns to Elohim, and says, ‘All of this you have shown to me.’”

Everyone completes the story now, “So may it be!”

***

The next morning, they load their packs onto donkeys to start their journey to Noam. Enoch uses one donkey for just his scrolls and tablets. Each one contains different information from the economic state of the city to an alphabet used to teach future scribes. Enoch double checks each one to ensure nothing is missing.

“Don’t forget my spices,” Edna reminds during goodbyes.

“I have it marked into my mind, woman,” Enoch replies. “Or would you rather I write it down on one of my scrolls as not to forget?”

She swats him away and turns to her younger son, Kenan, not yet fifteen years of age. “And you, stay with your brother,” she reprimands him lightly, then kisses him on the forehead.

“And *you*, stay out of trouble.” She gives Methuselah a hug, squeezing tightly with each word for added emphasis. Then her voice softens, “Watch after Kenan for me.”

“Of course,” he replies with a hug and smile back.

After each family member gets their chance to say goodbye, the trio starts out on their journey. They travel until well after dark, and then finally set up camp. Enoch and Methuselah take turns keeping watch throughout the night. Their group is so small that they shouldn’t attract any unwanted attention, but it’s better for them to be safe.

The nights are cold, so they keep the fire fed throughout the night, only letting it die down to embers in the early morning.

When the first morning rays touch the sky, they pack up and set out once again for another day of travel. They pass through grassy plains and deserts, always headed directly east. In some places, paths are worn and are easy to follow. Trade is quite common between the two cities. They even pass a caravan going in the opposite direction.

On the third day, they pass by something a little more unnerving. Cresting a rocky hill, they see what looks to be a giant round boulder. Looking closer, they can see it is a skull.

It lays on its side, crushed halfway into the ground. Its jaw is unhinged in a wide gape, and most of the rest of its body is gone.

Kenan stares, openly shocked at its size, the skull itself is his height. Enoch just stares straight ahead, however, with a set expression.

No one says anything about the skull. In fact, they don't say much of anything for the rest of the day.

Finally, on the fourth day, the first glimpses of houses can be seen over the sandy hills.

Cresting a dune, the city stretches out before them, curving along the bank of a river. The sand changes to grass and trees along the banks. Near the center of the city is the tall governing palace, surrounded by hundreds of stone buildings. The sounds from the city grow louder with their approach. The clamor is nearly overpowering as they pass by the outskirts of the market area.

The streets are narrower here, with cloths and banners draped across from one rooftop to another. From instruments to merchants yelling, to exotic animals for trade, around each turn is a barrage for the senses.

Kenan takes a step back, bumping into Methuselah when a hyena lunges at him. Its chain and muzzle stop it from causing any harm, but it does elicit a laugh from its owner at Kenan's reaction.

They quickly make their way around the busy market to the larger houses along the riverbank.

Stopping in front of one stone house, Enoch announces, "This is it!"

He steps up to the door and raps several times on the frame. A short and slightly plump woman comes to answer the knock. A thick mop of black curly hair clings around her face.

She stares silently for a second then exclaims, "Enoch! Oh, it's so good to see you!" She gives him a firm hug before turning to her other two visitors. "And Methuselah, look at how you've grown."

"Has it really been that long, Aunt Ardella?" he replies.

She smiles. "And what is your name?"

"Kenan," the younger boy answers seriously.

Methuselah musses up his hair and smiles.

"Well, please do come in. Reu will be so glad to see you when he comes back this evening." She ushers Enoch inside while Methuselah and Kenan take the animals to the stables.

After they finish unloading, they join their father inside where Ardella is preparing them something to eat.

"I've sent Aner to go fetch Reu." She nods toward Kenan. "You'll have to meet my son. He's about your age. You boys must be famished after your trip."

She sets down a plate of dried fruit and seeds in front of them.

"Where's the rest of the children?" Enoch asks.

"All gone," she says with a wave of her hand. "Married or on their own." She looks as if she might tear up for a second but then adds, "My girls are in the palace."

"What do they do there?" Kenan asks with a mouthful of fruit.

"Why, they serve," she replies with a slight laugh, then shakes her head. "Anyway, what about Edna? She is doing well?"

"Oh yes, she's sorry she couldn't make the trip, but with twins not yet six years old … well, let's just say she keeps busy," Enoch replies.

"Twins!" Ardella exclaims, placing her hands on her hips. "Well, all I can say is thank the holy angels that comes from her side of the family and not yours. I stayed busy enough with my twelve, but with Aner being the youngest, well, I can't say I do miss having some little ones around."

None of the men seemed to be fully paying attention, but if Ardella notices, she doesn't care. In fact, she seems content just to have some new ears to hear the chronicles of her life.

They exchange stories for a while, catching up on all the news. In the middle of one such story, they are interrupted by a booming voice from the doorway.

"Could it be that my brother has come to visit me?" Reu asks with his arms open. He resembles Enoch in the face, but the similarities end there. He is several inches taller and has a large square-shaped frame.

Enoch stands to meet his brother's embrace. "Reu! It's so good to see you again."

Reu squeezes his brother in an overwhelming bear hug and laughs loudly before letting him go.

The two brothers talk quickly, until Reu announces, "Well

hurry up, woman. Go fix them some more food. I'm sure they're hungry after their long trip."

Ardella stands up, reluctant to leave the conversation, but busies herself anyway.

"You might just starve between all the talking she does," Reu mumbles.

Another boy appears in the doorway. He has the tallness of his father but is much leaner than either of his parents. However, he does seem to inherit the curly black hair from his mother.

"Ah, Kenan, this is my Aner," Reu introduces.

Aner just shrugs and says, "I can show you my new bow." Then he leads Kenan through the doorway.

"Ah, Kenan don't go too far…" Enoch calls after the boys who are already disappearing out the door.

Reu sits heavily beside his two companions. "Now that it's just us men, let's get down to business. Tell me of the state of your city."

"We've barely stepped in the door, and you already want to talk about economy?" Enoch replies with a slight laugh.

Reu brushes off Enoch's comment and says, "We've had a rough year. The conditions are good for crops, yes, but there is a tribe of Nephilim that have moved in nearby. They expect us to help with their rather large appetites." He waves his hands in the air, then sighs and picks up a loaf of bread.

Methuselah raises a brow, seemingly not quite convinced his uncle isn't somehow related to the Nephilim.

Reu continues. "It hasn't been too bad so far, but anyone with eyes can see that we can't sustain them for too long."

"Why don't they plant their own crops?" Methuselah asks. When his uncle gives him a dismissive look he adds, "It's not like they haven't before."

"Different place, different time. They've figured out it's easier for them to have us do it," Reu replies.

"Easier?" Methuselah crosses his arms. "Why do we make it easier for them."

Reu sighs loudly this time, then grabs a handful of dried fruit before exclaiming, "Do you think they haven't made threats yet? Nothing to cause too large of a stir, but it's been more than just a camel or some sheep disappearing every now and again, I can tell you that." He points his finger at Methuselah with his last statement.

"Reu, if it's really that bad why don't you come to stay with us?" Enoch interjects in a barely audible voice. "They stay away from the mountain." He adds, "Well, at least for now they do."

"You were always more likely to think that way," Reu answers with another sigh.

Enoch clears his throat, about to defend his position, when his brother adds, "If we let them have our homes here, soon we will have nowhere to live. They may avoid the mountain now, but they have little respect for their fathers anyway. The Watchers may be the only ones strong enough to stand up to the Nephilim but, believe me, they pay little mind to the affairs of man." Reu leans back before continuing, "You are always around them, surely you can attest to that."

Enoch processes his brother's speech for a moment before answering.

"I am a scribe. I keep account of the days, trade, the movement of stars, and the language it's all recorded in. What the Watchers think about man or their own offspring is not my concern."

Reu laughs now. "It will be when their offspring is living on your doorstep."

CHAPTER THIRTEEN

NOT IN THE STARS

That night, Enoch tosses and turns in his sleep. A dream keeps haunting him.

Visions of destruction float around his consciousness. An ocean of fire becomes an ocean of blood. Next are the earthquakes, the ground splits in half below his feet. And from the darkness below comes screams from an innumerable number of voices.

It floods his mind, until all he can feel is horrifying darkness. And then he hears only one voice.

"Enoch."

He jolts upright. The room is dark, but his eyes quickly adjust in the dim light. He scans the room for his beckoner, but his only companions are still sound asleep—Methuselah and Kenan.

Enoch runs a hand through his short hair. The dark brown strands cling to his sweaty forehead.

He watches the rhythmic rise and fall of his sons' chests, before finally laying back down on his mat.

Sleep visits him again, and this time, the dreams allude.

That morning, he pulls Methuselah away before the family

gathers for breakfast.

"You want to leave?" Methuselah asks his father who has leaned even nearer to him in confidence. "We've only just arrived. Why are you saying this?"

Enoch looks past Methuselah to the rest of his family in the next room over. Ardella looks busy preparing a breakfast while simultaneously giving her husband some sort of instruction.

Enoch lowers his voice. "I had a vision last night."

"A vision? The scribe becomes a prophet?" Methuselah raises a brow at his father.

"I don't know what it meant, and it wasn't the content of the vision, but the feeling I got from it." He pauses. "I think we should leave as soon as possible."

"Father, how could a dream make you feel like this?"

"It wasn't just a dream." Enoch looks around, trying to find a better explanation.

Methuselah stays silent for a moment, then crossing his arms, says, "Well, how do you know that dream means we should leave? Maybe it means we shouldn't leave?"

Enoch leans his head back against the wall and closes his eyes, letting out a tired breath. "There is something wrong here," he finally manages to say.

Sighing, Methuselah tries a different approach. "Let's go into the city today. You can meet with the scribes, Kenan and I will check out the market, and tonight we will see what your dreams say. But you shouldn't be so worried about it."

This compromise is reasonable enough to Enoch and he agrees. Their resolution comes just in time too, as Ardella calls them into the other room for some breakfast.

Enoch and Methuselah stay quiet during the meal, mostly because they aren't in the mood for conversation, and Kenan stays quiet because he's rarely in the mood for conversation. However, Ardella and Reu provide enough discussion so that there is little silence.

Enoch pays little mind to them, as he still seems to hear the echoes of the voices crying out in anguish.

After they finish their meal, Enoch announces his plans to go into the city, and Reu and Aner agree to join them.

The city is even livelier in the mornings as they step out onto the dirt roads. Merchants and traders start out early setting up their tables, lined with everything from caged birds to furs and linens. The cloth banners hanging over the narrow streets provide a reprieve from the morning sun.

The smell is the only thing more overwhelming than the noise. The harsh odor from animals mixes with burning incense and herbs. If an animal isn't on a leash or in a cage, it is either sizzling over a fire or has its hide displayed on a table.

Some of the creatures Methuselah and Kenan have never seen before. One looks like a bumpy lizard with a long snout. Though it isn't very big, it has a leather strap around its mouth, binding it shut. A man with only a couple teeth holds the creature in his arms, rubbing his boney fingers over its tough hide.

The group presses through the throngs, practically shouting to hear each other over the clamor.

"Methuselah, you, Kenan, and Aner can explore the market, I'll try to make my trip quick." Enoch pats the scrolls wrapped under his arm. "Meet me back at your Uncle's later and keep a tight hold on your money," he warns Methuselah before Reu pulls him away.

With that, they split up, Reu showing Enoch the quickest escape from the crowd.

Finally evading the masses, they make their way toward the quieter governing palace. Palace might not be the best word to describe the building, but the large stone structure stands three times taller than most other houses. Although there is not as much of a clamor in this area, the atmosphere does not seem peaceful.

In fact, as Enoch looks up at the stone edifice, his uneasy feeling from before resurfaces. The looming edifice doesn't have the same effect on Reu, however, as he ushers Enoch toward the entryway.

The ceilings and doorways match the building in size, extending upward much farther than what is necessary for the average man.

Enoch knows exactly why those ceilings are so tall.

Passing through the entry, they head directly toward the library. The telltale sound of scratching on parchment is the first hint that they're heading in the right direction.

The library is a large, open room filled with wooden tables. Scrolls and tablets cover each table, and even more are stored away in the alcoves of the walls. There are scribes everywhere, many more than the few that occupy the smaller library in their home city of Armon.

In fact, Noam has grown so much over the past couple years and has become the trade center of the land, in both goods and knowledge.

Enoch is barely inside the entryway when a man comes to greet him.

"Enoch! Could it be?" The tall, thin man rushes over to clasp hands with his visitor.

Enoch nearly spills the scrolls from under his arm, but his excited greeter barely notices.

"How long has it been, teacher?" the man asks.

"Far too many years, I must confess." Enoch replies, returning the man's jubilant smile.

Enoch's student beckons him over to a chair, and they spend the next several minutes catching up. Reu follows too, although clearly disinterested in any of the scribe's works.

Enoch unrolls several of his scrolls, pointing out the things he's learned over the years. The thin man calls over some of his own apprentices who stare excitedly at the first man to create a written language. Enoch eagerly answers all their questions, quite comfortable in his teaching mode.

Both the students and scholars aren't sure how much time has passed before they are interrupted. Reu could probably give an exact amount, however, as he slumps back in his chair, staring blankly at the decorative ceiling tiles.

A servant woman appears beside them. She is dressed much more extravagantly than most of the other women in the city, with a dyed red dress and several beaded necklaces around her neck. A halo of beads is woven into her hair and her eyebrows are painted black. "Master would like to see you," she says.

Enoch exchanges a look with his brother, who asks, "Why? What does he want with him?"

The woman just smiles politely and indicates for Enoch to follow her.

"I'll come with—" Reu begins but Enoch silences him with a raised hand.

"It's alright, brother. I know how to be diplomatic in front of rulers," he says, adding in a halfway convincing smile.

He thinks back to the first time he met the Watchers. Back when their teachings were simple, and they did not hide away in their stone fortress.

When they had first come to the city below Mount Armon, they were always helpful, and encouraged Enoch in his work. They would refer to him as Enoch the Scribe and share with him important details about the world they live in for him to record in his scrolls.

After several years had passed, their teachings began to change. Instead of just teaching the patterns of the stars, their practices became something of obsession. They would instruct men on how to pull their futures from those lights in the sky, and men became so dependent on the practice that they wouldn't make even the simplest of decisions without first consulting the cosmos. Which is ridiculous, Enoch thinks, because the future is like something behind you, you can't see it.

Of course, this was just the start of changes. The Watchers demonstrated how to make all types of weapons, and this, too, became something of fervor. Simple land skirmishes became all out wars. People stopped being hospitable, preferring to become untrusting and callous.

It was not long after these changes that Enoch decided to focus all his time on studying. In a year, he had created a written form of their language, complete with an alphabet that creates a picture for each word.

It has become apparent that his fame precedes him, as even kings request his presence.

As they exit the refuge of the library, Enoch clears his mind by reviewing some of the basics of creating a word, a practice that has always served to compose him. He starts with the word "father." This is a very simple word, only two letters. The first is the image of an ox head, simply meaning strength.

The second is a picture of a tent, and in a tent, is a family. Putting the two letters together creates a word that literally means tent pole. Of course, Enoch knows the nuances of that word, and how a tent pole paints the picture of the strength of the family—the father.

"Mother" is very similar. It starts the same with the ox head, but next is the image of water. Enoch got this idea from the way they make glue, boiling the left-over animal parts until the substance rose to the top of the water. The father may be the strength of the family, but the mother is what holds it all together.

"Strength," he mumbles to himself. "The father is the strength."

Enoch is just about to move onto the word "son," when they stop in front of a massive wooden door. He exhales a breath as he feels his heart rate return to normal.

Following the servant's motion that he should enter, Enoch presses the door open a crack. Its groan reverberates way too loudly against the stone walls. All eyes turn toward Enoch, including a very large pair of eyes from someone sitting in the middle of the room.

The ruler sits back leisurely in his throne. Although he is definitely not the largest Nephilim Enoch has seen, he still stands twice as tall as the scribe. His limbs match the thick supporting pillars in the room, and his fists are boulders. A wide, protruding jaw defines his face, and Enoch can't help but notice that his skin almost has a red tint to it.

Maidservants stand on both sides of the throne, all dressed in bright fabric, with the same painted faces and braided hair. Enoch wonders briefly if any of them could be his nieces.

The guards in the room are all normal men, which makes their king look even more powerful, towering over them.

Enoch takes a step forward but stops at the sound of the governing Nephilim's voice.

"Could it be?" he says with a low voice that bounces off every stone in the room. "The original scribe, Enoch, has come to my city?"

Enoch feels that his throat is suddenly too dry.

The Nephilim motions to the side. "Please sit down."

Enoch lets out a sigh when he sees where one of the Nephilim's twelve fingers is pointing. There, parallel to the throne, is a solid stone chair, but its seat is above Enoch's shoulders.

"Oh, forgive me, please bring our guest something more his size." The Nephilim doesn't bother to conceal his smile as a servant helps Enoch with his seating arrangement. "I am Balaam, king of this city." He waits for some shocked reaction from Enoch.

When Enoch remains silent, he continues, though slightly irritated. "So, tell me, what is the reason you have graced us with your visit?" He lifts a goblet to his lips while waiting for an answer.

A servant has brought Enoch a stool that is more his size, and he situates himself. "I have students here who I have taught the written language. I have come to give updates and record news about the state of the cities surrounding Mount Armon," Enoch answers as a servant brings him a drink of his own. The servant keeps his eyes cast downward as he hands off the goblet.

"Ah, yes Mount Armon, you are a scribe for the Watchers are you not?" Balaam asks pointedly.

"Yes."

The king swooshes his drink around in his cup. "Now, there is a certain Watcher, I would like you to tell me about." Balaam rubs a hand over his chin, "Are you acquainted with Barkayal?"

Unsure where this questioning is going, Enoch stumbles over his words, but manages to say, "Yes, of course, he teaches the observation of the stars."

"And you have learnt that from him?"

"Some, yes. I've studied the patterns of the sky. The moon and stars." Enoch goes to take a drink but stops as he stares down at the thick, red liquid in his cup.

"Not to your liking?" Balaam asks with a slight smirk.

"I …" Enoch starts but feels the knot in his throat hinder him from answering.

"Don't look so alarmed," the Nephilim replies with a laugh. "It's from an ox. I wouldn't be so cruel as to give you the blood of your own kind."

***

"Can Aner and I go into the desert?" Kenan asks his brother over the sounds of the market.

The two boys look at him expectantly, and Methuselah reluctantly nods after a moment. "Yes, but be back at Aunt and Uncle's house *before* mid-day."

Methuselah barely confirms a reply before the boy's heads disappear out of sight in the crowd. Something quickly catches his attention before he gives them a second thought.

A pair of dark, painted eyes shadowed under an embroidered hood is all it takes to draw him over to a particular stand. The mysterious woman gives him a beckoning smile and he gladly obliges. She looks young, in her forties or fifties, and is dressed in a decorative manner.

Two thick braids peak out from under her red hood, and her ears are pierced with metal rings. Her prominent nose is also pierced with a gold hoop.

"Now, what could you be selling?" Methuselah asks, looking down at the blank table where the woman sits.

Directly behind her is a curtained doorway that gives no hint to her cryptic trade.

To answer, she holds out her open hand and asks, "Read your palm?"

He raises an eyebrow but places his upright palm in her hand. She examines it for several seconds, while he examines her thick lashes and tan complexion.

Finally, she proclaims, "You are a hard worker."

"And which line says that?" he asks leaning forward on his elbow.

She raises her brows and points at a callous. "This does right here."

"Oh, I see," he says drawing his hand away. "You're a fake," he says with a confident smirk.

She snatches his hand back before he can get too far and says, "You will have a long life."

He cocks his head to the side, leaning closer. "Won't we all? Now tell me something good or I won't pay you."

She gives him what seems to be a forced smile and replies, "Very well. You think you can use your looks to obtain whatever you want."

"You got that from my hand?"

"No, I got that from your well-kept hair."

Slightly offended, he runs a hand through his hair, making sure it's all in place. Before he can come up with a good rebuttal, however, another woman appears in the doorway with a swoosh of the curtain.

"Ah, I see our palmist here has piqued your interest." The tall woman offers a wide smile. She looks to be older, perhaps around two hundred, and her outfit is more elaborate than the other woman. Beads and feathers decorate her hair and match a layered necklace.

"You could say that," Methuselah mumbles.

"Perhaps you would like to learn more about sorcery?" the tall woman says with raised, thin brows.

Methuselah shakes his head. "Not really interested."

"Are you sure?" she pushes. "I can tell you have a strong spirit. You could learn it well."

"I don't—"

"Don't let us fool you." She claps her hands together. "We have learned the teachings of Samyaza and Danieal themselves. I can read the stars and the signs. I know the dividing of roots."

"We have actually traveled from Mount Armon," Methuselah replies when he hears the familiar names.

"Ah, so you are familiar with the Watchers!" she says with a spark of excitement in her gray eyes.

The woman sitting at the table also seems interested in the conversation now. "You have met him? Samyaza?"

"Not I, but my father has on several occasions. He is a scribe," Methuselah replies.

"Then surely your father must know sorcery," The older woman says.

Methuselah hesitates at first. "Our family tries to avoid it. My father says it is not Elohim's will."

"Is there anything on this earth that is?" the young woman says, more to herself than anyone else.

Methuselah decides it's best not to reply and just says, "Thank you, but I'm not interested. You have the wrong person."

"Well, I'm sorry I could not convince you, but we offer more than just sorcery. Perhaps you would be interested in something else? Herbs? Incense—"

"How much for the girl?" Methuselah indicates the woman sitting, then folds his arms across his chest.

Being sure to gauge her reaction, he notices that her expression goes from shock to a scowl in an amazingly fast amount of time. He gives her a smile, but that just increases her irritation.

"Why … no, I'm sorry," the older woman fumbles. "Edna is invaluable to me—"

"Her name is Edna?" Methuselah interjects.

"You don't like her name?"

"No, no Edna is a … a very good name," he says with

confidence even though she is still glaring at him.

"Still, I cannot go without her, I—"

Methuselah raises a hand, then digs a coin out of his money bag and tosses it on the table. "For the reading." He gives a nod, then turns back into the crowd.

***

Just outside the city, Kenan runs to catch up with Aner. The two boys jog on the rocky terrain, careful to avoid any thorny bushes. Stopping in front of one particularly steep hill, Aner slings his bow over his shoulder before starting his ascent.

"Come on, we can get a better vantage point from up here," he says as Kenan follows closely behind.

Cresting the top of the hill, Aner motions for them to crouch down. Kenan's eyes scan the valley below, where a little pool of water has collected. A dense row of trees lines the backside, and rough hills help keep the little pond secluded.

Aner places his finger over his lips, then points down into the valley. Kenan follows the motion until he sees a deer gingerly step toward the water. It sniffs the water a couple times, and Aner raises his bow.

The deer's ears flick back, and it raises its head to look around. Every muscle in its body tenses.

"Aner …" Kenan's voice catches in his throat as he pushes himself up on one hand.

"Be quiet!" Aner whispers harshly and lines up his shot.

"No, no, Aner, look!" Kenan frantically hits him and points down at the deer.

"What is …" Aner's annoyed voice trails off as he raises his bow a couple inches, pointed at the trees.

Hidden by the branches, a massive pair of eyes is stalking the same prey. Aner sees a row of jagged, pointy teeth.

His fingers slip. With a swoosh, the arrow shoots off, passing over top of the deer and into the woods.

The arrow seems like only a mild annoyance as the giant head rises out of the trees. What is more annoying, is that the deer is already long gone, scrambling off in another direction.

With teeth bared, the Nephilim towers above the trees. The tops of the branches barely reach up to his waist. A thick layer of orangey desert mud is caked all over his body, making his skin look decayed. He haunches over slightly and his eyes fixate on his new prey. His eyes widen as if he's gone insane.

The boys freeze into place, but it's too late. With one massive step forward, the Nephilim leaps toward the hill.

The boys scramble backward, narrowly avoiding a tree trunk of an arm that comes slamming between them. The Nephilim digs his claw-like fingers into the ground to help propel him forward.

Aner turns and bolts down the hill. The Nephilim follows suit, but slips, and slides down the hill on his back, letting out a scream of frustration at the same time.

Aner doesn't miss a step as he dashes forward.

"Stop! You'll take him back to the city!" Kenan calls after him but neither the boy nor the Nephilim gives him a second thought.

CHAPTER FOURTEEN

They Are Hungry

"Five pieces."

"Hmmm. I don't know." Methuselah rubs a hand over his chin as he talks with a merchant.

"These spices come all the way from Enos, you really can't expect a better price than this." The vendor holds out a jar full of sharp smelling leaves.

"Well, still …"

"Okay, okay, how about this." The man turns around and pulls a crate out from under the table. "I am the only merchant in the city who grows these." He sets the crate down with a dusty thud.

"What are …"

"From Egypt!" The man excitedly holds up an odd bulb-like vegetable.

Methuselah considers the peculiar vegetable for a second. "Alright, I will …" His voice trails off when he notices the crate on the table begin to rattle slightly.

Distant shouts draw his attention away as he scans the market for the source. He quickly pinpoints the cause of the chaos as he spots a massive head bob above the houses.

The panic quickly spreads through the crowd as people scramble for shelter. Tables topple and animals run free as people trample over each other, trying to escape the narrow alleyways.

"Kenan … Kenan!" Methuselah pushes forward in the crowd, running toward the last place he saw his brother. People slam against him as they run in the opposite direction.

Someone drops a crate full of doves and the birds escape through the broken slats, flying away from the fray.

The clamor only serves to draw the Nephilim's attention toward the market as he steps over houses. He stumbles forward like a mad dog, grasping at anyone close to him. He reaches into a crowd and snatches up the first person unfortunate enough to be in his way. It's a man, screaming desperately, trying to free himself from the Nephilim's grasp.

Ping!

An arrow bounces off the Nephilim's temple. The city's guards have finally acted. They barrage him with a shower of arrows, many of them doing little to no damage.

The attack does draw his attention away, however, and his grip loosens just enough to drop his captive. This proves to be just as unfortunate for the man as he plummets headfirst onto the ground below.

With an angry roar, the Nephilim jumps forward into the crowd, trampling, breaking, and snapping with every step. He lands on all fours, swings his arm into a line of guards, and smashes them against a building.

Those who are still on their feet scramble back, rethinking their attack strategy.

Methuselah frantically searches the crowd for any sign of his brother when something catches his attention. It's the girl from earlier—Edna. Though others are trying to clear out of the Nephilim's path, she steps directly in his way.

Methuselah sees her lips move as she appears to be repeating something over and over.

The Nephilim suddenly comes to a halt and clamps his hands over his ears. He lets out a vexing scream, then falls to his knees with his hands still firmly clasped around his head. Doubling over in pain, his yells of anguish ring off every stone.

The guards stand watching, too stunned for a moment to take any action. Finally, their captain orders them forward, rousing them out of their daze.

They capitalize on the Nephilim's distraction as they swarm in around him. Taking their long spears, they stab them any place they will go—his eyes, his throat.

Finally, a perfectly timed spear through his temple causes his screams to cease.

Edna's chants stop with him. She breathes heavily as if exhausted. With a few sways, she falls onto the ground. Methuselah runs up to her and lifts up her head.

"Methuselah!" Kenan runs up behind the pair.

Methuselah lets out a sigh of relief as he picks up Edna in his arms. "Come on, we need to go back to the house."

"But Aner—"

"We will find him, now come on."

"No, Methuselah—"

Methuselah finally stops to take a good look at his brother. He's trembling and his eyes are crazed and red. He looks as if he might keel over, so Methuselah readjusts the girl in his arms, and pulls Kenan away from the chaos.

"Aner … is he?" Methuselah doesn't have to finish his question because Kenan gives the most miniscule shake of his head. Kenan balls his hands into fists that shake as if they would explode.

Methuselah lets out a breath and turns his eyes away from his brother.

After a moment, he nods, and in a quiet voice says, "Let's go."

***

Blurry images start to come into focus. Edna's eyes flutter a couple times as she takes in her surroundings.

She's lying down, that much she knows. A wool blanket is pulled up to her chin. Some light streams in through the slats in the windows.

Sound begins to come back to her now. She hears some muffled voices that slowly grow into shouts.

"How do you not know?" an angry voice bellows above the rest. "What … how could this happen?"

Edna rolls over on her side and peers around the doorway into the other room. The movement causes her to bring a hand up to her head as she squints at the figures across the room.

A large man is yelling at a young boy. He grabs the boy by the shoulders and shakes him viciously. "What did you see?" he demands. "What did you see!" He smacks the boy across the face.

The man Edna saw earlier in the market comes into view, pulling the boy away from the man. An older man steps in as well, trying to dissolve the clash.

The large man just turns his anger to the older man and shoves him to the ground.

"Why did you teach them to be so weak?" he bellows.

The older man holds up a hand, signaling to the older of the boys to not come to his aid.

"Brother …" the older man starts.

"What's wrong with you?" The large man rages, clearly not interested in anything his brother has to say.

A woman comes up behind him and looks to the boy. "Is it true?" she asks as everyone falls silent.

The boy takes a step back but nods silently.

The woman clasps her hand over her mouth, letting out something that sounds like a sob. The large man's face crumbles and he sinks onto the floor. The woman follows suit, throwing her arms over the man and sobbing anew.

Edna's vision begins to darken around the edges as she watches the scene. Then she feels herself slipping back into the blackness.

This time when she awakens, everything is silent. She feels her senses sharpen as she focuses on the lamps flickering beside her.

It must be dark outside.

Her eyes then focus on a figure sitting near her feet, that same man from the market. He's leaning against the wall with his arms crossed.

"What …" She clears her throat and tries again. "What happened?"

He doesn't answer her, and instead gets up and steps over to a jar in the corner. He dips a clay cup into the jar and brings it over to her. When she doesn't make a move to take it, he sets it on the floor beside her.

"You didn't answer my question," she says as he takes a seat next to her.

"I think you should be answering that question. What's the last thing you remember?" he asks in a low voice.

She is about to answer when a woman appears around the corner. Her face is swollen from crying, and she keeps clutching her skirt in her hands.

"Oh, she's awake," she says in a weepy voice. "You're probably hungry. I thought I heard voices. I just couldn't sleep—" Her voice cracks and the man stands next to her.

"Please, Aunt Ardella, I'll take care of her, don't worry about it," he says.

She pats him tenderly and after a moment she says to him, "I know it's not his fault." Her voice is so low it's barely audible, but Edna still catches it.

Ardella manages to compose herself just slightly and turns to leave the room. "Something like this was going to happen eventually," she mumbles to herself as she leaves.

Edna's memory is suddenly clear.

"The attack ..." she blurts, sitting forward. "The Nephilim, he's—"

"Dead," the man finishes for her.

She leans back against the mat. "Good. It worked, then."

"What worked?" he asks, giving her a fixed look.

She scrutinizes him for several seconds, debating whether to tell him the truth. She decides there's no harm in telling him; it might even serve to her benefit.

"I called on a spirit to distract the Nephilim."

He blinks with a shake of his head. "What did it do to you?"

"Let's just call it payment," she says, almost letting a sardonic laugh escape, but thinking better of it.

"Payment for what?" he asks, unamused.

She folds her arms across her chest. "Everything has a price. Sorcery is just steeper."

"I thought you read palms, and the stars, or something."

"Perhaps I am stronger than you think," she says pointedly, staring him down.

He stands and leans his back against the wall. "If you're worried about your safety, don't be. I am, after all, the one who saved you and brought you here. Your … your companion didn't seem to be anywhere nearby."

She ignores his remark, so he changes the subject. "My mother's name is Edna as well."

She turns her head toward him. "Perhaps you should just call me Nan. That's what my mother used to call me, at least."

"Used to? Was that the woman at your stand?"

"And your name is?" She ignores his question.

"Methuselah."

"Well, Methuselah, you have my gratitude for making sure no harm came to me, but I will be taking my leave now."

"You're not going anywhere."

She freezes when he makes a move toward her, so he softly adds, "It's the middle of the night and everyone is on edge because of what happened earlier. You can at least wait until morning."

Nan doesn't look very happy with his answer, but she thinks it would probably be unwise to argue with him. As if reading her mind, Methuselah adds, "I promise you may leave in the morning, but it is dangerous for you to go out at night."

"Very well," she says, suddenly feeling too tired to argue. She settles back down into her bed.

***

The next morning, everyone sits quietly as they eat breakfast. Nan shifts on the floor, trying to eat as quickly and silently as she can. She notices that not everyone is here this morning. The large man from last night, which she has since learned is named Reu, is gone. The younger boy has also not made an appearance. Only Ardella, Methuselah, and his father are present.

Ardella hasn't touched any of the food before her, even though everyone else seems to be finished.

Deciding now is a good opportunity, Nan moves over to Ardella and kneels beside her. She bows her head down low and says, "I cannot repay you and your family for the kindness you have shown me. I ask that I may leave now, for I am very anxious to check on my family."

Ardella places her hand on Nan's hair and replies, "Of course, my child."

"No one is going anywhere," Reu interrupts as he suddenly appears in the doorway. "There will be more trouble."

"What's happened?" Ardella stands as her face turns white and she wobbles slightly. "Did you find anything?" she asks in a voice that's barely audible.

He shakes his head grimly, and then says, "There is another one."

"Not another attack?" Methuselah's father asks.

"No. But there could be one at any time. Another Nephilim has come for the one that was killed. Seeking revenge against the killer, I'm sure."

"But the guards killed him." Ardella tries to reason some explanation. "Surely king Balaam will not allow—"

"The king is with him now. He took the body but even with that he still won't leave ..."

Nan backs away slowly as she listens to the conversation. She knows how fast word can spread throughout the city, especially when people are desperate to pin the blame on someone.

She's just reached the back door when she decides what must be done. If she doesn't reach Mikah quickly, the consequences could be deadly.

Silently she pulls the door open just wide enough for her to squeeze out. To her relief, the family is still preoccupied with their conversation and doesn't notice.

Turning to disappear around the side of the house, she stops in her tracks when a hand clamps down on her wrist.

"Where do you think you're going?" Methuselah says, tightening his grip on her.

"Let me go! Didn't you hear what he said? That Nephilim is looking for the killer. I must find Mikah, and we have to leave." She emphasizes the last four words by struggling to pull away again.

"Mikah, the woman you work for? Is that your family?"

"Yes." She stops struggling.

"Fine." He loosens his grip slightly but still refuses to let go. "But please, just stay here. I will go and bring her back and then you can leave, alright?"

She narrows her eyes and with a shake of her head says, "Why would you do that?"

"Please, I promise I will bring her back to you."

She studies him for a few seconds then finally nods.

A look of relief passes his face, and he says, "Please just stay inside? I won't be gone but for a moment."

"Where we met at the market, she lives in the top floor of that house. She will be there." She swallows thickly as she says the words, willing them to be true in her mind.

Methuselah nods and lets her go. He stays for a moment to make sure she doesn't bolt, then disappears around the corner.

***

The city is eerily quiet as Methuselah makes his way through the alleys. There are no merchants or shoppers in the market today.

Instead, everyone is out picking through the rubble. It is apparent that many of them must have been out all night searching for any buried loved ones. Their hope of finding more survivors dwindles away as the sun rises further in the sky.

He doesn't pause to watch women wiping up blood that stains the streets and walls. He doesn't even pause to watch a line of people waiting to identify relatives from a pile of bodies.

Methuselah passes the spot where the Nephilim fell. A pool of blood staining the dirt road and a destroyed building is the only evidence left of his body.

So, the other Nephilim really did come take him. He must be just as big as the dead one, to carry the body away.

Just around this corner is where the house should be. Methuselah freezes in his tracks as he rounds the bend. Apparently, he isn't the first visitor to arrive. Several palace guards stand at the door.

Methuselah presses his back against the wall, peeking around the corner. Two guards go through the front door, while the others round the back, cutting off any escape.

Methuselah's attention is drawn to a window on the side of the house. The shutter silently opens, and he sees Mikah climb onto the windowsill. She drops down onto the ground, landing in a crouch. She lets out a tiny yelp and falls onto her side as she clutches her ankle.

Fortunately, the guards have not noticed her yet, but Mikah doesn't look like she can move very quickly as she winces in pain.

Methuselah considers his options. Casually, he steps out into the open and walks slowly in Mikah's direction. The guards waiting at the front door pay him no attention as he strolls over to the side of the house.

He catches Mikah's eye as she slowly pushes herself into a sitting position.

A guard comes around from behind the house and lets out a shout. He runs up to Mikah and grabs her, despite her feeble attempt to scramble away. Several more guards follow behind and drag her to her feet.

Methuselah decides this is a good time to switch directions and get out of the way of the guards. When it's apparent they aren't interested in him, he settles on the following-from-a-distance plan.

It becomes apparent they are heading toward the palace. Maybe if this woman can do one of those distraction things like Nan, she will be able to escape. However, Mikah doesn't make any moves. Methuselah churns through several different ideas as they come closer to the palace grounds, until finally he sees something that makes him lose his train of thought.

Another Nephilim, just as tall as the one who attacked, is pacing back and forth in front of the palace. He looks just as feral as well, with an armor of mud that seems to stay on him with the aid of thick body hair. He is almost twice the height of King Balaam, who is attempting to handle the situation, albeit not very well.

Methuselah doesn't have to get too close before he can hear their booming voices.

Balaam's relieved voice rings out first when the guards come approaching with Mikah. "Ah see! My guards have brought your brother's killer. Now, take her and be justified."

The Nephilim kneels, leaning in menacingly toward the woman and trembling guards.

"They tell me that it was a sorceress who killed my brother. Not the guards who drove spears through his skull." He directs his last statement toward the king, who plasters on a diplomatic smile.

"They were simply doing their job," Balaam says in a voice that's a little too soothing. "After all, your brother did kill several of my citizens. Please, just take the sorceress and we can be even."

This drags the Nephilim's attention away, as he slowly draws himself upward, overshadowing Balaam.

"Even? You treat us like animals. We scavenge for food. We can't even clothe ourselves so instead the earth is our covering." He almost seems to be laughing now. "Then, you think you can kill my only brother, and we're even?"

Balaam clears his throat while keeping a tight smile plastered on his face. "You can have the guards too. And we will give you more food. You won't have to live as wanderers—"

The Nephilim turns his attention back to the sorceress who is now cured of her muteness.

"Please! You have the wrong person," she argues frantically. "It was the girl. She works for me. She called a dark spirit to torment your brother."

The Nephilim snatches up Mikah as the guards dart out of the way. The woman's pleas turn more desperate. "You cannot have your revenge while his killer is still alive! Only I know where she is. I will bring her to you!"

She shakes with hysteria, but the Nephilim pauses. He considers for a moment, quite happy to be literally holding her life in his hands.

"Very well. You will find her, and you will bring her to me." The Nephilim bares his teeth and says, "And until you do, you will live as us, starving, naked, and with no place to rest your head."

Letting Mikah go, he watches her land hard on the ground below. She attempts to suck in a breath after the impact but is unable to move for several seconds.

The Nephilim ignores her and adds, "If anyone is caught harboring her, I will consider them part of my provision."

He displays his teeth in a smile that seems much more like a threat. He turns back toward the king. "I will accept your offer of the guards. I'm hungry."

He steps past Balaam who dodges out of the way to avoid getting run over.

"And one more thing," He turns and leans in close to the king.

"Your days are numbered. The strongest rule here, and I'm afraid that is no longer you."

CHAPTER FIFTEEN

A FAMILY

Satisfied that he's heard enough, Methuselah turns to hasten back to the house. He wastes little time upon his arrival, explaining the situation in a hushed voice to his father, who agrees they should leave immediately.

"Kenan, go get the animals ready. We are leaving as soon as it's dark," Enoch orders as they rush to collect their belongings.

"You're leaving …" Nan, who has appeared in the doorway, shoots Methuselah a confused look.

He takes her by the arm and pulls her to the side. She's already speaking before he has any chance at an explanation.

"You said you would bring her back," she accuses.

"Something's changed," he says, avoiding eye contact with her. "We have to leave the city now, and you're coming with us."

She yanks her arm out of his grasp. "I'm not going anywhere without Mikah," she says, not trying to hide her incredulous tone. "What's going on? Where is she?"

"Nan …"

"What?" she spits, already planning her escape route out of the house.

He straightens, finally looking her straight in the eyes. "She's dead."

Nan doesn't reply at first, staring at him with a blank expression.

He's beginning to think she doesn't understand him, when she says, "That can't be." She keeps her tone steady. "I had just seen her. She was right behind me." She shakes her head several times.

He places his hands on the sides of her arms. "She's gone. I'm sorry."

She backs away from him a couple steps and opens her mouth, but no words form.

"You're lying," she finally says.

"She was trying to protect you," Methuselah says, pleading. "That Nephilim's brother is looking for you. He will kill you too. We must leave."

He steps forward again, but she turns toward him with molten eyes.

"Then I will kill him first," she asserts, and darts toward the door before Methuselah has a chance to stop her.

Methuselah doesn't expect her to move so quickly and chases after her. He quickly learns, however, that she knows the city much better than him, as she eludes him down an alleyway. He has a good guess as to where she is heading, so he decides to take an alternate route and perhaps stop her before she does anything dire.

***

Nan pulls her hood up over her head as she races through the streets. She clears her mind, only focusing on the wrath that keeps her moving forward.

As she skids around a corner, she sees something that freezes her in place. Across several rooftops, she sees the head of the second Nephilim, and her courage begins to drain. Her rage dulls and is replaced with a new paralyzing emotion.

The Nephilim's pupils are constricted, making his eyes look almost completely white. His head turns, and he looks directly at her for a moment. Fresh bloodstains cover his mouth and drip down to his neck. He opens his mouth slightly, revealing strings of bloody saliva between his teeth.

Panic takes over Nan's body. Her breath catches in her throat, and she knows she cannot move, not even to save her life.

The Nephilim turns his head away, uninterested.

With the release of his gaze, Nan feels her feet loosen from the ground. She steps backward behind a building and slinks up against the wall.

She jumps when she feels a hand on her shoulder.

Methuselah pulls his hand away, looking unsure if he should touch her or not. She turns her unfocused eyes away from him as her breaths begin to come out in gasps now.

"She can't be dead," Nan whispers in an unfeeling voice.

Wrapping his arm around her shoulder, he says, "We have to leave."

She doesn't reply, but she also doesn't stop him from leading her back to the house.

***

Afterward, Nan stays quiet while they finish preparing to leave.

As the night draws in, Methuselah finally asks her, "Are you ready to go?"

A slight nod is all the affirmation she gives him.

The rest of Methuselah's family, however, is not so easily convinced. Enoch spent the rest of the evening trying to talk his brother into leaving with them, but Reu was firm.

"It doesn't matter where we go, we can never escape it … We can never escape them," he had said, turning coldly away from his brother, and Enoch gave up trying to change his mind.

Ardella was much more sorrowful, but she agreed with Reu. "We have always known …" Her voice trails off and she finally says, "We cannot leave our daughters."

Enoch's face turns grim at this, but he doesn't offer a rebuttal.

The last rays of sunlight disappear over the horizon and everyone says their solemn goodbyes. Nan notices that Reu keeps some distance from Enoch as they part, only giving his brother a tight-lipped nod.

The group of four head out the back way, silently leading the donkeys along the riverbank, then disappear into the night.

They don't stop at all the first night or the next day. But as the day draws to a close, they are satisfied that they are far enough from the city. The group stops to set up camp and let their animals rest.

They find an outcropping of rocks along a little stream and build a fire in one of the caves. Enoch and Kenan take the donkeys to the stream, leaving Nan and Methuselah alone.

No one has said much more than two sentences during their journey.

After several seconds of Methuselah mutely poking at the fire, he speaks up.

"I am sorry," he says then clears his throat. "That I couldn't save her, I mean."

She draws her legs up to rest her chin on her knees.

"No. It's not your fault," she says with a voice not much louder than the cracks of the fire. "She was not yours to protect."

Methuselah stares at the charring wood, avoiding her gaze.

"The fault is not yours either," he says carefully, then throws a stick on the fire and watches the sparks rise in the air. He finally meets her gaze.

She shakes her head slightly and makes a noise halfway between a laugh and sob. "Yeah, nothing is ever my fault."

Not sure how to reply to that, Methuselah hesitantly asks, "Why do you do it? The sorcery?"

She lets a short breath out of her nose. "Because I'm tired of running." She stares into the bright tongues of fire. "Tired of leaving everyone behind to die."

Methuselah directs his eyes downward again. "Nan, Mikah was—"

"I'm not talking about her," she says then quickly silences as Enoch and Kenan come join them in the rocky hollow, settling down in front of the fire.

"Well, this isn't as nice as our comfortable home, but it will still work, huh?" Enoch asks, sitting between his sons, and quite oblivious to the previous tension.

Methuselah lets out a sigh, stands, and says, "I'm going to take watch."

For the rest of their trip home, Methuselah doesn't hound Nan for any more details, and she makes it clear that she does not intend to offer up any more information.

On the fourth day of traveling, he announces to her that they will arrive shortly. Before their house is even in sight, the rest of Methuselah's younger siblings come to greet them. The twin boys run up first, followed quickly behind by two other sisters.

"The boys are Judah and Tovi, and my two younger sisters Dinah and Martha." Methuselah whispers to Nan as they approach.

The little kids become overly excited at the new big sister their brother brought home, but the older girls stare with shocked expressions.

"Father, what is this? Who is she?" Dinah asks, crossing her arms and openly staring at Nan.

Enoch attempts to calm everyone down with a raised hand. "Girls, this is Ed—"

"Nan," Methuselah interjects. "You can call her Nan."

"She's pretty," Martha whispers, but Dinah just continues to scrutinize.

"How many siblings do you have?" Nan asks as the little boys run around her, attempting to sword fight each other with sticks.

"Nine. Six at home, and two older sisters and one younger who are already married and no longer live here," Methuselah answers.

"And here he is, the oldest brother and still not married." A slightly younger man steps up beside Methuselah and puts him in a headlock.

"Oh yes, I forgot about this one," Methuselah says, straining under the pressure of brotherly love. "Nan, this is—"

"Lamech." The man answers, nodding in introduction with a half-smile.

"My *younger* brother," Methuselah interjects with a sigh.

"Also, yet to take a wife," Lamech says, releasing his brother and taking Nan's hand in one smooth movement. He raises her hand up between them. "Nan, it's an honor to meet you." He gives her a wink and Nan smiles slightly at the over-the-top display.

"Alright." Methuselah places his hands on the top of Lamech's shoulders. "Perhaps you should go let Mother know we've returned. I'm sure she's eager to see us." He emphasizes his words with a tight squeeze that turns Lamech's smile into more of a grimace.

"Oh, but there's our mother now," he replies pointing to Edna making her way toward the group.

She stops to greet her husband first. "You're back already? What happened?" She doesn't wait for his answer, and instead wraps him in a hug.

She pulls away when she notices the extra female presence.

"Who is … I did not think you took my request to bring Methuselah back a wife seriously," she says with a shocked expression.

"What? Oh, no," Enoch replies with a laugh. "It's not like that. It's … well …" He pauses for a moment as if something had just occurred to him. "Methuselah are you taking her as a wife?"

"No." Both Methuselah and Nan reply at the same time, then shoot each other a look.

"Hmm," Edna replies, then looks over to where Methuselah and Lamech are standing.

The two brothers stand shoulder to shoulder, both appear to be in some unseen competition over who will stand closer to Nan.

"I guess that's good because it looks as if you should have brought back two," Edna mutters under her breath to Enoch.

Edna ushers everyone toward the house as she interrogates the group. "Well, tell me quickly what has happened that you returned so soon."

Enoch begins to explain then drops to hushed tones as he notices that the littlest ones are listening. He pulls Edna to the side, describing the rest.

A look of pity crosses Edna's face as she looks back over the group.

"I am thankful you are safe," she says finally and turns to Nan. "Of course, you must stay with us. Please make this place your home."

Nan bobs her head politely in return. "Your family has shown me such kindness. I am forever indebted to you."

Even though she wasn't expecting them back so soon, Edna still prepares a large meal for them that night. No one asks any unnecessary questions about their trip. Instead, they all eat quietly and turn in early for the night.

As everyone is getting ready for bed, Edna takes Nan to the side and explains that she can sleep with the girls. "I've put down extra bedding for you. I'm sure you'll be comfortable." She takes Nan's hand in hers. "Methuselah explained to me what happened. I'm so sorry. You are welcome to stay with us for as long as you like. Whatever you want to do is alright with us," Edna says, giving her a smile.

"Thank you," Nan replies and takes a linen nightdress Edna offers to her.

As she enters the girls' room, the two sisters both fall silent.

Martha is the first to offer any greeting. "Nan, you can sleep on that mat there."

Nan nods her head and then quietly begins to change into her nightdress.

"How do you get your hair to look like that?" Martha asks as Nan removes her scarf.

The sudden question catches Nan off guard, but she replies, "You mean this?" She holds her intricately twisted braid between her fingers. When Martha nods, she replies, "Oh, I just braided it."

"Could you show me how?"

"Martha, you would look like a harlot," Dinah finally speaks, narrowing her eyes at her sister.

"I would not! I like it. I think it looks pretty." Martha smiles at Nan. "Please, show me how," she asks again.

Dinah just rolls over on her mat. "Leave her alone. Can't you see she doesn't want to talk to us?" she mumbles under her breath.

Martha ignores her sister and pats a spot next to her on her mat, indicating for Nan to sit down.

"Well, you have to start with two pieces of hair at the top of your head." She takes a handful of Martha's hair, dividing it in half.

"Don't mind Dinah." Martha turns her head, whispering to Nan. "It just takes her a little bit to get used to new people. But I know she thinks you're pretty."

Nan smiles and nods in reply, then continues to say, "Your hair is curly, so it will look very nice like this."

***

The next morning, the girls are up before the sun.

"We always go down to the stream to bring up some fresh water for the day," Martha explains, as the girls get dressed. "Does my hair still look good?" she asks Dinah.

Her sister looks over the several pieces of curly hair sticking out from the braid. "Yes, it still looks good," she answers but can't help a small smile.

Nan follows behind as the girls get one of the donkeys to take down to the stream.

"We hang these pots from either side of the donkey, and she carries them back for us," Martha explains as she hangs the two clay pots over either side of the animal's back, then grabs a much smaller jar that will be used to fill the big ones.

Then, they lead the animal behind the house and down a grassy hill to the riverbank. The water is no more than a foot deep, but Martha explains how it would rise a couple feet more during the rainy season.

The sheep have also come down to drink while the sun is still just below the horizon.

Nan turns her head up toward the sky to let the morning rays bathe her face. The cool air refreshes her, and she feels the tension she didn't realize she was holding ebb slightly.

She turns when she hears the twins come running down the hill behind them. One of them, Nan thinks it is probably Tovi, takes a tumble. He quickly recovers, however, and catches up to his brother at the bottom of the hill.

"Nan, come play shepherds with us!" the one who didn't take a tumble says. Yes, he's definitely Judah, Nan thinks as she notices the distinctive freckles on his left cheek.

"Boys, Nan can't play right now," Dinah says, then quickly adds, "She has to help us."

"I promise I'll come play later," Nan says with a smile and the boys disappear between the sheep.

"They surely like you." Martha laughs.

"Yes, all the men in this family seem to," Dinah says under her breath as she dips one of the smaller jars into the stream.

By the time the girls have almost finished filling up the jars, the boys come running back again. However, this time instead of their voices being excited, they are anxious.

"Come quick! She had her baby but something's wrong!" they say in unison.

"What? Who?" Martha asks, but the boys are already leading them through the tall grass.

Through a parting in the grass, they see one of the ewes with her head bent over a lump on the ground. Nan realizes that lump is a newborn lamb. She steps up beside the baby and her fears are confirmed when she sees he isn't breathing.

"What's the matter with him?" Tovi asks.

Nan places a hand on the lamb's still wet body and is slightly relieved when she feels he is still warm.

She starts by rubbing the lamb firmly all over his chest and neck. Lifting his head up, she sticks a finger into his mouth and begins clearing his airway.

Everyone is totally silent as she works, even the mother sheep watches quietly.

After cleaning out the mucus and birth sack, Nan puffs a couple breaths into his mouth, but the lamb is still lifeless. Without missing a beat, she continues to rub his chest and neck, repeating the breaths every few seconds.

"Come on, little one," she whispers, but he stays unresponsive.

Dinah places her hands on the twin's shoulders, drawing them closer to her. "Boys …" she begins.

"He's breathing!" Nan exclaims as the little lamb sucks in a breath. He coughs several times, and she continues to rub him while he recovers.

After a moment she sets him down next to his mother and he lifts his head. The mother sheep begins to clean off his face, licking him all over.

"You saved him! You saved Eve's baby!" the boys yell excitedly.

Nan sits back, attempting to clean off her mouth with her sleeve. "The ewe's name is Eve?"

"Yes, we named her that," Judah starts.

"After our mother, Eve," Tovi finishes.

Nan can't help herself, and she clamps a hand over her mouth and begins laughing.

"What's the matter? Do you think she wouldn't like it?" Tovi asks.

Nan shakes her head, still smiling, "No, I'm sure our mother would love such a … a fine sheep to be named after her." She then starts laughing even harder, and before long Martha joins in.

The boys follow suit, and even Dinah can't help but snicker as well.

"We better leave our new mother here in peace," Nan says when her laughter subsides.

After a few more moments, the lamb starts to stand, and they move him so he can nurse. The boys offer to stay and watch for a little while longer so the girls head back to their task.

"Where did you learn that?" Dinah asks, as they leave mother and baby behind.

"My family used to raise goats when I was much younger. I learned a lot from them," Nan replies and is relieved when Dinah doesn't ask any further questions.

CHAPTER SIXTEEN

Can You Hear Me Now?

Samyaza's footsteps echo through the stone hallway. While passing by one of the large, open courtyards, something makes him pause.

He takes a step out into the yard, but all he sees is the columns lining its perimeter. He scans the sky above, and even the birds seem to be absent. "Hmph." He turns to leave.

Someone is standing behind him.

He is wearing a black-jeweled crown that eclipses one of his eyes. His skin is almost totally white but has no glow. His eyes have the palest yellow tint, and a gray cloak shrouds the rest of his figure.

"What are you …" Samyaza begins, but his words catch in his throat.

"Is the earth not my kingdom still?" Lucifer asks as he takes a step forward. He circles around Samyaza who turns with him. "Besides I got the feeling that I was welcome here." He smirks, giving Samyaza a pointed look.

“What do you want?” Samyaza asks, keeping his voice steady.

Lucifer notices the Watcher nervously tapping his fingers against his leg.

“I’ve heard some rumors …” Lucifer begins.

Samyaza straightens, and Lucifer takes note, amused at the Watcher’s discomfort.

“It seems to me, that Earth has become altered.” He studies Samyaza’s reaction as he speaks.

“The earth has been altered for years. Your revelations have come too late.”

“It is just astonishing, how much darkness has spread on the earth, with so little effort on my behalf.” Lucifer’s voice echoes throughout the courtyard’s expanse. “But then again,” he takes a step closer to Samyaza. “Who am I to question one of Elohim’s holy angels?” He bows gallantly in front of the Watcher.

Samyaza eyes the stooped figure, then decides to take the opportunity to exit.

A pale hand shoots out and snatches him by the wrist. He takes a step back in surprise as Lucifer examines his arm.

“But what is this?” Lucifer points to the thin red line wrapping around Samyaza’s wrist. “An oath?” Feigned shock spreads across Lucifer’s face.

Samyaza tries to pull his arm away, but Lucifer’s grip only tightens.

“This really is astounding.” Lucifer digs his nails into Samyaza’s wrist, pulling him closer. “But a bit of advice, coming from someone who has turned away from … Him.” He points a jeweled finger upward as his voice drops to a whisper. “You’re making too much noise.”

With that, he releases Samyaza and takes a step toward the doorway. Samyaza looks down at his shaking hand and sees red marks where Lucifer grabbed him.

“Oh, in fact,” Lucifer pauses, “here comes some of that noise right now.” He disappears before Samyaza can reply.

Samyaza whips around, in dread of the next surprise. The courtyard is still silent, but he senses the difference. A low rumble in the ground every couple of seconds is the tell.

The rumble grows louder until finally, he sees her. A Nephilim emerges at the opposite end of the courtyard. She’s one of those that dwarfs even the tallest cedar trees.

The Watcher catches her eye, and in just a couple steps, she's crossed the length of the yard.

She snatches Samyaza in her hand, pinning him to the ground and shattering the surrounding stones at the same time.

Thick mud covers her body and long matted hair, giving her more the appearance of a reptile, rather than human. Although only a fool would refer to something like her as human.

Her eyes constrict and she snaps her teeth at the Watcher.

"J-Jezebel." Samyaza struggles to breathe under the pressure of her hand.

She leans in closer with a snarl. "Father, am I not your only daughter? Is it right for you to not invite me into your home?"

"The beasts of the field are not welcome in my home, and neither are you," he says as she pushes in a little farther into the ground.

Ignoring his quip, she says, "We're starving. The humans aren't providing enough food for us." Her voice is grating, not much different than an animal.

"Then maybe you should till the fields yourself … If the humans can survive on their own … then so can you." He gasps out between his gritted teeth.

She releases him and sits back on her heels. He sucks in a breath of air with the crushing weight removed.

"You have no idea what it's like for us, do you? After everything we've built and created. Now we are dogs surviving on scraps."

"The humans cannot produce enough food to feed all of you," he says disdainfully as he pulls his body out of the ground. "You are pathetic parasites."

"Do not think I am asking you. This is a warning." She bares her teeth as she speaks. "If they cannot provide for us, then they will become the provision. We have been lenient with them for too long." She gives a menacing smile. "I thought you would want to know that, considering you have such a special place for them in your … heart."

In a flash, Samyaza moves from his place on the ground up to Jezebel's head. He points a sword up to her temple.

"I may look like a man, but do not forget, dear Jezebel, I

certainly am not one." He pushes the tip of the blade into her skin, causing a large drop of blood to bubble to the surface. "You may be able to force those weaker than you to do your bidding, but I can still kill you. I have adapted to this world. My abilities extend beyond the other realm."

If his threat has any effect on her, she doesn't show it. Instead, with a sneer, she replies, "You're fortunate that man has fallen. If it wasn't for the cursed blood of my mother running through my veins, I would have destroyed you long ago."

After a moment, Samyaza pulls the sword away and lowers himself back to the ground.

"You're not welcome here." Not bothering to look back, Samyaza disappears through the doorway, leaving her alone in the silence.

***

Jezebel watches the Watcher go, then stands to her feet. Turning to look at the city past the courtyard, she wonders if she should make good on her threat right now. However, she knows the timing is wrong. She doesn't have to look up to the upper levels of the palace to see the eyes she already feels watching her.

She knows the other Watchers are there, in those stone rooms built into the side of the mountain. She straightens and keeps her head high. She does not show them the fear others do.

Stepping toward the end of the courtyard, she heads to the other side of the mountain, away from the city.

The terrain changes beneath her feet, shifting into the rocky desert. She passes by some travelers whose animals startle at the sight of her. They look as if they don't know whether to freeze or flee, but she just ignores them. Her appetite has waned.

She does smile slightly at the thought of the mercy she showed them. Most others would not have been so fortunate.

Jezebel doesn't stop until she's crossed over the river and reaches the jagged hills on the other side. This spot gives her the perfect view of the city in the distance.

The buildings almost look pink, reflecting the sunlight that casts off the side of the mountain.

Before she settles down, a guttural noise catches her attention. She cocks her head toward the sound. It's animal in nature, a mixture of cracking and sloshing.

Silently, she steps down the hill to look behind some large boulders. As she peeks around the corner, the source of the sound becomes grotesquely apparent.

Another creature like her, except about half her size, is leaning over the carcass of a wild camel. The Nephilim is eating away at the camel's midsection, snapping ribs like sticks.

When the Nephilim notices her, he crouches back and lets out a defensive growl. He is no defense against her, Jezebel knows. She could easily overpower him.

But there's something about the sight that makes her pause. She takes in the strings of red meat still hanging from the Nephilim's teeth.

It occurs to her that the sight should repulse her. Creatures of power should never eat from the ground.

But then she smells the blood.

As she looks at the smaller Nephilim before her, she enjoys his uncertainty. Perhaps he's thinking that if he runs now, she will leave him be and just scavenge off the camel.

But he doesn't seem willing to give up his meal, even under his matted body hair she can see he's extremely thin. Most likely he's starving, and with starvation comes desperation.

Good. It's disappointing when they die too easily.

***

"Where did you go?" the woman asks, a clear smile in her voice as she leans over Samyaza, and he focuses on her.

"Hmm?" He angles his face toward her, absentmindedly pushing a lock of her black hair out of her face.

"Lost in thought again?" she teases, and then presses some gentle kisses across the side of his face.

"I can't be lost for too long when you're around," Samyaza answers, eliciting a laugh from her.

She settles down beside him, a hand resting on her rounded belly.

"Ah, he's been kicking relentlessly today." She groans, adjusting again to a more comfortable position.

"Has he?" The Watcher asks, suddenly eager. He runs a hand over the bump as well.

Taking his hand in hers, she presses it over a particular spot on her belly. A wide smile breaks out across his face as he feels the flutters beneath his fingertips.

And then the world begins to fade.

Samyaza focuses on the man standing in front of him and shifts in his seat. The throne beneath him suddenly feels stiff and uncomfortable.

"It would be a terrible waste," the man before him says. "My brother is a drunkard, squandering his inheritance."

Samyaza taps a finger on the armrest.

The man tries a different approach. "The land is rich, fertile. It will produce a bountiful harvest."

Samyaza lets his eyes drift over the room. Others wait to make their pleas, lined up against the back wall. A scribe sits adjacent to the throne, scratching down important points from the discourse.

Movement in the far corner catches Samyaza's attention—long black hair swaying with the turn of a head.

It's just one of the servants, Samyaza reminds himself. Not her.

"Even the signs in the sky point to a bountiful harvest this year, my lord," The man continues. "The great Barkayal himself has said it is so—"

"It is your brother's birthright." Samyaza cuts the man off in a dismissal.

The man is not so easily deterred. "Ah, yes, but you can change that, my lord." He takes a step forward. "Give the land to me, and I assure you, the fruits that we reap from it will be a great help for your servants." As if suddenly remembering something he adds, "Of course, I am not asking for your charity my lord …"

He motions behind him, and a girl steps forward.

"Do this for me and, please, take my daughter to live in your household as a concubine."

He pushes the girl out in front of him. She keeps her gaze cast downward, not meeting the Watcher's scrutiny. She is young, very young. Most likely not over twelve years of age.

Samyaza begins to tap his finger again, then motions for one of the servants to step forward.

"Take her to the others," Samyaza instructs, boredom clear in his voice.

The servant gently takes the girl by the arm and her father gives her an encouraging push forward. She looks back briefly at her father before casting a cautious glance in the direction of the Watcher.

"I will grant your request," Samyaza says, standing.

"Oh, thank you, thank you, my lord." The man wrings his hands together in gratitude.

Samyaza pays him no mind, however, as he steps away from his throne.

The rest of those waiting in line are visibly disappointed, but they don't dare to voice it as the Watcher takes his leave.

Samyaza paces down the hall, only stopping when he reaches the astronomy room where he knows he will find Barkayal.

This room is noticeably much darker, with no windows to keep out the daylight. In the middle floats projections of the stars and planets. Miniature versions of the celestial bodies give off an ambient glow, staining the room in a blue tint.

Barkayal stands in the center, an unfurled scroll floating next to his right hand. He moves his left hand and the star cluster in front of him rotates. This elicits a new note to be made on the scroll.

"Barkayal—" Samyaza starts.

"So patient, aren't we?" Barkayal interjects, not taking his eyes from the cosmos before him. He writes down another notation.

Samyaza clenches his jaw but waits for the Watcher to finish his recording. Finally, Barkayal waves his hand, and the scroll rolls up. He hooks it onto his belt and turns toward Samyaza.

He steps through the heavenly projections and asks, "Yes, Samyaza?"

"Have they changed?"

"Hmm?"

"Are they still foretelling the same outcome?" Samyaza clarifies, slowing down his words.

Barkayal's mouth twerks up in a half smile. "Are you asking if the stars have changed?" A slightly incredulous tone is evident in his voice.

"I did not come here for your ridicule," Samyaza counters.

Barkayal lets a moment of silence pass then says, "Why don't you look for yourself." He moves to the side, reaching out his hand.

Samyaza hesitates for a moment, then strides up to the cluster of stars next to Barkayal's outstretched fingers. He stares down into the glowing orbs while they lazily rotate. They almost seem to have a magnetic pull as he feels himself drawn closer.

The corners of his vision darken as the illuminated specks are all he can seem to focus on, the roar of white noise growing louder in his ears.

The stars begin to move closer to him, their light bleeding away. They turn to jagged dark rocks and rush forward.

A scream snaps Samyaza out of his daze.

"What is it now?" Barkayal asks in a way that indicates he's not really interested in an answer.

Samyaza blinks several times, then pushes past the other Watcher, making a beeline toward the scream. As he steps out into the hall, he can see a crowd has gathered at one of the large balconies that overlooks the city below.

Approaching, he can now see that the scream has come from one of the maidservants. She's on her knees next to the balcony railing, reaching up toward a woman crouched on the edge.

"Please, mistress," the maidservant begs, "Please come down."

A few other Watchers and servants have gathered, taking in the spectacle.

Samyaza eyes the woman perched precariously on the edge. Her eyes are bloodshot, recessed behind dark circles. She clings onto her extended stomach.

"I won't let him become one of them!" she cries out in a shaky voice.

Out of the crowd of Watchers and servants, Danieal steps forward. "Ahya," he states in a firm voice, "Get down."

She just shakes her head, refusing to look in his direction. She wobbles, eliciting a stifled cry from the maidservant.

Samyaza steps forward, and the crowd turns their attention to him. The woman watches his approach warily, she runs her hand over her stomach again, shaking.

Silently, Samyaza reaches out his hand and caresses the side of her face. She brings her eyes up to his, her breaths coming out in ragged pants.

Samyaza leans in closer as if to whisper into her ear and drops his voice.

"Ask him if I'm making enough noise."

The woman's eyes widen slightly, and Samyaza puts his hand on her chest, pushing her backward.

She lets out a gasp, and tumbles over the edge. The maidservant shrieks, clamping her hand across her mouth.

Samyaza turns and sweeps his eyes across the crowd. Danieal sets his lips in a tight line but doesn't say anything further.

Samyaza stalks away, recessing into the shadows, and leaving the crowd behind.

CHAPTER SEVENTEEN

My Brother's Keeper

Exactly forty-nine days after the barley is ripe, the wheat harvest season begins. The yield is especially bountiful this year. Nan, Dinah, and Martha all help gather the wheat after it's been cut.

All the girls have their hair braided back to help keep it out of their faces, something Dinah was reluctant about at first, but with some convincing from Martha, she finally gives in and is quite happy with the results.

As Nan finishes tying together a sheave of wheat, she leans over to Martha and asks, "Who is that?" She nods her head toward a boy currently talking to Dinah.

"Oh, that's Eder. She's spoken to him before. He obviously wants to take her as a wife," Martha replies without even looking up.

Nan raises a brow. "So, why doesn't he?"

"She says she's too young to leave home. I think she feels like she needs to stay, at least until the twins are old enough," Martha replies thoughtfully, then adds, "But perhaps now that you're here, she will feel like she has more freedom."

"They could marry and live here, couldn't they? I'm sure it would improve his living."

Martha laughs in reply. "His family is wealthy as well. I'm convinced the only reason he is here helping is to get to talk to her."

The girl's conversation is interrupted when Methuselah and Lamech approach, scythes in hand.

"You girls are going to have to tie faster than that if you want to keep up with us," Lamech says, with a rakish smile.

Martha bends down to take a handful of wheat and mumbles under her breath, "We won't get anything done if you don't start paying attention to the wheat and less to Nan."

Nan ignores Martha's grumble and instead says, "It seems like you're challenging us."

Methuselah scoffs slightly, "Oh, come on Nan, we're just—"

Nan cuts him off by placing her hand over his holding the scythe. "Trade with me?" she says with a smile that renders Methuselah only able to utter, "W-what?"

She turns her smile toward Lamech. "If you want a challenge, then I will finish cutting half of this field before you."

"But then I'd have to tie …" Methuselah says when he is able to speak again.

Nan doesn't reply and instead stares at Lamech expectantly.

"Very well," Lamech says after a moment. "And when we've just finished one row and you are too tired to continue, Methuselah can take over for you."

Nan just smiles, then takes the scythe from Methuselah, who protests. "Don't listen to him, you're not accustomed to this type of work."

"Am I not?" she replies casually and marches over to a new row of wheat.

"No, you're not." Methuselah's retort is ignored as she adjusts her grip on the scythe.

Lamech takes his place beside her and says, "You say when to start."

Nan grips the long wooden handle awkwardly at first, but nonchalantly looks at how Lamech is holding his and adjusts her grip. She nods and swings the curved blade in front of her. It takes her a couple times to figure out the best angle to cut the wheat, but she finally gets the hang of it.

However, as soon as she's gotten the rhythm of the motion, she begins to realize just how hot it is outside. Not wanting to give Lamech any satisfaction, she ignores the heat and continues forward, even when her hair begins to stick to the back of her neck.

By the time they are halfway done with this field, she wishes she had just kept her mouth shut. She shoots a glance over at Lamech who, much to her relief, seems to be struggling almost as much as her.

"I think you both need to take a break," Methuselah shouts behind them, but neither one of them acknowledges him.

Nan grits her teeth, more determined than ever to prove them both wrong. She stares daggers at the wheat in front of her, trying to develop some sort of hatred toward the stocks, thinking that might help motivate her.

With a burst of energy, she swings the scythe forward. However, she swings too low and hits the ground with the blade. The momentum sends her tumbling to the side with a tiny yelp, before she slams ungracefully into the ground.

Before she is even aware of what happened, Lamech is over top of her, concern evident on his face.

"Are you alright?" he asks, putting a hand on her arm.

"I'm—"

She doesn't get to reply more because Lamech is wrenched backward, disappearing from her sight as Methuselah takes his place.

"You fool!" Methuselah snaps at his brother. "She could have seriously hurt herself, why do you always do things without thinking?" He kneels beside her. "Are you …" His voice trails off when he notices her palms. "Your hands. They're bleeding."

Nan hadn't even noticed until now the large blister on her palms. Ignoring the sting, she snaps back just as harshly. "I'm fine. You don't have to be so cruel to your brother."

He just grits his teeth. "I certainly do if he's going to act this … this reckless."

She scoffs and then begins to protest when Methuselah lifts her up in his arms. "Put me down! What do you think you are doing?"

"You can quit struggling because I'm not going to let you go," he says with his jaw set.

Too exhausted to protest further, she lets him carry her away, him grumbling about Lamech with every step. He takes her down to the stream where he finally sets her down next to the water.

She slowly lowers her hands into the stream and grimaces slightly at the sting.

Methuselah notices and says, "You know he was just teasing you—you don't have to prove anything."

"Oh, now you're angry at me? I said I'm fine. I'm not going to die," she replies, scowling.

He doesn't respond, and instead sits down next to her, untying his sash from around his waist. He dips the cloth into the water, then lifts it up to her face.

"What are you doing?" she asks but makes no move to stop him.

"I'm sure you also got too hot," he says, wiping the cool cloth across her forehead.

"The heat is one thing I'm used to."

"Still," he says, concentrating intently on her face. He presses the cloth to the back of her neck. Brushing her hair out of the way, he traces his fingers along the curve of her face while he's at it.

Noticing his very deliberate touch, Nan brings her cupped hand out of the water and splashes him in the face.

"What was that for?" he asks sitting back in surprise.

She laughs. "I thought perhaps you were feeling too hot."

Her eyes then widen as he scoops her off the ground, holding her over the stream. He then dunks her into the shallow water right as she screams, "Put me down!"

While she's in the water, she makes sure to splash around enough to completely soak him as well. Wriggling out of his grasp, she sloshes out of the stream, scaring a few curious sheep at the same time.

"I think you're right. I could use a break," she says, untying the top of her dress. She removes the overdress, leaving on the linens she's wearing underneath.

She hangs the overdress on a branch to give it the opportunity to dry.

"Might as well go for a real swim then," she calls back over her shoulder as she makes her way up stream to where it's much deeper.

Methuselah stands there dumbfounded, but it only takes a few moments for him to follow her, and unceremoniously strip off his now soaking outer layer.

Nan jumps into the pool, right below a small, bubbling waterfall. She bobs back up to the surface after only a second, stretching her arms out around her. She leans back, letting the sun shine down onto her face as she tranquilly floats.

Upstream, the others have apparently gotten the same idea. Lamech wades into the water, splashing at Martha and Dinah on the shore. The girls shriek and laugh.

Dinah runs after Lamech, and unsuccessfully attempts to push him over. Instead, Lamech wraps his arms around her, pulling them both down into their watery demise.

Dinah screams and claws her way back to the surface. She playfully shoves Lamech, which he pays little mind to, laughing.

Martha keeps her distance, wading in the shallows.

Methuselah steps up to the edge of the pool, watching Nan as she floats on her back, lazily waving her arms around her.

With a splash, he jumps in next to her.

Nan squints against the sunlight, waiting to see where he will pop up. When a few seconds pass and he doesn't resurface, she scans through the ripples, trying to pick out his figure from the depths.

She feels a hand wrap around her ankle and drags her under. Before she can react, she feels an arm go around her waist, pulling her back up.

They both surface at the same time, and she shoots a glare at Methuselah.

"It's a good thing I was here," he says, ignoring her scowl. "You could have drowned."

"Ah, so you do know how to have fun. And here I was thinking it was all seriousness and scowls from you," she quips back, then realizes he still has his arm wrapped around her waist.

For what seems like a long moment, neither of them says anything. She scans over his face, then becomes painfully aware of how quickly her breaths are coming.

She then smiles and says, "I guess I should thank you for saving me then."

She leans in even closer, placing her hands up on his shoulders. Then with all her might, she presses down, shoving him below the surface, before swimming toward the edge of the pool.

***

As Methuselah bobs back up, he watches her climb out onto the edge of the pool. She lounges back on the smooth stones, letting herself dry.

Methuselah can still hear his siblings' voices in the distance. Lamech laughs at something, no doubt teasing one of the girls.

Sloshing out of the water, Methuselah sits beside Nan. Her eyes are closed, and the sunlight filters through the trees onto her face. It moves in patches across her skin, changing with the breeze.

Methuselah reaches a hand toward her hair. It hovers there for a moment, then he just barely caresses one of her curls with his fingertip.

"How are your hands?" he asks.

She opens her eyes, raising her hands in front of her face.

"They do sting a bit, but it's not too bad."

Methuselah nods mutely, watching the glint from the sunlight reflect on the water below.

"You know," he begins, "you don't have to prove anything."

She doesn't reply at first, but squints her eyes open, tilting her head back to look at him.

After a moment, she closes her eyes again. "Oh, so you're saying I don't need to earn my keep?"

Methuselah shakes his head, but a small smile spreads across his face.

"I would like it," he starts, "if you were to stay here."

With just a hint of a smile, she replies, "Well, I'm not sure there's many more places for me right now." She looks at him again. "But perhaps I will think about it." She then sits up, saying, "We should probably head back to the others. We don't want to cause too much gossip."

For the rest of the day, Nan helps Martha and Dinah tie the wheat, with her hands bandaged in thin cloths. Before much longer, they finish the harvest, and the threshing process can begin.

***

In the days immediately following, the surrounding field owners prepare a feast to celebrate the completion of harvest.

All day long, the girls help Edna prepare their contribution to the celebration. When all types of breads and sweet treats topped with dried fruits are ready, the girls begin to ready themselves.

This time, Dinah doesn't need any convincing when Nan offers to style her hair. As Nan finishes tying back a final braid on top of Dinah's head, she takes a step back, offering Dinah a small mirror.

Dinah holds the mirror outstretched, examining Nan's work. A small smile breaks out across her face as she runs a finger over the locks of hair that hang down over her shoulders. She then turns her head to the side to see the intricate twists and braids pulling half of her hair back and finished with a colorful scarf.

"Do you like it?" Nan asks.

Dinah nods, still smiling, then dropping the mirror down into her lap, she tentatively asks, "Nan, would you paint my eyes like yours?"

"Of course," Nan replies with a broad smile, then turns. "You too Martha?"

Martha looks unsure for a moment. "I …" she starts, then nods. "Why not?"

As the girls approach the feast, they can see it is illuminated by a large bonfire in the center. Getting closer, they can hear the celebratory music that wafts through the air.

Many of the local farmers and their families are gathered in groups, talking and laughing amongst themselves. Others make circles around the fire, dancing together hand in hand.

Lamech notices the girls' approach and jogs up to meet them.

"Well, don't you girls look …" His voice trails off for a second when he notices Nan behind Martha and Dinah. "Beautiful," he finishes with a wide smile.

Without waiting for a reply, he motions for them to follow. "Come, join us." He waves a hand, and the girls follow behind.

Nan spies the source of the upbeat music—a small group of musicians sitting next to the fire. Each one holds a different instrument with various sizes of drums, flutes, and stringed instruments.

The lively beat is enough to convince most to join in on the dancing. Nan notices that the way they dance is slightly different than she's used to but seems simple enough to catch on to.

She scans the rest of the crowd, and finally spots Methuselah sitting some distance away. He doesn't seem to have noticed her yet, and another girl that Nan doesn't recognize is talking to him.

The girl standing next to him laughs at something he says, and Nan raises a brow.

Lamech's face suddenly appears in front of her, and he extends a hand toward her. "Care to dance?"

Nan shoots one more glance over in Methuselah's direction and reaches out to take Lamech's hand.

He leads her closer to the fire, then spins her around a couple times as they dance together as a couple.

Lamech places a hand on her lower back, pulling her in close to him. He gives her a wink, then spins her out again, holding one of her hands. He then reaches out to the person next to him, and Nan does the same as they join a dance circle.

The group spins around together, then swing their arms as they move in toward each other. They raise their clasped hands in the air before spreading back out into a wider circle.

Nan laughs as they repeat the steps of the dance. She glances over at Lamech and returns the smile he's giving her.

***

Not too far away, Methuselah watches the group spinning with the rhythm. He had spotted Lamech dragging Nan into the jubilance, and now taps his foot in annoyance as he watches the pair.

The girl standing next to him takes notice of his agitation and looks over the delighted fray. Turning back toward him, she asks, "Would you like to dance too?"

Methuselah looks up at the girl. He knows she told him her name when she approached him this evening, but for some reason, right now it doesn't seem important to remember it.

"No, I'm good," he says with a smile that he doesn't quite feel.

She crosses her arms across her chest looking less pleased, but still doesn't make any move to leave.

Methuselah's attention is drawn away, however, as he spots his parents leaving one of the dance circles.

One of the field owners approaches Enoch. The man grasps Enoch on the shoulder then leans in to say something. It's obvious that the man is having to yell to be heard over the bustle.

Enoch nods and smiles, waving his hand in the air in a dismissive gesture. This doesn't deter the man any, and he continues to talk, waving his arms around in a way that would seem like he's telling an interesting story.

Most likely he already has had too much to drink, Methuselah thinks.

Then something else grabs his attention. At the very edge of the crowd is the leading Watcher, Samyaza.

No one else seems to have noticed the Watcher as he looks over the festivities with a bored expression.

Methuselah looks back to his father to see if he has noticed.

Enoch is now taking half steps away from the man between each sentence but isn't showing any acknowledgement of the Watcher's presence.

When Methuselah looks back, Samyaza is gone. He scans the crowd, seeing if perhaps he has moved, but the Watcher is nowhere to be seen.

As the musicians finish off the melody, the dancers slow their spin, taking a brief respite before the next song.

***

When the music ends, Nan notices that Lamech is still holding her hand and he gives it a squeeze before releasing.

Martha and Dinah appear behind Nan. Martha links her arm with Lamech's, and Dinah steers Nan to the side.

"I think there is someone else who would like to dance," Dinah says to her.

Nan turns to look, knowing exactly who she's talking about.

She spots Methuselah staring at her. Turning back to Dinah, she says, "He seems a little busy."

Dinah just rolls her eyes, and with an encouraging push, mouths, "Just go."

After another hesitation, Nan rolls her shoulders back and marches toward Methuselah.

When he sees her approach, he stands, stepping toward her and leaving his companion behind. Nan sees him mumble something to the girl, who shoots a scowl in Nan's direction.

The musicians are just starting a new melody as they meet. They stand for a second not saying a word, then Nan clears her throat.

"I don't mean to interrupt …" she starts.

"No" is all he says.

"Would you like to—"

"Yes."

She doesn't get to finish her question as he replies.

He holds his hand out and after only a second, she takes it. He draws her into him, and she looks around at the other dancers for a cue.

"I don't know this one," she says after a moment.

"I can show you," he replies in a low voice.

The corner of her mouth quirks up at that. "Ah, so you know the couple dances well, then?"

He smiles back at her and, leaning in close, answers, "I know this one."

"What's it called?" she asks, hyper aware of his proximity but not moving to distance herself.

"The covenant dance." He takes her hand, pressing their palms together between them and raising them up in front of her face. Bringing their hands back down, he takes a step back, their fingertips flexed toward each other.

The music begins to pick up, and Nan feels her confidence build. Snatching one of her hands, Methuselah spins her in front of him.

The fire kicks up sparks that float around them, coloring a golden halo around Nan's hair. She watches the sparkling reflections in his eyes as they continue to sway and spin.

She can feel herself getting lost in the music, taking small cues here and there from the other dancers. They join the others in lines, arms linked together, then pair off into partners again.

This time when they link up again, the dancers grasp hands and start to move to the side. They begin to circle back around, and Nan thinks that perhaps they will create a circle.

Instead, the line begins to cross over itself. Nan fears that the dancers will collide. But they drop hands as they cross, perfectly timing their movements as to not run into each other.

Nan feels herself being pulled closer to the crossing, but with the timing in sync with the rhythm of the music, she easily passes through without issue.

She then follows along as the line begins to curl around a second time, and it dawns on Nan that they have created a perfect figure eight. The line of dancers continues to crisscross each other, forming the perpetually moving symbol that loops over itself.

Colorful fabric reflects the orange and red glow of the fire as it flows around the dancers. The cascade of the garments makes the symbol they've created with their bodies look almost as if it were made of molten flames.

They continue this movement for quite some time, and then begin to spin as they split off again. Nan closes her eyes, letting the melody wash over her in waves. She moves with Methuselah in sync, until finally he pulls her in close to him.

It takes Nan a moment to realize that the song has ended. Neither of them makes a move for several seconds as they stay pressed together once again.

Nan realizes he's looking at her differently now. When he held her in the water, his look was much more playful, but now it seems … intense.

Looking around self-consciously, she unceremoniously strips herself from his grasp.

Stepping back, she takes in some of the curious nearby glances. "Well, there will definitely be gossip now," she whispers, offering up a smile.

Much to her relief, the intense look melts from his face and is replaced with a smile in return.

"Come on," he says, offering his arm. "Let's find the others."

***

As the season changes, Enoch must return more often to the palace below Mount Armon as the Watcher's make more demands on his time. He secludes himself in the records room as much as possible. Hiding behind shelves and tables, he only makes conversation when necessary.

During these conversations, Enoch mostly replies in nods or "hmm," focusing on the precise marks he carves into tablets.

At the end of the day, Enoch quickly organizes his work area, being sure to arrange everything so that it will be easy to find later.

Leaving the records room, he steps out into the dim hallway, only lit by a few oil lamps. His footsteps echo against the stone floor. Passing by an open doorway, he jumps slightly when he sees Samyaza standing in it. The Watcher was so still, he hadn't noticed him at first.

Samyaza's eyes focus on Enoch as if he were coming out of a trance. It takes a couple seconds for the glint of recognition to pass across the Watcher's face.

"The scribe," he says in a way that makes it seem like he's confirming that bit of knowledge in his mind.

He doesn't wait for Enoch to reply, instead he turns halfway in the door and says, "This way."

Enoch lingers for a moment as Samyaza disappears into the dark room. Finally, with a sigh, he follows.

He isn't sure what to expect, but what he sees catches him off guard—a room, complete with household furnishings. There's a sleeping mat in the middle of the room, piled with extravagant blankets and pillows.

Enoch wonders briefly if the Watchers even need to sleep. He has seen them eat on occasion, but for some reason the thought of them sleeping seems bizarre to him.

He shifts from foot to foot in the doorway, waiting for Samyaza to break the silence.

If the Watcher notices the unease, he doesn't seem to care.

"Tell me," he says while staring at the wall, "How has the harvest been this year?"

Enoch stumbles only slightly before answering. "Very well. In fact, it's been more bountiful than last season."

"There will be enough then," Samyaza says, still not taking his eyes from that spot on the wall.

“Most definitely, the city will not be in famine this year,” Enoch replies with a sigh of relief.

Now it’s Samyaza’s turn to look uneasy. He opens his mouth to speak but nothing comes out. Finally, after what seems like some great effort he says, “If it is so bountiful, perhaps we could use the extra to feed the others …”

“The others?”

“Those on the outskirts. The ones who do not call Armon their home.”

Enoch tries to swallow but realizes he can’t. The Watcher finally turns to look at him, and Enoch wishes he had just kept staring at the wall.

“They …” Enoch begins. “They wouldn’t agree to that.”

“Who?” Samyaza asks, taking a step closer.

“Th-the people in the city. And the field owners,” Enoch answers, taking a half step backward.

“They doubt our wisdom?” The Watcher doesn’t stop his advance, closing the distance one step at a time.

“No, it’s just that hasn’t been done since—”

“Since when?”

Enoch bumps against the doorframe. His tongue stubbornly refuses to move as he tries to answer.

Suddenly Samyaza stops, like another thought has occurred to him. His voice drops so low that it is barely audible. “Do you remember her?”

Enoch presses his hands into his robe. Against his will, they tremble slightly. “Wh-who?”

“The first one.”

Enoch turns his eyes to the floor and shakes his head. “No.”

“It was only a century ago. Has your memory failed you?” Samyaza is now about only a foot away. The Watcher suddenly turns away. “No one else seems to remember her either.”

It takes Enoch a moment to realize that the conversation is over. As the Watcher stays silent, Enoch slips out of the door and back into the empty hall.

***

“Well, I’ll guess I have to admit you are an … adequate hunter.” Lamech crosses his arms as he watches his brother pull an arrow out of a freshly killed deer.

“An adequate hunter? And how many beasts have you killed so far?” Methuselah asks as he slides the arrow back into his quiver. “And I thought we would have to head back empty handed. But looks like we will make it back in time for sacrifices.”

Lamech looks down the embankment where they are standing. Kicking a rock with his foot, it bounces down the rocky cliffs into the shallow stream below. “Well, I did want to make sure that there was not too much to carry back.”

“How thoughtful,” Methuselah mutters, taking out his hunting knife to prepare the deer. “I … I did want to ask you something.”

“I know you are an old man, but I will not carry back more than my fair share,” Lamech quips, examining his bow string.

“No, I’m … I’m going to ask Nan to be my wife,” Methuselah replies, turning to look at his brother.

Lamech stays silent for a moment, tapping the end of his bow on the ground.

“Well, I think that might be one of the only good decisions you’ve made.” Lamech looks down the embankment as he answers.

“You’re not angry?”

“How could I be angry at my brother?” Lamech finally looks up at him.

“It’s just … I know you have feelings for her.”

“And you?” Lamech replies. “How do you feel?”

Methuselah taps the blunt side of his hunting knife against his palm. “Like I don’t want to continue my life if she’s not in it.”

Lamech gives him a pointed look, and Methuselah nods in resignation.

“Still,” Methuselah says kneeling down before the deer, “it’s not like you to give up so easily.”

Lamech shrugs. “Like I said, you’re an old man. You’ll return to the dust before long, and then she’s mine.”

“Be quiet,” Methuselah says harshly, standing to his feet.

“It was merely a joke—”

“No, no, I mean be quiet,” Methuselah says in a tense whisper, and then points into the woods behind them. He takes a couple silent steps back toward his brother and freezes in place.

Neither of the brothers moves an inch as they both scan the tree line.

"What?" Lamech mouths to him, but Methuselah just shakes his head.

Other than the breeze rustling tree branches, the forest is totally silent.

That's what's wrong. The silence. The birds have stopped singing. The whole forest seems to be stuck in time.

"Did you feel that?" Methuselah asks in a barely audible voice. He slowly takes an arrow from his quiver and notches it onto his bow. For a long moment, they both stand, waiting.

Crack!

A Nephilim comes crashing through the trees, snapping trunks as if they were twigs and towering above the branches as she lunges forward.

She snatches out at the brothers as they reel backward.

Methuselah steps back too far and teeters on the edge of the embankment. Lamech reaches out to him, but it's too late. Both brothers go tumbling down the rocky bank.

With vision blurred, Lamech tries to take in his surroundings. They are both now in the ravine. Methuselah is beside him, but he doesn't appear conscious.

"Methuselah!" Lamech calls out to him in a harsh whisper and starts to crawl over to his brother. He doubles over in pain as he moves his leg.

Looking down, he sees his ankle has been snapped in half, and his foot is hanging limp to the side.

He turns his eyes up to the top of the embankment, and sees the Nephilim reach down and grab the deer. She lifts it up to her mouth and, with a crunch, bites it in half.

Fighting off the wave of nausea, Lamech digs his fingers into the loose gravel and drags himself over to Methuselah.

Blood spills out of a gash across his brother's head.

"Wake up. We have to get out of here." Lamech gives Methuselah a shake, but his brother remains unconscious.

As he looks back up, he sees Jezebel eclipsing the sun. She's just finishing off the deer and will be coming for more.

With a burst of strength, he grabs Methuselah and starts

dragging him away from the stream. Darkness creeps in around his vision as he fights to stay conscious. He makes slow, painful progress up the rocky embankment, until he finds a concave on the side of the cliff.

It isn't a permanent solution, but the space should conceal them for a few precious seconds. He pushes his brother under the eave, then crawls in beside him.

A thud shakes the ground, and he knows the Nephilim has jumped down into the riverbed and is looking for her prey.

Lamech places a hand up to his brother's nose. He's still breathing.

Lamech's pulse slams in his head as he looks out from under the rocky overhang. She will find them soon. He looks down and sees that the concave extends down several yards along the cliff-face.

He turns back to Methuselah and starts to say something, but just nods his head instead.

***

In the riverbed, Jezebel scans for where her meal went. A streak of red catches her eye. She crouches down and sees a blood stain on the stones. Her eyes follow it up to a little cave in the cliff face.

Jezebel's blood-splattered mouth twists into a smile as she stalks up to the hide out. Placing her hand on the rock wall, she leans down to peek inside of the cave, but a noise draws away her attention.

Her head whips around and she sees one of them stumble over some rocks. This one has a broken leg. She watches for a few seconds as he attempts to crawl away.

Easy prey.

CHAPTER EIGHTEEN

My Strength Comes From

Methuselah wakes up with a start. Blinding light streams in from the sides of his hiding place. He squints, trying to see through the rays, and feels an intense stabbing pain behind his eyes.

So instead of trying to see, he lays back and listens.

A stream. He can hear a stream.

He darts up again, which is a mistake, as darkness creeps around the edges of his vision. A wave of nausea rolls over him, and he turns to the side retching up whatever is left in his stomach.

"Lamech?" he whispers hoarsely. "Lamech!"

After a few painful moments, he gingerly makes his way out of the crawl space. The sun is in the same position in the sky as it was before. He looks up and down the ravine, but there is still no sign of his brother.

He teeters back and forth as he stands, then places a hand on the rock wall.

A few small bloodstains are the only clue he sees to figure out what has occurred while he was unconscious. Squeezing his eyes shut, he brings a hand up to his head and delicately feels around the gash in his hairline. He can feel the blood that runs down the side of his face already starting to dry.

He spends the next several hours painfully searching along the river. But as the sun begins to dip in the horizon, he already knows that his search is futile. He sits by the edge of the water and stares into the streams that glimmer in the sunset.

It can't be time to give up.

The ground seems to beckon to him, inviting him to curl up and close his eyes.

It can't be time to give up.

He digs his fingers into the gravel, nearly crushing the small stones in his grasp.

He stands again, but this time, he starts the walk home.

The moon hangs in the sky by the time he finds his way back. Cresting over a familiar hill, he sees the house in the distance, a small oil lamp burning in the window.

He stops at the door frame, debating, then lightly knocks.

His mother is the one who opens the door. She takes in the dark blood covering half of his face and pulls him inside.

"What happened?" she asks, then looks past him expectantly. "Where's Lamech?"

Nan, who was apparently waiting up as well, steps over to Methuselah and gently places her hand on his forehead. Her eyes travel from his wound down to his expression. Comprehension dawns on her face and she shoots a look over at Edna.

Stubbornly, his mother shakes her head, "No. Methuselah, where is he?"

Methuselah finally notices his father at the other end of the room. Enoch takes a step forward, the dim light from the lamp illuminating his face.

Edna's voice raises. "Where is—"

"He's gone," Methuselah says flatly, staring down at Nan with a hard look.

Nan takes a step back and grabs onto his arm.

Edna lets out a mixture of a shriek and a sob, clamping her hand over her mouth.

"How? What happened?" Nan asks as she searches his face.

Methuselah falters, grabbing onto Nan's hand.

Dinah and Martha rush into the room, Kenan not far behind them.

"Mother?" Dinah asks.

"It was one of them," Methuselah says, raising his voice so everyone in the room can hear. "I think ..." He trembles, lowering his voice again. "I think he was trying to save me."

"What is this?" Enoch asks, stepping forward. "Where is your brother?"

"I—" Methuselah shakes his head, his vision blurring with the movement. "It came out of nowhere. I ... I hadn't noticed it stalking us or—"

"Lamech is dead," Enoch states, and Methuselah looks squarely at his father.

"Yes," Methuselah answers then turns as his mother's cries intensify.

Before he can speak, his father strides up to him, grabbing his son by the arm.

"How could you let this happen?" Enoch accuses.

"I ... I tried—"

"Well, you didn't try hard enough. He was your brother. Your younger brother, Methuselah!" Enoch tips each word with venom. "You were supposed to take care of him."

The words hang in the air as Methuselah's breath becomes labored. "Me?"

"Yes, you."

"I was supposed to take care of him?"

"Yes."

Methuselah takes a step back, pulling out of Nan and his father's reach. "And what about you?" he asks.

Enoch angles his head at his son as if to provoke him to continue.

"Yes, what about you, Father? What about how you sit in their palace every day, bowing to the Watchers as they kill and rape." Methuselah raises his hands in the air. "But oh, it is the will of Elohim, and His holy angels."

"I did not say it was His will," Enoch shoots back.

"Then, what is it?"

"Do not speak of Elohim's will."

"Fine," Methuselah snaps. "Then let us speak of your will, Father."

"My will?"

"Yes, tell me, how many of your family members must die, must be *eaten* by their children, for you to stand up and do something?"

"Enough, Methuselah." His father's face is a stormy mask now.

Methuselah waves a hand toward his sister. "Or perhaps you will wait till they take Dinah to breed one of their cursed offspring? So, after it claws its way out of her womb, she can be its first meal."

"I said enough!" Enoch shouts and everyone falls silent.

Methuselah stares his father down for a long while, his lips pressed together in a tight line. Finally, he turns and leaves the room.

Edna sinks down to the ground, her sobs starting again. Her younger children gather in around her.

Enoch stares after his son, before finally turning and heading in the opposite direction.

***

Nan decides it's best to wait for a bit while everyone settles. She busies herself with making an herbal poultice for Methuselah's wound, then after a few minutes, heads down the hall to where she knows she will find him.

Pushing the curtain covering the door aside slightly, she knocks gently on the doorframe. He doesn't beckon her in, but he also doesn't send her away, so she enters.

Methuselah is sitting on his mat, his back toward her. Silently, she sits down next to him.

"I need to clean that," she says, lifting a damp cloth to his forehead. Her hand hesitates in the air for just a moment as she studies his face, then gently begins to dab the wound.

She removes any debris and is relieved to find that the cut is not too deep.

"Does your head hurt?" she asks after she's satisfied that it's sufficiently clean and begins to apply the herbal poultice.

He doesn't answer, so she lets the silence hang between them for a while.

Trying an alternate route, she speaks up again.

"I've felt that before … that feeling you could have done something. Or should have."

She starts to say more, then stops. After a few more attempts, she finally says, "I was very young. But I still remember what it was like." She stares hard at his wound, not letting her gaze drift down to his eyes.

"We moved around often with our herds. It was just us and several other families all living as nomads. Life was meager, but still, it was safe." She presses a clean cloth onto his forehead and begins to bandage the area.

"I had never seen one of them before." She drops her voice. "I had heard the stories though. All the boys would recount tales of giant monsters with jagged teeth and horns—trying to scare me."

She dares a glance down at his face. He's still staring at the wall, so she continues.

"It was the middle of the night when it happened. My mother dragged me out of bed." She rattles this part off as if she were recounting a story someone else had told her. "It was so confusing at first, but then I started to hear people screaming. She took me by the arm and pulled me out of the back of the tent. I kept asking where Father was, but she would just tell me to be silent.

"She took me to where we kept the animals and put me on one of the donkeys. I just kept asking where we were going and why Father wasn't with us, but finally she said, 'We have to run.'

"I knew then what was coming for us." Nan pauses, realizing she has stopped bandaging him. She quickly finishes wrapping the cloth around his head and ties it off.

"That's when I saw it." She lets her arms fall to her lap as she speaks. "It was maybe three times our height, but to me, it was the biggest thing I had ever seen."

Nan pauses for a moment and Methuselah stays silent. She furrows her brows together and continues.

"It was worse than the stories. The teeth and horns aren't what scare you, it's not even the size. It's the eyes."

She stares at him, and he finally meets her gaze. "They look at you and you can't move, you can't breathe. You never feel so helpless so … powerless, than you do in that moment. You know what it's like to be the weak ones. There is no comfort in knowing they are stronger than you, they have no compassion or mercy. All they do is destroy and devour."

Nan feels her throat tighten.

"She didn't follow you, did she?" Methuselah finally speaks up, and Nan shakes her head.

"I ran away. I didn't stop until the animal was nearly dead with exhaustion. I thought I would die too. But then a caravan found me. They were going to learn the teachings of Danieal. And that's when Mikah took me in. She took care of me, taught me sorcery, and in return I worked for her. I had a new family."

Some time passes, and Methuselah reaches out a tentative hand. He takes her hand in his, running his thumb across it.

She gives a shaky smile, lacing her fingers in his.

After a moment, she turns his palm over, looking at it intently and tracing one of the prominent lines with her finger.

Suddenly, Methuselah snatches his hand away from her grasp.

Startled, Nan stands and quickly says, "I'm sorry. I didn't mean …"

She shakes her head and gathers the supplies she brought with her then turns to leave. Looking back in the doorway, she sees that he's gone back to staring at the wall.

***

Nan awakens much earlier than normal. She squints her eyes open to see that the sun has not yet risen enough to shine through the cracks in the window shutters.

Looking over, she notices that Martha and Dinah's sleeping mats had been made up already, so she gets up and dresses quickly.

Going outside, she finds where the family has gone. Dinah and Martha stand under a tree, watching as their father and Kenan assemble an altar.

She joins the girls and observes as the large stones are aligned on top of each other, forming a circle.

After it is built up high enough, they lay planks of wood on the top to create a flat surface.

Once they finish, the twins approach their father, leading a ram behind them.

Judah speaks first. “Father, we would like for our ram to be the sacrifice for this year.” Tovi nods solemnly in agreement.

Enoch kneels before his two sons and places his hands on their shoulders. “Are you boys sure about this?” he asks.

With set faces, they both nod and hand their father the rope tied around the animal’s neck.

Watching the exchange, Nan looks over to Martha in confusion. “That’s the lamb?” she whispers. “That’s their pet, why would they give it up to be killed?”

Martha shakes her head and says, “They know what it means.”

Edna has finally made an appearance. She approaches the boys, holding an empty bowl in her hands.

She places the bowl below the ram’s neck, and Kenan holds its head to keep it in place. Taking a knife, Enoch runs it along its throat, letting the blood spill down into the bowl.

The twins stand stoically as they watch their ram being placed on the altar. The lamb that had returned from the dead, now lies silently, asleep once more.

As the sacrifice is lit, Edna walks around the altar. Using an olive branch, she dips it in the blood, then sprinkles it into the flames.

***

While the sacrifice burns, Enoch looks up into the smoke-filled sky. The white smoke burns his eyes as he waits for something. For anything.

“Elohim,” he says under his breath. “Where is your justice?”

The sky stays quiet.

He looks over at the house and sees Methuselah standing in the doorway. The smoke blurs the image of his son, but he sees him cross his arms over his chest.

Enoch stands there until the fire consumes the rest of the sacrifice. He doesn’t move until there’s nothing but ashes and bones left, and even then, he remains unmoving.

Later, as nightfall comes, Enoch returns to the house to lay down on his mat. Edna is turned on her side, the blanket nearly covering her head.

Enoch stares up at the ceiling. But then, all at once, sleep overcomes him.

"Enoch."

There's that voice again.

"Enoch!"

The visions come back.

Enoch bolts upright. The sun's rays are already peeking through the wooden shutters on the window.

He quickly untangles himself from the blankets as he rushes to get up.

"What is it?" Edna asks, confused.

"There's something I have to do," he says hurriedly as he throws on a cloak.

"What?" she asks, concern rising in her voice.

He doesn't answer and instead, rushes out the door.

CHAPTER NINETEEN

BESEECH THE JUDGE

Samyaza paces back and forth in his room. He barely notices when a servant enters his sanctuary, instead he becomes fixated on the mesmerizing patterns of the tapestry on the wall.

"Master?" the servant asks, staying in the doorway.

"What?" he snaps.

"Enoch the scribe would like to—"

"What?" The Watcher stomps to a halt, but still taps his fingers on the side of his robe. He gets his answer, however, when Enoch appears behind the servant.

Samyaza openly stares, as if he's not sure what he's looking at. He is even more confused when he sees Enoch is staring right back, contrasting the servant that shrinks farther away.

"What do you want?" he asks in a more timid voice than he meant, and in recovery gives Enoch a scowl.

"You're being sentenced," Enoch manifests.

The Watcher blinks a couple times, his expression remaining blank.

"Sentenced?" He takes a couple steps forward, but Enoch stays unaffected by his approach. “For what?”

“A great judgment has gone forth against you. You will not be able to obtain mercy or peace,” Enoch answers without falter.

This freezes Samyaza into place. His restless fingers ball into fists.

“Because of you the earth has been filled with blood. Even the souls of the dead cry out. And their cries ascend from their sanctuary in the earth all the way to the courts of heaven.”

“The dead are no fault of mine,” Samyaza retorts, then wonders why he’s even arguing with this scribe. He pushes aside the thought that, for some reason, this man’s words chill him to his core.

“You have abandoned your purpose and polluted yourselves. Because of your transgression you will watch your offspring be slain and you will be bound within the earth.”

Samyaza takes a step back, astonished. He rubs a hand over his wrist. “You can’t possibly know this,” he concludes. When Enoch doesn’t reply, he adds, “And if it were true, then I will beseech the Judge myself.”

“You will no longer be able to address the court yourself.”

“That is a lie!” Panic begins to rise in his voice. “How can you sentence me?”

He lunges toward Enoch, but the scribe disappears. Samyaza spins around, but his target is nowhere to be found. He paces back and forth clenching and unclenching his fists.

“That wasn’t real,” he mumbles. “It’s him. He’s trying to trick me.” He pauses, half expecting pale, boney hands to lash out and strangle him.

Finally, he turns and darts out the door. In a flash of light, he’s at the base of Mount Armon. He stares up at the lofty peak.

With a bound, he races up the mountainside. Reaching the icy top, he uses it to launch into the air. He jumps upward, but something is wrong. His body moves slowly through the air, as if he is traveling through thick mud.

He reaches up his hand, but he falls. With a resounding thud, he crashes back down onto the mountaintop. Sucking in a breath, he stares up into the sky.

A frozen mist colors the stones around him white. Sealed under a gray prison, he is unable to go any higher.

As he lies there, a voice comes back to him. “You must be more careful." He can't quite place the owner of the voice in his memory, but it fills him with urgency. A nearly uncontrollable impulse to flee rushes through his limbs.

Yet all he can do is stare in shock at the sky.

He isn't sure how much time has passed when he pulls himself out of the ice-covered terrain. He can't feel his body at all. It occurs to him that maybe someone else is moving him. Or maybe he's just a frozen corpse with blue lips and white eyes.

When Samyaza finally returns to the palace, he finds he's not the only one present. The rest of the Watchers have gathered. They all talk fervently amongst themselves, but then turn to stare at Samyaza as he enters.

He stares like a cornered rabbit, afraid to move lest it trigger their killer instinct and they pounce on him. He steps to the side slowly, willing himself to not make any sudden moves.

Danieal is the first one to approach. He steps in front of Samyaza, thwarting any getaway.

"Something must be done," Danieal urges.

Samyaza notices the Watcher's wide eyes and paled skin. His breaths are hurried, and Samyaza realizes that he has never seen the Watcher look so afflicted.

He then tilts his head to scan the rest of the faces. Their expressions mirror each other—tense muscles, constricted pupils.

Samyaza has seen that look before. Not in the Watchers or humans, but in the beasts and cornered animals. And he knows the danger of a wounded creature just trying to survive.

His initial fear turns to a cold, sickening dread as he turns back to Danieal. His heart feels like a heavy rock inside his chest. "What do you suggest?" His voice has dropped to a whisper.

"The scribe must make a petition for us."

The leading Watcher takes a step back. "Why is he continuing to be involved in this?" he asks through gritted teeth.

"He hears from Elohim," Danieal insists. "We can no longer beseech for ourselves. We have no other choice." He leans in closer and whispers, "You have seen yourself, we cannot leave."

His eyes suddenly dart from Samyaza to behind him as someone else has entered the room.

Enoch steps through the entryway and all eyes turn toward him. The room is totally silent for a few seconds, and Danieal shifts from foot to foot.

With a frustrated sign, Samyaza approaches the scribe. He leans in toward Enoch and drops his voice till it is barely audible. "Diligent scribe, we have all gathered here to ask you if you will plead for us to the heavenly courts."

Enoch just stares back at him with tight lips, so the Watcher clears his throat and tries again. "Please, we plead to you. Give us a voice."

After a few uncomfortable seconds pass, Enoch affirms with a curt nod. "I will write a prayer for you."

Relief floods back into the Watcher's face. He is about to reply when Enoch speaks up.

"There was once a man who met a dragon."

Samyaza raises his brows but doesn't interrupt as the scribe continues his story.

"The dragon said to him, 'I can give you a gift. Make a deal with me and I will grant you eternal life.'

"The man replied, 'What must I do in exchange for this?' The dragon simply said, 'Forever you must run from God. He will chase you, but as long as you run, you will live forever.'

"The man agreed and from that day on, he ran. He could never see God, but he could always sense him close behind. The man went to the mountains, but he could not find sanctuary there, so he ran to the desert, but still there was no place for him to rest. He went to the forest, but the trees gave him no covering.

"Finally, he ran to the sea. He said, 'My body is tired and weak, let me throw myself into the sea and there I will meet God.' The man let the waves overcome him, and soon he began to drown.

"However, it was not God he met in the sea, it was the dragon. Confused, the man asked, 'Why did you say God was chasing me when it was you all along?'"

Enoch suddenly stops his story now, and Samyaza leans in.

"What did the dragon say?" he asks.

Enoch eyes him for a moment, then turns to leave. Danieal says something to the Watcher, but he doesn't hear him. Instead, Samyaza focuses on Enoch's disappearing form.

"What did the dragon say?" he asks again, but his words are lost in a sea of voices.

***

Jezebel steps along the rocky terrain. Only the moon lights her path as she follows beside a sheer mountainside. Behind her is a vast grassy plain, barely visible in the dim light.

She keeps close to the mountain until she finds a gorge between two cliffs. This is where the others will be spending the night. As she rounds a corner, she sees the dark silhouettes of her own kind.

Some of them are hiding amongst crags in the rocks. They bare their teeth and growl slightly as she passes. Jezebel ignores them and keeps her head forward. She steps straight toward a muddy pool at the end of the gorge.

Another Nephilim is already kneeling by the water as she approaches. He lifts his head to sniff the air then says, "Jezebel. Already you have returned?" He sits back leisurely and smiles at her with pointed teeth that look blue in the moonlight.

She stalks up to the pool and sits across from him. "What, Daeva, you thought you would have more food without me?" She dips her hand into the water.

"Hunting trip?" another Nephilim, Aeshma, asks as he slinks out from the shadows. His yellow eyes stand out in the dim light, which also illuminates two horns that sprout from either side of his head, curling back like those of a ram.

Daeva gives him a low growl, but he ignores it.

"You could say that," Jezebel replies, not offering any more information. She lifts a handful of water up to her mouth. Pausing, she stares into the stagnate liquid for a moment. "I think I should go to Egypt." When neither of her companions replies, she adds, "I could become a god there."

As she speaks, another Nephilim, much smaller than her, cautiously approaches the pool. Jezebel bares her teeth at him, and he quickly backtracks.

She continues speaking unperturbed. "I've heard they treat us with respect there. You don't have to live like dogs, and you would be far from the reach of the Watchers."

"We could have respect here," Daeva speaks up. "Just start eating everyone and they will give us whatever we want." He offers a twisted smile.

"The Watchers would never allow that. If we take away all their women, they'll take out their wrath on us," Aeshma replies. "That's why we should leave. I've heard a group of us took over a city not too far from here. Ate the king, and he was a big one. I'm sure he lasted a couple days."

Jezebel stays silent, and Aeshma soon loses interest in the conversation. He gets up to leave but leans over to Jezebel and says, "Next time you go hunting, remember to bring me with you."

After he leaves, Jezebel moves to sit next to Daeva. She waits until Aeshma is out of earshot and says, "I think you're right."

"You do?" he says, crossing his arms.

"I'm not afraid of the Watchers." She leans in closer to him. "I think they should know their place," she states with a confident grin. He looks at her skeptically and she adds, "Have you ever heard of a Watcher killing his own offspring?"

"What are we to do?" he asks.

"I think we should take over this city."

"What good would that do for us?"

Jezebel grits her teeth, but then plasters a smile on her face. "He's a fool," she says, inclining her head toward their departed companion. "We are more than strong enough to defeat the Watchers and rule every city within a week's journey from here."

When he still looks unconvinced, she adds, "I need your help. It would be like we are two gods ruling together." He looks at her appraisingly, and she quickly adds, "I am, after all, looking for a mate."

He appears much more open to the idea after that.

"It's too dangerous for us to discuss our plans here," she says, giving a wary eye to the other Nephilim nearby. "But they are easily manipulated. They needn't worry us too much."

As if to illustrate her point, she stalks over to the smaller Nephilim who had been sticking close to the pool. She backs him up against the rocks, and he desperately searches for some way to escape. Then, he makes his fatal mistake. The smaller Nephilim lunges toward her, but she grabs him at the neck, slamming him against the rock wall.

The sudden noise draws the attention of the surrounding Nephilim. They gather around and this panics the small Nephilim even more. He snaps his teeth and jumps at them, but it's too late.

They circle around him and Jezebel steps back to watch. The Nephilim descend on him in a frenzy, and his shrieking cries soon fall silent.

The rest of the Nephilim then begin to fight over pieces of him as they tear him apart with their teeth and claws. They growl and snap like wild dogs over a fresh carcass.

Daeva steps up beside Jezebel. He looks at her with a wicked grin and asks, "Should we join in?"

She matches his smile, and they both jump into the fray.

***

The next evening, Enoch follows along the river Dan. His sandaled feet make a crunch with each step on the loose gravel.

The sun is just beginning to set and casts rays of light onto Mount Armon in the distance. The snowy peaks look like streams of light in the glow.

Enoch holds a scroll in his hand. He has suffered over writing it all day, a repeating process of writing one sentence, then throwing it out and starting again. Now that he is finally somewhat satisfied with it, he unfurls the scroll before him.

After clearing his throat several times, he begins to read off its contents and keeps up his pacing at the same time. It's a memorial of the Watcher's request, starting off with a list of all the accusations.

"… Polluting the bloodline of man, creating a chaos filled world by teaching sorcery, by teaching the fabrication of weapons …"

He pauses for a few moments and stares at the sunset glow on the river. Continuing, he reads their supplication. "That they might obtain remission and rest …"

He lets out a pent-up breath as he reaches the bottom of the scroll. Quickly, he rolls it back up, then stands still and waits. His eyes scan the horizon expectantly while he rocks back and forth from foot to foot. Nothing happens.

Unrolling the scroll once more, he looks back down, grazing over the words with his eyes. Maybe he needs to read it again.

He repeats the mantra out loud once more, then waits. Still

nothing.

A flock of birds fly in formation overhead, and the sun is now dipping into the horizon, but still, only silence. He decides to take a seat next to the river.

Holding the scroll out formally before him, he repeats the words once more. His body seems to be heavier now, and the words blur together on the page. He blinks his eyes a couple times, trying to focus.

He shakes his head, but that doesn't help any.

He slowly lies down next to the river and falls asleep.

***

Enoch blinks his eyes open, but then quickly squeezes them shut as the bright sunlight beats down on him. It must be morning now. He lifts his hand above his face, trying to block out the rays.

"Enoch."

That isn't the sun.

Squinting, his eyes adjust slightly to the harsh light. Pushing himself up on his elbow he takes in his surroundings. The radiance isn't from something natural, instead it emanates from three beings before him.

He jumps to his feet.

They have the appearance of men but stand a couple feet taller.

The first one speaks again. "Enoch, you must come with us." His voice is commanding.

Michael.

The other two have a more asterial manner, one of them smiles at him.

Gabriel and Aziel.

Michael takes another step forward. The brightness grows and soon envelops them. Then everything turns white.

CHAPTER TWENTY

VISITORS

"He didn't come home last night," is all Dinah and Martha can get out of their mother when they try to talk to her.

"Father has had to stay at the palace for days in the past," Martha tries to reassure, but it seems to little avail.

After that, the rest of the family stays quiet and indoors. Dinah gives some leftover dinner to the twins but they only stare at their food, tearing off a few pieces of bread here and there.

Dinah sighs and crosses her arms "You have to eat something," she snaps.

Nan intervenes and suggests that maybe a game with the boys will encourage an appetite. Sitting down in front of them, she dances around one of their wooden figures, giving it a funny voice to match. Soon the boys come up with a storyline for her to act out.

After a minute, Methuselah comes to join them, sitting down next to Nan.

"Are you—" Nan begins but Methuselah interrupts her with a raised hand.

"I'm fine." He holds up one of the carved toys and dropping to a deeper voice says, "Come on, men, we must kill the dragon before that wretched beast destroys the city!"

The boys add in with excited voices, rallying their troops.

Methuselah glances up at Nan, a small smile tugging at the corner of his mouth.

She gives a tentative smile back, and in a low voice says, "About before … I shouldn't have—"

"Don't worry about it," he replies simply, his gaze roving over her face.

"I think, perhaps …" Before Nan can finish, the front door slams open.

They look up to see Kenan in the doorframe, his arm around a stooped figure. A ratted cloak conceals the figure's identity.

Edna stands to her feet. "Enoch …"

Kenan shakes his head. "No, she needs help." He guides the woman forward and Edna takes her other arm.

Kenan continues, "I found her by the stream. She looks close to death."

They escort her over to a chair where she sits down heavily.

"Thank you," the woman says with a hoarse voice.

"Nan, get her some water, please," Edna orders.

Jumping up from the floor, Nan hurries over to the water jar and fills a small cup. As she turns and steps toward the visitor, she drops the clay bowl and it shatters on the floor.

All eyes turn to stare at her, startled by the sudden noise. Nan freezes into place, staring wide-eyed at their strange guest. She hesitantly takes a step forward.

"Mikah?" Her voice is barely above a whisper.

The woman finally looks up. Her eyes are hollow, but they light up with a glint of recognition when she looks at Nan.

"It can't be …" Mikah says, looking almost entranced. "I thought it was false hope—"

"Mikah!" Nan rushes forward, wrapping her arms around the woman's neck. A few happy tears start to well up in her eyes. "I thought you were dead! How…" Her tone changes from joyful to troubled. Releasing Mikah from her embrace, she turns around hesitantly.

"You told me she was dead." She shakes her head, staring at Methuselah, confused.

He steps over to her. "Nan, let us talk …" He reaches out for her, but she jerks away.

"I don't understand. You told me she was dead," she accuses. "You lied to me?"

"There is more to it," he insists.

"Really? What, did you think she was dead? Did you see her die?"

"No, it's—"

She raises her voice. "Then what?"

"She was going to betray you. I heard her, Nan. I heard her say she would find you and give you to that Nephilim. She was going to let you die."

Mikah speaks up before she has time to answer. "Edna, you know that's not true. He's been deceiving you. I would never betray you."

Nan looks back and forth at them.

Mikah adds to her testament. "Edna don't let them trick you. I raised you. I gave you a home." Standing, she grabs Nan's wrist. "Please, come with me."

"Where are your belongings?" Nan asks quietly.

"What?" Mikah shakes her head, confused.

"I asked, where are your belongings? Why are you here, starving with no place to stay?" She takes a step back, but Mikah doesn't let go of her.

"Because I've been looking for you. We lost everything in that attack."

"It didn't make it that far. I stopped it. How did we lose everything?" Nan finally pulls her arm away.

"You weren't there, Edna. You don't know what it was like after—"

"Well, you found me. I guess if what you're saying is true, then you won't mind if I stay here," Nan says, straightening.

Alarm starts to edge into Mikah's voice. "No, you have to come with me."

Nan turns away. "Why? If we lost everything, wouldn't it be just as well if we start our new life here?"

Mikah's eyes dart toward the ground briefly before she swoops down to the ground and snatches up a shard of the shattered bowl. Nan jumps back in surprise, but Mikah still manages to wrap her arms around her.

Kenan and Methuselah rush forward but freeze when Mikah places the shard against her captive's throat.

"We are not staying here." She pushes the fragment into Nan's skin.

"Stop!" Methuselah yells, but then he notices Nan mumbling under her breath.

Suddenly, Mikah's hand begins to shake, and she drops the shard. The woman doubles over on the ground with a groan. Nan is speaking out loud now, repeating an unrecognizable chant. She towers over Mikah as the woman clutches her head, crying out in pain.

"Nan, stop it!' Methuselah dashes forward.

Her chant suddenly ceases, and she rocks back and forth on her feet for a moment. She stares straight ahead, unmoving.

"Nan?" he asks cautiously.

Finally, she blinks and looks down at the crumpled woman at her feet. A slow smile begins to creep across her face.

Nan reaches down and grabs her by the neck. Mikah stares up at her, panicked, as she slowly lifts her up off the ground. With one hand, she raises Mikah above her head.

Everyone takes a step back, too shocked to speak.

Mikah squeaks out some sort of plea, but Nan isn't listening. Without blinking, she slams Mikah's body back onto the ground.

Kenan runs up behind Nan, wrapping his arms around her. She struggles for a few seconds, but then her power seems to wane. A laugh that is most definitely not her own comes out of her mouth.

"What's happened to her?" Kenan asks.

"We need to restrain her," Methuselah yells, then all at once Nan goes limp.

***

Enoch follows the Archangels. Their light illuminates the grassy plain around them. Suddenly, something in the shape of a sphere appears in front of Enoch. It's golden and has two rings around its circumference. The outer ring is lined with white shining lights that blink as if they are eyes.

"Eremiel, it's time to go," Michael instructs.

And with that, the sphere begins to expand. It opens and ribbons of gold wrap around Enoch and the angels. The ribbons spin so quickly that they look like liquid flames of fire.

Lightning strikes, spreading around the orb. Instantly, they start moving. They lunge upward at an incredible speed, but Enoch is still able to stand upright. The sphere has grown to encapsulate them and is now their apparent mode of transportation.

The outside world is unrecognizable, flashing by in one solid stream of light.

Enoch looks around at his companions. Michael stares straight ahead, totally focused on the imminent task. Aziel, on the other hand, gives Enoch a warm smile.

Enoch gives him a small smile and nervously nods his head.

"Hello…" Enoch starts, then looks to Gabriel who is reading an unfurled scroll.

The parchment hovers in front of the Archangel, who places a hand on his chin while he reads.

Enoch stares at the scroll, then blinks in recognition. He looks about his person. "Isn't that the—"

He doesn't have time to finish as they abruptly come to a stop.

The sphere seems to disperse around them, then reappears in its smaller version and hovers between the Archangels. It gives a whirl of satisfaction and then zips off in another direction.

Enoch hardly even notices the angels anymore as he takes in his surroundings. Directly in front of them stands a massive building made from clear crystal stones. Even when Enoch cranes his neck all the way back, he can barely see the top of the building.

He can see, however, that the sky above is an ocean of water.

"This way," Gabriel instructs, as the scroll rolls back up and he takes it in his hand.

They step toward the doorway and Enoch hesitates.

The door itself is like a solid sheet of light, somehow contained within the doorway.

Gabriel gives him an expectant look, and so he steps forward. Walking through the door, he is seized with an assault of sensations. The room is burning hot and freezing at the same time. A sudden pressure has come over him, and each step forward is more difficult.

This area appears to be a large hall leading to another room. The floor is crystal, the same as the walls, and is bright, almost white.

Up in the lofty heights of the ceiling, Seraphim whirl around. A large pair of wings keeps them aloft while a smaller pair covers their faces. Their bodies decorate the ceiling like stunning paintings with golden wings and iridescent fabric. They are all singing in a low voice, almost sounding like one being.

The group stops before they enter the room at the end of the hall.

Gabriel turns to Enoch and says, "Welcome to the heavenly courtroom."

As they enter the room, a bright light overwhelms Enoch. He shields his eyes from the center of the room where the light derives.

The pressure doubles, and Enoch feels his knees buckle. He knows that his companions want him to move forward, so he decides the best course of action is to stare at the floor and go one step at a time.

The floor itself has the appearance of bright molten liquid. It's a warm color and has bright white sparks swirling through it. Wherever he steps, it leaves a white imprint of his foot, then slowly fades back to its normal amber color.

As they approach, he realizes the light is giving off the pressure. Just when Enoch feels he will collapse if he takes one more step, they stop.

He pants as sweat beads around his forehead. Through squinted eyes, Enoch can see a singular throne sits before them. It's too bright for him to make out anything further.

Looking to the side, he notices that the pressure also affects the Archangels with him.

Aziel has moved behind a marble table and has a large book open in front of him. Enoch keeps his eyes on Aziel, since looking anywhere else is too overpowering.

A voice emanates from the throne. "Enoch, scribe of righteousness, hear my voice."

Aziel begins taking notes in the book as the one from the throne speaks.

The voice continues. "You have brought a supplication from the Watchers. Go to them and say, 'You ought to pray for man, and not man for you.'"

Enoch isn't sure, but he thinks he sees Aziel grimace as he jots down that note.

The voice has its own power, and each word is like a gust of wind. "Ask them, why have you, possessor of an immortal life, defiled yourselves with the mortal? Men die, so I give them wives so they may have sons and daughters. But you possess a life that is not subject to death.'

"Now, as for your impious offspring, who have been born of both spirit and flesh, a dark spirit will proceed from their bodies. And they will be forced to wander the earth. They will be hungry and thirsty, and they will rise against men and women because they were created during the days of slaughter and destruction." One final judgment is given, say to them, 'Therefore never will you obtain peace.'"

Enoch feels as if he should probably say something, but the words refuse to come out. All of this is happening so quickly that he can hardly process the words being said.

As Aziel finishes writing the verdict, something happens to the words. They begin to glow a bright red, then fade back to black, sealing them into place.

Aziel gives a nod to Gabriel, who comes over next to Enoch.

"This way," the Archangel says, indicating for Enoch to follow. They lead him out of the courtroom.

As they leave the building, the pressure is suddenly relieved, and Enoch doubles over. He gasps for air and the angels wait for him to recover.

"Here, eat this." Aziel holds out a red-colored fruit.

Taking it in his hand, Enoch turns it over several times, inspecting it with a raised brow.

"It will help restore your strength," Aziel adds. "See, you cannot handle the power as well as we can. You have a body in the other realm, so the real you—"

"Let's not overload him with too much information," Gabriel reprimands gently, and Aziel nods.

Enoch takes a tentative bite of the fruit and gives a muffled "Mmph!" when it gushes juice over his chin. He reaches up a hand, but then realizes that the juice has disappeared, and hasn't left any stickiness at all.

He then notices that what Aziel has said was true. Not only is his strength restored, but he feels twice as strong as before.

With his new vigor, he feels brave enough to ask some of the questions he's kept bottled up.

"That room … the courtroom. That voice, was that …?"

"It was," Michael answers.

"Oh … oh my." Enoch places a hand up to his forehead and lets out a breath.

"Do you need another fruit?" Aziel asks with raised brows.

"No, no. I'm fine," he replies, then is suddenly struck with a thought. "Wait … are you the ones who gave me the visions? Who made me talk to the Watchers? What did you do to me?"

"We did nothing to you," Michael replies sternly. "If you are talking about your sudden ability to be authoritative and speak to the Watchers in such a bold manner, you can thank yourself for that."

"What? But I didn't—"

"We need to keep moving," Gabriel interrupts. "There is still much more we must show you."

Enoch silences and follows behind them. He notices several more angels around this area. They look like beams of light, but then, when they please, they change to have the appearance of men. Some also look like women.

This place is like his home, with trees and tall grass, but everything is more alive and blooming. Flowers grow everywhere, and Enoch takes notice of some white ones clustered together on a bush. As he leans closer, the flowers turn their blooms toward him.

Enoch jerks his head back slightly, but the flowers just continue to bob their heads. After a second, he realizes they all appear to be dancing together. In fact, there is some sort of music everywhere, and all the flowers nod along with it.

As they walk beside a river, Enoch begins to hear voices. He looks around, trying to pinpoint the source, then realizes that the sound is near his feet. As the lively waters babble along, they create a sort of humming sound. Listening closer, he notices each little wave and ripple has a voice of its own. The river is alive, like a stream of watery phantoms, all laughing and singing amongst themselves.

Enoch points down to the water. "Say, that's—" He cuts himself off when he looks up and sees that the Archangels are continuing ahead of him. He quickly jogs to catch up and makes a mental note to not get so distracted.

"Where are you taking me?" he asks as he follows his companions.

"You are not here just to testify but to bear witness as well," Gabriel replies but doesn't offer up any more information.

Suddenly, the same sphere from earlier appears in front of them. Eremiel, they had called him. He expands like an unfurling ball of yarn, and they step inside of him.

Before Enoch can even wonder where they are going now, everything blurs. When the view comes into focus, he can see they are hovering over the earth. The mountains and rivers are visible below, but they are still very high up.

"Look, that's where you live," Aziel says suddenly, pointing down to a certain place on the globe.

Enoch places his hands on the glasslike walls of their transport to get a better look. "This … this is the world we live in?" he asks, pressing his face against the glass.

"That's right," Aziel answers. "But our current destination is more … inward." He cryptically raises his brows.

Gabriel makes a noise that seems halfway between a sigh and a scoff.

Enoch decides the best course of action is just to go along with them and wait for his questions to answer themselves.

Suddenly, they drop, and Enoch feels his stomach lurch up into his throat, but the Archangels don't appear alarmed at all. In fact, Aziel looks quite excited. Michael, on the other hand, just stares straight ahead with a set jaw, and Gabriel clasps his hands peacefully in front of him. The only effect the drop has on them is their hair flying upward.

The sphere keeps dropping faster as the ground rushes toward them at an alarming speed.

Enoch clasps at the sides of their transport.

"Fear not," Aziel replies with a wide smile. "We'll be alright."

The treetops are visible now. Just a couple seconds more and they will hit the ground. Enoch braces for impact.

The earth rushes up to them, and everything goes black.

It takes Enoch a couple seconds to realize that they're all still alive and well. They are still traveling downward, but everything outside of the sphere is totally dark.

Could they be underground?

Just when Enoch is about to ask, they enter a cave. A glow begins to emanate from them, illuminating the smooth walls of the chasm.

The cave is like an abyss, separating two other open areas. One side is bright and sits on a cliff-face with a stream running along its ledge. The water spills over the side of the cliff and disappears into the blackness below. The wall that sits behind the stream is lined with several tall archways. Even though this area is stone like the rest of the cave, sparkling flecks of precious stone can be seen embedded in the wall.

The other side, however, is not so inviting. It is an open area, like the other side but, is shrouded in darkness. The dark is like an entity of its own, overwhelming any light spilling from the opposite side.

Upon a closer look, Enoch can see what looks like black blobs moving through the darkness. The blobs turn into shadowy bodies, crawling around each other like a pile of worms.

The forms barely look human. Instead, the mass of decaying bodies appears to morph together into one putrefied creature.

Even at their distance, Enoch can hear the wails and shrieks that constantly emanate from the darkness.

"What is that place?" Enoch asks, moving away from the side of the sphere.

Michael is the one that answers this time. "That is Sheol. The resting place of all souls who are unrepentant."

Enoch nods slowly, then indicates to the other side. "And that place?"

"That is for the departed souls of those who are covered under sacrifice."

"Those souls who are covered by sacrifice … come here," Enoch says to himself, but then Aziel adds, "For now."

Enoch is about to ask Aziel exactly what he means, when something catches his attention. There is someone walking along the stream on the illuminated side.

"Who is that? And what is he doing?" he inquires.

"That is Abel," Gabriel replies, "who was slew by his brother Cain. And he is making accusations against his brother that rise all the way to heaven."

Abel paces back and forth without rest. Enoch watches him for a couple moments, then goes back to an earlier question. "What did you mean 'they are staying here for now'?"

The three angels look at each other. Michael answers, "That is something that even we don't have full knowledge of."

"But soon, you will," Gabriel says, staring directly at Enoch. He then pulls a scroll out from his robe and hands it to Enoch.

"What do I—"

"Open it," Gabriel instructs.

Enoch examines the scroll. It's made of parchment, far finer than any he's seen before. In the middle is a blood-red seal stamped with a figure eight.

"Go ahead," Aziel encourages.

Enoch breaks the seal, and the scroll unrolls itself. Its inside is glowing with light. The light starts to grow, and then it consumes Enoch.

***

"Don't go in there," Edna pleads as Methuselah paces tirelessly. "And please sit down."

"I can't just leave her in there, bound up like some animal." He looks at her with concern. "Maybe the spirit has left her."

"Methuselah …" She steps up to her son and places a hand on his face. "She may not live." Edna nods over to a still unconscious Mikah.

Martha has managed to stop the bleeding from where the woman's head hit the floor and now uses a wet rag to clean the blood from Mikah's hair.

Methuselah eyes Mikah's limp body. "That is not of great concern to me. It might be of benefit if she does die."

Dinah speaks up, "You know Nan wouldn't want that." All eyes turn to her. "Nan wouldn't care what that woman's done to her. She wouldn't want her dead."

"Well, that's obviously not Nan in there right now," Methuselah answers, pointing to the door leading into the next room.

Edna shakes her head. "Your father would know what to do."

Methuselah ignores her comment and pinches the bridge of his nose. The pounding in his head has only grown worse in the last few hours.

"Maybe we can make a sacrifice," Methuselah reasons to himself.

"We make sacrifices to protect ourselves as our fathers have taught us. I've never seen anything like this." His mother lets out her breath and drops down into a seat. "The teachings of the Watchers truly are dark," she surmises.

"I think we've come to that conclusion," Methuselah says, not slowing his pacing before spinning on his heels.

He steps deliberately toward the other room, ignoring the "Wait!" from his mother.

He stops in the doorway. Nan sits with her head slumped over, leaning against the supporting post where she is tied.

"Nan?" he ventures.

"She isn't here," Nan replies, but it doesn't sound like her at all. The voice is much deeper and guttural. "And she's not coming back," she adds, looking up at him with a leer.

"You need to leave her," Methuselah says, then clears his throat.

"What authority do you have to tell me to leave?" She tilts her head to the side, then laughs wickedly at his lack of response. Suddenly, she rushes toward him, stopping just inches away as her binds hold her back. "Do you really think these ropes can hold me?" she snaps at him.

"Nan …" He absentmindedly reaches out toward her.

Her dark hair has fallen out of its usually neat braid and now sprawls around her face in messy clumps. Methuselah takes a strand in his fingers, but then notices that Nan seems to be shrinking away from him.

It takes him a moment to realize that he's the one moving as he feels himself being yanked backward out of the room.

"What are you doing?" Kenan asks, pulling his brother out and slamming the door behind him. "Do you want her to bite your hand off?"

"There has to be something we can do," Methuselah argues.

"Of course, but going in there and talking to that … that thing isn't going to help."

Methuselah strides over to where Martha is taking care of Mikah.

"We will have to find out what will help then," he says, taking the bowl of water Martha was using to clean Mikah's wound. He dumps it over the woman's face, soliciting a stern rebuke from his sister.

"Wake up." He gives the woman a stiff shake.

After several seconds, Mikah blinks her eyes, then places a hand up to her head and groans.

Impatient, Methuselah shakes her again. "Get up!" he snaps.

She glares back at him but doesn't retaliate. She then looks around the room as if to get her bearings.

"What's happening?" she mumbles after a second, and then presses her hands against her head again.

"Why don't you explain what happened to Nan?" Methuselah replies, crossing his arms.

A look of realization crosses Mikah's face as she slides herself up into a sitting position.

"Give her a second," Martha chastises.

Mikah rubs her eyes then leans her head back against the wall. She squints up at Methuselah and asks, "Where's Edna?"

"What did you do to her?" Methuselah asks, not bothering to answer her question.

"What did *I* do? I'm the one lying on the ground with blood pouring out of my head." She gingerly presses her fingers to the wound on the side of her head and winces.

"Don't touch it," Martha warns.

"She's been possessed," Methuselah states. If he was expecting a reaction out of her, he doesn't get one, instead she looks around the room as if planning her next move.

He squats down to her level. "How do we get the spirit to leave her?"

Now forced to look at him, she just furrows her brows together and answers with a snappy, "I don't know."

She flinches as Methuselah makes a move toward her, but he stands instead. He stiffens, however, with the sudden pain in his head from moving too quickly.

Although he tries to hide the pain, his mother notices and steps in front of him. Edna reaches down and takes Mikah by the arm, pulling the woman upward. She then drags her over to the door leading to the other room, not letting go of her firm clasp on Mikah's wrist.

"You will look at her and tell us if anything can be done," Edna orders.

Mikah looks much paler now but doesn't protest as Edna cracks the door open slightly.

Tentatively, Mikah peeks into the opening.

Nan just stands in the center of the room, her eyes focusing on the floor. Her matted hair obscures her face, and she speaks without bothering to look up.

"The one who kills her students," the grating voice says. "Have you come to draw the blood of this girl too?"

Mikah stumbles backward, slamming the door shut at the same time. She somehow looks even paler now as her breaths come in rapid bursts.

"What's wrong with her?" Dinah asks.

Suddenly, Mikah's eyes roll to the back of her head, and she collapses onto the ground.

"Is she alive?" Martha rushes over, an edge of panic in her voice.

They lean over the woman when a snapping sound interrupts them.

Methuselah rushes to open the door, stepping over Mikah's limp body.

All that greets him is an empty room.

"Where did she—" Kenan begins, stepping up beside his brother.

Methuselah walks over to the frayed ropes on the ground, then directs his eyes to the broken shutters on the window.

Grasping the doorframe in alarm, Kenan looks to his brother. "Now what do we do?"

Before Methuselah can answer, a voice from the other room cuts through the air. They both look to see Mikah is indeed alive on the floor, her eyes wide in horror.

"She must be killed, there is no other way! He has come for her. He will not let her go!" Her words intermingle with sharp inhales. "Fear the darkness that comes, for it will overtake us all!"

CHAPTER TWENTY-ONE

Fear and Trembling

Screaming. He can hear screaming. It's faint, and almost sounds dreamlike. Distant wails and shrieks of panic rise and fall like waves.

"There you are. How long have you been here?" Danieal asks, marching over toward Samyaza.

The Watcher doesn't respond. Instead, he stays lying down amongst an excess of blankets and pillows and stares with fixed eyes up at the ceiling.

"What's wrong with you?" Danieal stands over him and sees the absentminded Watcher holding a hand over the red line on his wrist.

"Do you have any idea what's been going on?" he asks, crossing his arms.

Samyaza blinks a couple times, then shifts his gaze over to the invader of his privacy. "What …?"

Danieal just lets out a sigh and turns to leave the room. Samyaza lifts his head out of his plush resting place and manages to say "What are you …" before the other Watcher exits the room.

He quickly gets to his feet and follows behind. Danieal stays silent as they walk through the empty corridor. They come to a hall lined with several open archways that give them a view of the city below.

Samyaza squints as the outside world is much brighter than his previous refuge. When his eyes adjust, he takes in the view below.

"What happened …?" His voice trails off at the sight of crumbled buildings. Many of them have just one wall standing or are nothing more than a pile of wood and stones. Dust is still thick in the air, and several roads are defaced with red splatters. One section of the city is almost completely destroyed.

"You really have no idea of what's going on?" Danieal shakes his head and almost laughs. "You haven't even heard their cries." He points downward to where the main entrance to the stone palace is.

Hundreds of people from the city are gathered around, banging on the wooden door. They cry out, shouting variations of, "Why do you not deliver us?"

Some of them are just screaming. He notices one woman is just standing there, covered head to toe in blood.

Samyaza doesn't seem to find the situation funny. Although, he doesn't quite find it disturbing either. In fact, as he looks over the disarray, all he can manage to feel is the desire to return to his room.

"It was them. Wasn't it?" he asks.

"Of course, it was."

He calmly observes the ruin and crowd for another second then says, "What happens to man is no longer a concern of ours." He turns to leave, but Danieal grabs him by the wrist.

"It should be. Because this is a gift to us." Danieal's eyes widen as he speaks.

"How—"

"This is why we were cursed to begin with." Danieal inclines his head out to the destruction. "The spilled blood, the dead souls crying out for redemption." Samyaza doesn't attempt to leave now, so he continues, "Now they cry out to us."

He places both of his hands on either of Samyaza's arms and

straightens. With an exhale, he says, "We have to kill them all. Then our wrong will be righted, and Elohim will have mercy on us."

"What?" Samyaza takes a step back in surprise.

"The scribe may have written a supplication for us, but you know that this is what we need to do."

Samyaza grabs the Watcher's hand, flashing his wrist to him. "Have you forgotten this?"

"It was our oath that brought our cursed offspring into this world. Maybe if we destroy them all, our oath will be annulled," Danieal replies, then shakes his head with a smile. "Don't you see? This is our way out."

He is smiling, and it unnerves Samyaza more than comforts him. He stares at him for a good while, then leans to rest his arm on the archway. He slowly lets the idea of Danieal being right wash over him.

With the idea, a stark reality seizes him. He can no longer hide, sealed away in his palace, hoping that the eye of Elohim passes him by. All must come to judgment. In some way, all must answer for their sins. But maybe now, he could give the judge a different reply.

He then looks back at Danieal and says, "Well then, we should probably go inform the others."

With a placid smile on his face, he steps away from the view of the city and shuffles back into the palace. The hall before him seems longer now and unfamiliar. In fact, every room or passageway he passes seems foreign.

The decorative patterns on the walls blend, making shapes that almost look like faces when you don't directly look at them. But other than the haunts in the walls, no other souls appear to occupy the massive palace.

Somehow this doesn't panic Samyaza, even when the hallways become more and more confusing. Some dead end, and when he turns around, his pathway is different from where he just came.

Finally, he finds a large open room filled with the other Watchers. They all flock together in groups, probing each other for answers.

Samyaza notices Danieal at the edge of the crowd.

"There you are," the Watcher says to Samyaza.

"Tell us what you are planning," someone says from the crowd.

Danieal begins to explain his proposal to them. Samyaza listens quietly but keeps his back to the others.

"They must all be destroyed," Danieal instructs. "It is the only way we can obtain mercy."

"Can we do that?" Barkayal speaks up.

"This realm is different," Danieal answers. "Perhaps since they are our offspring, we can take their mortal bodies."

"We have to try." Samyaza turns to face the crowd, but his determined look fades from his face when he sees who else has entered the room.

Enoch steps through the doorway and clasps his hands in front of him as if he is waiting for something. Samyaza feels his throat tighten. He opens his mouth to speak, but nothing comes out.

He cannot be here, not yet.

Enoch breaks the silence for him. "I have brought your supplication before the courts of heaven."

Everyone strains to hear now. None of them even breathe.

"Your request has not been accepted, and you have been cursed."

Samyaza feels all the air leave his body, yet somehow finds his voice at the same time. "What?"

"We just need more time," Danieal insists.

Enoch ignores their protests and adds, "Secrets have been revealed to me, and I have seen the end. You will meet an end as well." He doesn't falter once as he speaks. Instead, he stares them down with a serene demeanor.

The manner of the Watchers couldn't be any more different. The whole room is filled with voices as they question each other about what this end might be.

Enoch relays the exact message from the courts and the panic only heightens. Certain words stick out to Samyaza, mostly the phrase, "Never obtain peace."

The room almost seems surreal now and spins as he turns to Danieal, but only to catch a glimpse of him leaving the room.

"What are you doing?" he questions, chasing after him.

Danieal ignores him and keeps marching forward. He steps out onto a balcony and jumps up on the railing. He is kept in place, however, when Samyaza grabs the end of his cloak.

"Our fate is sealed. There's nothing more we can do," he says, but the words seem to hit him harder than Danieal.

Without a look back, Danieal pulls himself from Samyaza's grasp and leaps into the air.

***

"That's it?" Daeva hardens his expression at Jezebel. "There was nothing stopping us. We could have taken over the entire city."

"We need to feel out the Watchers. Not all of them are just going to sit passively," she spits back. "We have to see how they react."

They have retreated to the wooded area after their trial attack. The trees are tall enough to reach their heads in this part of the forest. Daeva isn't grateful for the cover, however. He would much rather turn right around and head back to the city to finish what they started.

Jezebel looks him over, her jaw tightening with each second. His muscles are tense, but not from alertness. Instead, it's obvious he needs to expel the energy trapped inside.

She turns away from him, but he grabs her by the arm. "The humans will be preparing for us next time. They will run away," he says with a tight squeeze on her wrist.

"Are you really concerned about men?" She laughs at him. "You're pathetic. Our goals are much bigger than them."

He yanks her toward him. Reaching up with his other hand, he grabs her by the hair.

She tenses from the pain but subdues her reaction as he speaks.

"Do you think you can speak to me like that? You said you needed me, but now you make all the decisions?" He bears his still bloody teeth at her.

Jezebel clenches her fists. She takes a couple breaths and, after a few seconds, places a hand gently on his arm.

"You're right," she says quietly. "I should have listened to you." She gives him a small smile, ignoring the sharp pain from his grasp.

His harsh expression softens slightly. Quickly, she adds, "You still think we should use the others? Those who are weaker than us? They can still be helpful to us."

Daeva nods and releases his grip. "That, I will agree to."

She doesn't take the opportunity to back away, instead she inches closer, purses her lips, and says, "You go ahead. They should know your leadership before me."

He smiles and places his hand gently on the back of her head. "Just stay here. I'll be back soon." With that, he turns to leave and disappears into the trees.

She watches him and waits till he is out of sight, then exhales forcefully. She decides to go down to the river and mull over her plan a little more.

The trees part, and she steps down the hill to the stream below. Sitting down next to the water, she places her hand in the flow. The hardened mud on her fingers begins to loosen and drift away in the stream. The water turns slightly red from the layer of blood that flows downstream.

Her eyes shift focus on the reflection of her face. She studies her appearance. Clumps of her hair lie over her shoulders and are caked with the same dirt covering her body. Her eyes are just a dull gray in the daylight, not bright yellow like Daeva and others of her kind.

The coppery taste of blood is still prominent in her mouth as she picks up a chunk of hair and twists it between her fingers.

"A bath in the Dan might help," a rough voice beside her says.

Jezebel jerks her head back in surprise. She looks and finds a young woman sitting on a rock next to her.

She scoffs at the girl. "A human? What's wrong with you?" She leans closer, menacingly baring her blood-stained teeth. "Fortunately for you, I've just eaten."

"On second thought, keep the filth. It fits you," The woman says in a deep, grating voice. "Also, don't be a fool. I may look human, but this is not my body."

Jezebel looks the girl up and down once more, and wonders if she should just go ahead and kill her. Or maybe just bite off her arm.

She sits back and realizes that this is the first conversation she's had with a human in a very long time. Perhaps she will just see where this conversation with an insane girl is going.

The woman seems to be giving her a once over as well. She shakes her head and says, "I wouldn't think you would know me. We have met before, but I doubt you'd remember." Her eyes suddenly morph into black orbs.

Jezebel's vision also goes dark, and she brings her hands up to her face. "What's happening?" she cries.

Images begin to flash before her—memories, but not her own.

A mother with long black hair and a beautiful smile. She looks down at her pregnant belly and gently rubs it. But something's not right. Her skin pales and she's far too thin. Her eyes are hollow, and her bones protrude. Her black hair has lost its luster, and all that is left is the sickly, deformed figure of a once beautiful girl.

There's someone else with her. He has his arm around her, holding her like a dying bird, but there's nothing he can do.

Jezebel gasps in recognition. This is all so familiar to her, although she knows there's no way she could have seen this before. Then the visions change. A baby. Not a human, however. And not just one baby, but two. The second one is stillborn.

The visions vanish and Jezebel gasps for air. She digs her nails into the ground and focuses on the flowing water before her.

Still short of breath, she turns on the woman and says, "You … you're my—"

"Brother," she answers. "Didn't know you had a twin, did you? Well, it wouldn't be like our father to mention it."

"How are you … why are you—"

"I was fortunate, I guess you could say," the girl says with a shrug.

Jezebel swallows thickly. She has no memories of her mother, and the thought of her having a sibling never crossed her mind. At least not from the same mother. "What's your name?"

"Jadal. However, this body is obviously not my own. It belongs to a woman called Nan, but she matters not now."

Before she can reply Jadal adds, "Oh, and sister, I think you can do a little better than your … companion."

Jezebel starts to laugh. She's not sure why, but it just seems to fit the situation. "Oh, I see … brother." She raises her brow and looks at her brother in girl form. "You're here to tell me what to do," she says, then scowls. She never laughs, and the fact that this girl, or spirit, or whatever made her laugh so quickly, makes her uneasy.

Nan's body steps forward, but her eyes remain black. "I'm not here to tell you what to do. I'm here to help you."

***

"He's back!" Kenan shouts, looking through the window. He rushes to open the door, right as Methuselah bursts through it, then doubles over, panting.

"What happened? Why are you back so quickly?" Edna asks, placing a hand on her son's shoulder.

Methuselah straightens and drops his voice as he talks to his mother. Her face looks as drained of blood as he feels.

"They've attacked the city," he says, and she places a hand over her mouth. "You and the younger kids should leave now," he adds.

"What?" Kenan steps up beside his brother. "Where are we supposed to go? And what about you?"

Methuselah keeps his voice soft as he replies, "I don't know what provoked them to attack, but we can't just stay here until we know what's going on. Take mother and the others to the caves by the river."

"You can't …" Kenan raises his voice. "You're going back out there?" There is a sharp cut to his words.

"You know I have to find her," Methuselah says. "She's a part of our family too."

"We've known her for a season. Lamech was your brother for forty," he spits, then quietly says, "And he was my brother too."

Methuselah quickly steps toward him, and he braces, ready for a blow. But it doesn't come. Instead, Methuselah places his hands on his brother's face, forcing him to look his way.

"Lamech died so that I didn't have to," he says, then his grip loosens. "Do not think I wouldn't do the same thing for each one of you. For you, for mother, for Dinah, Martha, Judah, Tovi, and, yes, for her too."

Kenan is unable to meet his gaze anymore. He turns away but doesn't protest Methuselah leaving anymore.

Edna steps up to Methuselah and eyes him for a long time. He withstands her scrutiny without uttering a word, but he knows his mother is doing much more than just memorizing his face. She is reading him, like his father reads a scroll. But she does it without papyrus, words, or even an alphabet.

Somehow, just by looking into his eyes, she can see anything she wants to know. Finally, she nods mutely.

He draws her into a hug and says, "I will return to you."

She nods against his chest once more, and he looks to his brother.

Kenan turns away from his gaze. "Take a weapon at least," he mumbles.

Methuselah replies, "I will."

He releases his mother and straps a spear onto his back. Before he steps out the door, he turns to his family and says, "We will all be together again soon." And then he leaves.

***

As he shuts the door behind him, Edna turns to her children and announces, "Girls, gather everything we might need. We can no longer stay here."

"What about her?" Dinah asks, indicating a mute Mikah who is lying on her side on a mat in the corner and hasn't said anything since her episode earlier.

With a sigh, Edna replies, "We're taking her with us."

CHAPTER TWENTY-TWO

Those Who See the Light

Daeva has gathered the Nephilim before them. Jezebel looks over the troops he has assembled—if you could even call them that. There are no more than thirty, but their numbers should be of little consequence with their task at hand. They are all smaller than them, a safety precaution, of course. But they are still large enough to easily kill any human that would get in their way.

Most of the Nephilim give Jezebel and her mate wary stares. Jezebel grits her teeth, frustrated at how pathetically untrusting they are. Perhaps it's the way Daeva keeps snarling and snapping his teeth at the smallest ones.

Daeva doesn't seem bothered by their suspicion. Instead, the idea of convincing them to rally together seems to excite him.

He smiles as he begins. "The Watchers have shown no interest in protecting man. Earlier today we killed dozens of men, and the Watchers just stay on their mountain without retaliation. That means the humans are ours for the taking."

This immediately excites the gathered Nephilim. The prospect of so much food is too good of an offer to turn down.

"As soon as mankind is subdued, you will be able to live peacefully under our rule. We will treat you as equals, not as dogs like men and the Watchers do. And you will never scavenge or go hungry again."

Jezebel steps in with a heinous smile and adds, "You may eat those who you wish, the rest will be our slaves."

The group frenzies now, many of them growling and roaring. They claw at the ground, ready to tear into the forest at a moment's notice.

Daeva releases them, raising his voice above the uproar. "Now go and drink the blood of men."

They don't need any more convincing as they dash through the trees, running toward the city. They shake the ground as they go, and Jezebel can't help but smile at the thought of how terrified those in the city will be. When they feel the tremors in the ground, they will know that nothing can save them from a gory and brutal death.

She steps toward Daeva, giving him an approving look.

"It's exactly as you planned," she says, "Now, even if the Watchers have any rebuttal, they will take the blunt of it and we will remain safe." She wraps her arms around his neck. "And it's all because of your plan."

"Our days of hiding in the dark are no more." He gives her a fanged smile and pulls her closer.

Just as she feels his warm breath on her skin, a growl interrupts them. "Let her go."

They turn to see Aeshma stepping through the trees.

"Aeshma. What are you—" Daeva starts.

"I think that's what I should be asking you." He bears his teeth. "I said let her go."

Jezebel backs from them, and Aeshma turns his attention to her. "What did he do to you?" he asks.

Daeva steps between them. "You must leave this place," he threatens, then reaches out to take Jezebel by the arm.

He draws her towards him and isn't expecting when Aeshma springs into action. Aeshma lunges forward, tackling Daeva and taking out a line of cedars in the process.

The ground quakes as the two Nephilim smash into the forest floor. Daeva quickly rebuttals by grabbing one of Aeshma's horns and yanking back his head.

In return, the Nephilim swings his arm down, catching his opponent's jaw and snapping the bone. Daeva lets out a roar in pain as blood gushes out of his mouth. He doesn't let go of the horn, however, and yanks his attacker to the side, rolling him off him.

Daeva scrambles up to his feet, clutching his hanging jaw. He doesn't get any relief, however, as he is quickly lunged at again. Daeva is quick to step out of the way and rushes off in the opposite direction with the other Nephilim on his heels.

In a massive leap, Aeshma grabs him from behind, tackling him to the ground once more. He flashes his teeth, then bites down into his opponent's neck.

Daeva's vision begins to blur as he feels sharp teeth sinking into his neck, then shoulder. Blood squirts out, spraying into his eyes until all he can see is red.

Daeva turns his head to the side, blinking at Jezebel. He reaches out toward her with fingers clawing at the air. "Jezebel!" he cries. "Help me!"

But she doesn't help. She just stares as Aeshma sinks his teeth once more into Daeva's skin, crunching on bone. She watches for a couple more seconds, then slowly backs away into the trees.

Daeva's eyes go wide as he watches her go, until she disappears in the thick foliage.

Jezebel turns and runs through the forest, leaving the bloody scene behind. She hears an animal-like shriek, then all she hears is the sound of her footfalls, shaking the forest floor.

She doesn't stop running until she reaches a break in the trees. Sliding to a halt, she surveys the city below.

It takes her a couple seconds to realize something's wrong. It's far too silent.

She takes a few steps forward and finds her answer. A river of blood flows through the streets, far too much blood.

Her army of Nephilim lay scattered through the city. Several of them are beheaded or have massive holes in their chests. Some bear large claw and teeth marks as if they'd fought each other.

She steps forward, her mouth gaping. Dazed, she walks onto one of the streets, stepping over detached limbs.

In the back of her mind, she knows she shouldn't be here, that she should run. But for some reason the sight glues her in place.

One Nephilim appears to still be moving. He looks up at her, a look of shock prevalent on his face.

He tries to speak but can't. Instead, he reaches up a hand toward her. Then his fingers curl, leaving one pointing up to her head. Jezebel stares down as she tries to figure out why he's pointing at her.

Then something slams into the back of her head.

The impact sends her flying forward. She lands on her chest, snapping her head back painfully. Dust flies up around her as bits of stone sink into her skin.

Sucking in a breath, she struggles to flip over, knowing that lying there would mean certain death. As soon as she turns on her back, however, she feels something heavy on her head.

It's one of the Watchers, Danieal.

He pushes her head into the ground and holds a sword in his two hands, ready to bring it down into the middle of her forehead.

He swings his arms down to pierce her skull. Just before the sharp tip breaks her skin, a flash of light blazes across her face.

Suddenly the pressure is gone, and she feels the rush of blood return to her head. She scrambles up, scanning for her attacker, and finds him in a struggle of his own with Samyaza.

The Watcher has Danieal by the throat, lifting him into the air. With a spin, Danieal manages to free himself. Grabbing Samyaza by the arm, he hurls him to the ground.

"What are you doing?" he yells but is ignored as Samyaza lunges after him again.

Jezebel feels her frozenness release as blood rushes back into her limbs and her heart slams against her chest. As instinct takes over, there is one thing she is quite sure she can do now—run. She lunges in the opposite direction. In single steps, she jumps over the houses, escaping the city as quickly as possible.

Suddenly, she feels her feet go out from under her. She must have stepped in a pool of blood as she slips and smacks into the ground.

She looks behind her as she scrambles up, but the Watchers are still preoccupied with each other.

Turning forward, she sees something else approaching.

It's not a Watcher this time. Instead, it's a massive wall of sand filling the air. The cloud of dust rushes forward, rolling over the landscape. It stretches out farther than her eyes can see as it cloaks any building or tree in its way.

Jezebel doesn't slow down, however. She pushes forward, welcoming the dusty cover. It blows over the city, turning the air an opaque brown. She leaps into the fray. The biting sand doesn't affect her hardened skin, but she holds her arm in front of her eyes as she runs through the city.

***

The sandstorm overtakes the two Watchers as well, stealing away their vision. Loosed from his attacker's grasp, Danieal takes off after the last place he saw Jezebel. Samyaza follows closely behind, grabbing him by the foot.

Danieal turns his sword onto his opponent, but Samyaza blocks the blow with his arm and grabs Danieal by his cloak. He then spins in a circle, letting Danieal go when he's aimed at the ground.

The impact shakes the ground and cracks the stone road.

The blow keeps Danieal glued to the ground for several seconds. He stares up at the Watcher but can barely make out the dark figure of Samyaza through the dust in the air.

He squints and realizes that there is a bright light glowing behind his opponent. The light grows brighter and brighter, until finally, it hits Samyaza.

He goes flying, slamming face first into the ground besides Danieal.

The light doesn't stop coming toward them, however. In a panic, Danieal realizes it's coming for him too.

The light grabs him, yanking him off the ground. He is then dragged off, flying into the sand with the light, leaving Samyaza behind.

Danieal cranes his neck to see who is taking him away. His eyes widen in fear when he recognizes who is omitting the light.

They exit out of the sandstorm, but don't stop. The terrain begins to change underneath them. They're going out into the desert.

The wind pounds against the Watcher's ears as they travel. The rocky ground passes below in a blur.

Finally, they stop, suspended in the air, and Danieal can clearly see Michael clutching him.

The Archangels eyes are bright white, and they leave a streak of light behind as he turns his head toward Danieal.

The Watcher's throat tightens. He realizes he can't breathe.

"You will never see light again," Michael says with no emotion. In fact, he says it as if he was simply making an observation.

Then, without another word, he lifts Danieal above his head and slams him down into the rocky ground below.

The blow creates a crater in the dirt. The sound, like a massive explosion, rocks the desert. An immense pressure holds Danieal down, making it impossible for him to move. He isn't sure how it's not crushing him.

Suddenly, chunks of rocks and boulders begin to rise out of the ground. They float up in the air as if they are weightless, breaking through the sandy surface and ascending to Michael.

They circle around the Archangel as he hovers above. There are so many of them that they start to block out the sun.

Finally, with the most minuscule movement of Michael's fingers, the rocks plummet downward.

With a dust raising crash, they slam into the earth, burying Danieal beneath them. Danieal sees the outline of Michael blocking the sun before a boulder covers his face, sealing him in the darkness.

***

Jezebel doesn't stop running until she's out of the city. The dust filled wind still hasn't died down. In fact, now it seems to be blowing in from all directions.

She slides to a stop as she reaches the edge of the cliffs before the desert. Panting, she shields her face from the biting storm but keeps a watchful eye out for anyone who could be following her.

She coughs, trying to rid her throat of the coating of dust. As she wheezes, something causes her to look in the other direction. She spots the outline of someone walking toward her. The figure comes into view out of the dust and stands near Jezebel's feet, looking up at her massive form.

"What are you doing?" Jadal shouts through Nan's body. "The Watchers are gone. Now is your opportunity." Nan's neck is craned all the way back to look up at Jezebel, and she appears to be rocking back and forth.

Jezebel sits down on her knees to talk to her brother. "I was almost killed. It isn't worth dealing with them anymore."

Jadal scoffs and yells over the howl of the wind. "You have nothing to fear from death."

***

From the tree line, Methuselah ducks behind a tree, observing the exchange. He had spotted Nan pacing around the outskirts of town and followed her here.

He draws out his spear, gripping it tightly as he watches her converse with the Nephilim. The Nephilim leans down closer to her, and Methuselah feels his heart slam against his chest. The stabbing pain behind his eyes blurs his vision, and he squeezes his eyes together to try to focus.

Much to his confusion, the Nephilim doesn't seem threatening. He takes a chance and steps closer, hoping to catch part of their conversation.

"They're gone," Nan insists in that grating voice. "They have met their judgment."

The Nephilim shakes her head. "What does that mean?"

"It means there's nothing more stopping us."

The Nephilim opens her mouth to reply, but Nan suddenly whips around, scanning the sand filled air. Her eyes focus in Methuselah's direction, and he freezes in place.

"Someone's coming," Nan says.

The Nephilim tenses as she stands to her full height. Her eyes go wide as another noise comes over the howl of the wind.

Rhythmic thumps shake the ground, and Methuselah turns his head to see a bloody Nephilim running toward them.

***

Daeva steps over Methuselah and lunges toward Jezebel.

She jumps back, but he's already on top of her, tackling her to the ground.

The momentum causes the two Nephilim to slide across the dirt, stopping dangerously close to the cliff's edge. Her head leans backward over the steep drop, and she catches a glimpse of the abyss below.

She can feel his rage as he crouches over her. His neck and shoulders are almost black from his wounds, and fresh blood spills out from his exertion.

He is much stronger than her, but she hopes that perhaps his injuries will slow him down. She grabs his arms, intent to push him off, but he brings his head down onto hers. With a dull thud, his headbutt breaks the skin on her forehead, causing her vision to go dark for a second, and she feels her warm blood drip down across her temple.

She realizes that it's too much to hope for his wounds to affect him. He seems to be in a rampage, unable to feel pain, and with only one goal—to kill her.

She manages to grab his throat as he rears his head back. She digs her claw-like fingers in, and with all her strength, pushes him to the side. Scrambling up, she presses her hand over her head and feels the blood covering her face.

Daeva recovers quickly and catches her by the foot as she tries to run away. Falling forward, she claws at the ground, digging her nails into the dirt.

In horror, she feels him yank her backward, dragging her closer and closer to the cliff. She grabs at a tree, but the weak trunk breaks off in her hand. Frantically, she kicks at him with her other leg, but the blows don't affect him.

Her fingers tighten around the tree trunk, and she has one last idea. She twists to the side, and with the rest of her strength, pitches it at him.

The jagged wood sinks into his midsection. He lets her go, and with a scream, grabs at the tree impaling him. He yanks the wood out and looks up to see Jezebel lunging toward him.

With a shove, she pushes him over the cliff, and Daeva disappears into the sandstorm below.

Jezebel wobbles on her feet as she stares down into the dusty chasm. She presses her hand over the gash on her head, and closes her eyes, finally breathing a sigh of relief.

Suddenly, a sharp pain shoots up the back of her leg. A human has stabbed his spear into her ankle and yanks it to the side.

She whips around, sending her attacker and the spear flying in opposite directions. Although the stabbing is more of an annoyance, her quick movement causes her to lose her balance.

Loose rocks shift below her feet, and she slips over the edge.

Her chest hits the cliff's edge, and she digs her fingernails into the rock. Clawing into the stone, she scrambles to pull herself up. Her feet scrape against the sheer wall, unable to find a secure foothold.

***

Methuselah jumps back up to pick up the spear, but freezes in his tracks as someone else grabs it first.

Nan gives him a dark smile as she brandishes the weapon. She steps toward him, aiming the bloody tip at his head.

"Nan …" Methuselah raises his hands, trying to calm her, but she still advances forward.

"I knew someone was following me," the deep voice that isn't her says as she circles around him.

Methuselah's eyes dart from the possessed girl to the Nephilim who is still clinging to the rocks.

"You can't stay in her," Methuselah says, keeping a distance between them.

"Actually, she's the one who invited me," Nan corrects. "And do you really think she would want to come back to deal with this? To face the murderer who she's considered a mother for so many years?"

The Nephilim finds a handhold in the rock and drags herself up a little higher. She'll pull herself up soon, and Methuselah realizes he has very little time left.

Nan takes a couple steps closer to him and presses the spear against his chest. He racks his brain for everything he knows about dark spirits. His father was always so tightlipped about these matters, so to say his knowledge is lacking would be an understatement.

"You underestimate her," he replies, keeping his tone even.

He did know, however, that somewhere Nan was still inside. She was not truly gone.

She scoffs and raises her weapon back, ready to kill. Her eyes suddenly shift from Methuselah to something behind him.

She sees another figure emerge through the storm. Her eyes widen, and she freezes. Her breaths come out in short bursts as she clutches the spear in her hands. For a moment, time doesn't exist. Nothing exists except for the two with eyes locked, and the now distant howl of the wind.

Then Nan straightens. She lunges, weapon pointed forward.

The metal tip pierces through the Nephilim's neck.

The Nephilim's eyes widen in shock. She looks down at Nan pushing the spear through her throat.

"J-Jadal …" she gasps as dark blood spills out of her mouth.

"He's no longer here," Nan says, twisting the spear.

The Nephilim's tight grip on the rocks loosens, and she slides backward.

Nan releases the weapon as both it and the Nephilim fall over the side.

She drops down to her knees, breathing heavily. Methuselah rushes over to her side, placing a hand on her shoulder. She turns to look at him.

There are so many things he wants to say, but nothing comes out. Instead, he just nods, and a smile breaks through Nan's heavy panting.

"Are you alright?" he asks.

"It's gone," she manages to say, breathing in deeply though her nose.

"The spirit—"

"It didn't stop me," she interrupts. "The fear …"

She gives him another smile, then turns to look at the figure behind them.

Methuselah turns to look as well. "Father …" he whispers.

Enoch steps toward them, but Methuselah rushes up, meeting him halfway. He pauses only for a moment, then wraps his father in a hug.

Nan approaches too, and Enoch reaches out an arm, welcoming her in. She joins them, then they sink to their knees, still embracing.

"The sand…" Nan says after a second.

The trio looks around, realizing that the winds have disappeared. A layer of dust covers everything, but they can still clearly see the sun, just setting on the horizon.

CHAPTER TWENTY-THREE

Awaken

At the bottom of the cliff, Jezebel's body lies in the sand. A pool of blood spreads around her head from both the spear through her neck and her cracked skull.

Her eyes open.

With foggy vision, she pushes herself up. A ringing pounds in her ears, and she realizes she's lying in a lake of blood. Slowly her senses come back. The first thing she feels is a hot burning in her throat.

She then realizes that her senses seem to be heightened. The dust, the hot liquid she's lying in, and the red sky above all overpower her.

Something large next to her blocks the rays of the setting sun. She turns her head to see that it's a body. Her body.

She pushes herself up with a start, staring up at the massive corpse. As she stands, she can barely see over the Nephilim's head. The body already looks decayed, with dark bloodstains mixing with the caked dirt on its skin. Its dead eyes stare upward and are almost completely white.

The mangled body is almost unrecognizable. With a sick feeling in her stomach, Jezebel knows it belongs to her. Dumbfounded, she stares at the corpse. Gritting her teeth, she feels her throat tighten even more.

"It's an odd feeling," a voice comes from behind her.

She blinks, and jerks around.

"What's happening?" Her voice sounds thin. She swallows thickly, trying to focus on the owner of the voice.

His face comes into focus. He stares at her with his hands folded in front of him. His pale, almost translucent skin contrasts to the dark brown robe he has draped over his shoulders, and his eyes are gray and vacant.

"Who are you?" she asks, swaying slightly.

He smirks. He moves toward her gracefully, almost gliding. Tenderly, he places his hand on the side of her face, then like the strike of a snake, he grabs her by the throat. His nails dig into her skin, sinking several inches into her throat.

Jezebel grits her teeth, and her eyes go wide in shock. She rears her head backward until all she can see is the maroon sky.

"Don't be weak," he says in a tone that almost seems encouraging.

Her chest rises as she sucks in a breath and closes her eyes. The robed figure leans in, scrutinizing her face, then slowly releases his hold on her. He doesn't leave any wounds behind on her neck, but she can still feel a throbbing pain. She keeps her eyes closed as her breaths calm. Slowly she tilts her head forwards.

"Lucifer," she answers her own question.

When she opens her eyes, a vision appears before her. It's the girl again. The beautiful girl with the long black hair. Her mother.

She smiles and laughs, then picks up her skirt to run away from something. The perspective shifts to what's chasing her. Samyaza. He laughs as he runs after her, always a few strides behind.

"My parents ..." Jezebel says as she watches the images before her.

"He loved her, you know," Lucifer says as the vision changes to when her mother is pregnant. "He couldn't stand to see what it was doing to her."

Her mother is dangerously thin, apart from her oversized, protruding stomach. She looks nearly dead already with a shallow complexion and lifeless eyes, the skin sinking in around her collarbones and arms. Samyaza hovers over her with concern as she takes frail breaths.

Lucifer's voice sounds distant. "Finally, he decided he had to save her. He cut out the babies and tried everything to heal her but nothing worked. You were the only one who lived," he explains as the visions fade away.

He stares unnervingly into her eyes. "Your parents could have been happy. But everything they had was torn away from them."

Jezebel's expression turns hard. A sense of clarity washes over her. The questions she couldn't answer in her life now become evident in her death.

She plays over the flashbacks in her head. They were happy at one point, but it couldn't last. Because that was how this world works and every other world that exists. If there is any light, it will get snuffed out.

There's something else in the visions, however. Something Jezebel can't see. There is a difference between the images replaying in her head and another reality.

Her mother laughs and runs away, however, her smile turns to shock. She isn't laughing … she's screaming.

"Looks like someone wants to see you," Lucifer says, interrupting her thoughts.

Jezebel turns to see someone standing behind her. His skin is gray, and his legs resemble a ram. One of his legs seems to be longer than the other, so he leans to the side as he steps forward. His arms are also unusually long and hang limply to his sides.

"Jadal …" she says, instantly recognizing her brother.

"We finally meet as our true selves," he replies with the same guttural voice that Jezebel has heard before.

"Wait." She whirls around. "Where is—"

"Don't worry," Jadal says. "He's gone. For now, anyway. See for yourself." He lifts one of his long arms and points a black finger to around Jezebel's corpse.

She steps around her massive head and sees Daeva's body. He has landed in an unnatural position, head-first with the rest of his body bent to the side.

There seems to be no sign of the real him, however, and Jezebel relaxes. With one last disgusted look at his body, she turns back around. Only Jadal is standing there with her now. The robed god has disappeared.

"Come with me, sister." Jadal says, stepping up next to her. "There is much I need to show you."

***

Samyaza awakens with a start. He sucks in a breath and feels dust coat his lungs. He pushes himself up into a sitting position and coughs as the smell of sulfur overpowers his senses.

It's dark now. The Watcher blinks, trying to adjust to the dimness. He looks up to the sky but then realizes it's gone. Above him is a rock ceiling, low enough that he can't fully stand.

With eyes beginning to adjust, he scans his surroundings. It must be some sort of cave. Staggering forward, he feels around in the darkness. Then he hits something. He wraps his hands around rough metal bars.

His eyes focus on them and give off a slight yellow glow in the darkness. It's not just a couple bars but a whole row of them, keeping him in a stone cell. Giving them a rough shake, they don't budge.

Panic begins to rise in his chest. He whips around the room looking for another way out, but everywhere he meets either solid stone or thick bars. His breath quickens, but then freezes when he hears a sound.

Taking a few tentative steps forward, he stares through the bars into the blackness. A rustling noise cuts through the silence once more.

"Who's there?" he asks warily but is met with no reply. He concentrates on the dark, trying to find the source of the sound.

Suddenly, a white hand grabs the bar in front of his face. Samyaza jumps back in surprise, and a face appears next to the hand. The face is shallow and has dark hollows under its eyes.

Samyaza blinks. "You're—"

"So, you do recognize me," the sudden apparition says. "It's been a long, long time since I've seen someone. From before."

"Samael …"

The figure before him barely resembles the once asterial Power.

The beam of light that had encircled his head is long gone, leaving behind hollow, white eyes.

"Hmm, yes, I guess you wouldn't know what I'm called now," Samael replies.

"W-what do you mean?" Samyaza asks, trying to back as far away as possible, but his head thuds against the rocks behind him.

"I am death."

"You. You became death?" Samyaza swallows as he realizes that this angel of death has an even more eerie appearance from a distance. His eyes glow white in perfect circles, and his figure looks unnatural and contorted in the dimness.

Samael nods and his bones make a sickening popping sound with the movement.

"Wh-why am I here?" Samyaza asks, fighting off the wave of nausea in his throat.

The angel of death presses his face through the bars, pulling on his skin. His eyes bulge out even more, and his skin looks as if it might be ripped off his face.

He smiles. "I guess you share the same bonds as me."

This can't be right. Samyaza places a hand up to his head. How can he be here with one of the betrayers? He tries to focus, but everything seems out of place. He remembers getting hit by that light that dragged Danieal away. The memory flashes in his mind. With a cold, sick feeling, he remembers that same light returning for him.

He backs up to the stone behind him and then sinks down to the ground. He places his hands over his eyes and presses. When he dares to look up again, he sees the angel of death still staring at him with a vacant expression.

Death seems to appraise him for a second.

"Why are you staring at me?" Samyaza manages to ask.

"It's very interesting," he replies simply.

Samyaza shakes his head, and desperately tries to come up with something else to focus on.

"Tell me," Samyaza suddenly says, "Have you ever heard a story about a man who makes a deal with a dragon?"

Death angles his head upward as if to consider the question. "I've heard a story like that. How does yours go?"

Samyaza swallows before answering, "The dragon tells the man that he must run from God. But in the end, it was the dragon who was chasing him, not God."

"Ah." The angel of death blinks his round eyes. "That one I do not know."

Samyaza sighs, but suddenly his attention shifts. He focuses on someone else. Behind Samael is a black form, cloaked in the shadows.

Hesitantly, Samyaza asks, "Who is that?"

Death turns his head slightly, cracking with every movement. Then, almost mechanically, turns back to face the fallen Watcher.

Smiling, he replies, "Death is always accompanied by Hell."

***

"There really has to be some sort of irony to the fact that I really am better off dead," Jezebel mumbles as she stares at her reflection in a golden mirror.

She takes a piece of her long hair and arranges it with her fingers so that it lies perfectly with the rest of her curls.

"Well, no one ever really dies," Jadal says from across the room. He leans against the rock wall, crossing his long arms.

Jezebel casts a look his way. "Everyone is already dead," she states, then turns back to examine her dress. "Hmm, what do you think … red? I do like this whole black idea." As she speaks, the material changes its color to midnight black. She flashes a heinous smile at her new ability.

Her brother audibly sighs. "You know, it's really not the best thing in the world."

She knows that he's not talking about the dress. But she's not going to let anything he says distract from the new fun she's having. "And what's so bad about this situation?" she replies with a grin. "Did you know this is the first time I've ever worn clothing? Those humans think they're so special with their adornments, but I can change my appearance however I want."

Then, as if to emphasize her point, she holds out her wrist and two beaded bracelets appear on it.

"I can be the most beautiful girl in the world if I choose to." She looks back at her reflection. Her yellow eyes look even brighter contrasted by the black surrounding them. Thick, curly hair matches the dark shadows outlining her face. As she tilts her head down, she parts her painted lips in a smile.

Her whole life had always been about survival. What a fool she was, she realizes, to hang onto something so pathetic, to try to extend her wretched life.

"No more covering myself in dirt, no more scavenging." She cocks her head. "Speaking of, I feel like I'm starving. What is there to eat?"

Jadal lets out another long breath. "Nothing."

"What do you mean?" she says turning around, whirling her hair and skirt in the process.

"I mean there is nothing for us. You will always feel hunger and thirst and there is nothing you can do about it."

Jezebel ignores the sharp pangs in her stomach and replies, "Well, fine."

"The pain does get worse," he adds. "But somehow the more of it that comes, the more you get used to it."

"I can deal with pain."

"It's not physical like you're used to," he says and takes a step forward, leaning sideways in his awkward walk. "It's a type of pain that comes from hate. The more you feel it, the more hate you need. It is the only reprise you can get. And that's how it will always be."

He stops a few inches from her, and she studies his face. His skin is dry and cracked. In some areas it seems to be falling off his face. He's completely hideous with his unbalanced form and part-human, part-animal features.

"Why do you make yourself look like this?" she whispers.

He leans his head back. "This is who I really am, sister. You will come to know who you are."

Turning away from her brother, she says, "There's someone I need to go thank for this … this gift they've given me." She steps away and adds, "You can follow me if you want." And with that she steps through the rock wall, and into the outside world.

As she enters the city, she hesitates for only a moment, then steps confidently onto the stone street. She looks down and frowns at her bare feet. In a second, golden sandals with jewel accents appear, and she continues to stride forward.

She watches in amazement as she walks past people without them even noticing. She stares at their faces, but no one even looks in her direction. Everyone is busy cleaning up the damage from the most recent attacks. She notices some of the Nephilim corpses and keeps a wary eye out for any other dead friends she might encounter.

She notices some shadowy figures hiding along rooftops and disappearing around corners. Most of them look like cloaked apparitions and they watch her warily from a distance. None of them seem very eager to approach her.

Something black flies past her face.

She jumps back in surprise, letting out a little squeak. She sees some sort of bat-like creature disappear between two houses.

A laugh comes from behind her. "Frightening out here, isn't it?" Jadal says shuffling up behind her. He's wearing a dark hood that he keeps pulled over his head, so that she can only see the lower half of his face.

"They can't see us," Jezebel says as she nods to some of the nearby humans.

"For now." He pulls his cloak tighter around his shoulders.

"You look like an old woman in that thing," she says, eyeing his choice of attire.

"Well, do you know what you look like?"

"Actually, I have a few ideas," she replies with a smile, and Jadal just silently walks beside her.

They come to a place where one Nephilim fell over part of a house, crushing the wood beneath him. The residents of the house dig through the rubble, pulling out any valuable items they can find.

As Jezebel stops to watch, she notices a dark creature crawling through the debris. It climbs on all fours and is about half the size of Jezebel. Its skin is black and scaled like a snake.

"What is that?" she inquires, narrowing her eyes at the creature.

"Not direct offspring of the Watchers," Jadal answers. "I guess you could call them, second generation. They are lower ranking and mostly just make suggestions."

"How so?"

As if to answer her question, the low-level spirit crawls over to one of the women picking through the rubble. It steps up behind her and places its clawed hands on her shoulders. The creature then leans toward the woman's ear and begins talking to her.

The woman visibly shrinks, distress apparent on her face.

"What did he tell her?" Jezebel asks, but Jadal just shrugs.

"Can I do that?" she asks.

"That and more."

A wide grin spreads across Jezebel's face and she steps forward, scanning for a victim of her own.

She spots two girls picking through the rubble and circles around them, settling on one of the girls who has just picked up a jagged piece of wood.

Jezebel leans in close and whispers, "Stab her."

The girl pauses for a second, then gives a minute shake of her head. She goes back to gather wood, seemingly unaffected by the spirit's advice.

Jadal laughs once and it sounds more like a cough. "Excellent first try. Couldn't have done better myself."

Jezebel glares at him, then turns back to her victim and yells, "I said stab her!" But the girl doesn't even seem to hear her this time.

"What happened to my sister with such well laid plans? Has all your patience gone?" Jadal asks as Jezebel begins to seethe. "First, you obviously don't know anything about her," he continues.

"What does that have to do with anything?" she asks, grinding her teeth. The shadows under her eyes appear especially dark and several veins pop up on her face.

"Fool," he mumbles, then says to her, "Take your time, pay attention to your environment, and suggest the right things."

Jezebel looks as if she might boil over, but she watches Jadal demonstrate for her. He picks the other girl, the one who is slow about her work, and keeps glancing up at the giant corpse crushing her house.

"It's only a matter of time before everyone you know is dead," he whispers to her, and the girl casts another glance at the dead Nephilim. "They will return, and next time, the Watchers won't be here to save you."

The girl places her hands up to her face and lets out a whimper.

Taking notice, the other girl reaches her hand out to comfort her friend. "No, it's alright," she says gently. "Everyone in our family is still alive, and we will make it through this."

Her friend just shrugs away and wraps her arms around herself.

Jezebel steps in. "You know she won't survive this," she

whispers. “If she’s this weak now, imagine how she’ll be when someone actually dies?”

The girl’s expression hardens, and Jezebel laughs.

“It worked,” she says, turning to Jadal with a wicked grin. “I see. You need a little … tact.”

Her brother doesn’t share her excitement and instead appears bored.

“This is not the limit on your abilities,” he says. “But it is refreshing to cause suffering wherever I can.”

Jezebel doesn’t stick around to hear anything else he says. Instead, she jumps up onto one of the rooftops and looks over the city. With renewed energy, she leaps from one house to the next.

“Now where are you going?” Jadal calls after her.

“To visit the little witch who killed me,” she replies with a smile.

***

Nan sees Edna at the small opening to the cave, watching their approach.

“They’re back,” Edna calls back to the others behind her.

Kenan pushes past his mother to get a look for himself. “They’re back!” he repeats loud enough for the whole family to hear.

He is the first one to run to his returning family. The others are not far behind, spilling out of their cramped hideout. Enoch greets his children first, then wraps his wife up in a hug.

“I hope you did whatever it was you had to do,” she says.

He chuckles once, then replies with, “We’re safe now. We can go back home.”

She doesn’t reply. She doesn’t have to. Instead, she just buries her head into his chest.

The girls approach Nan cautiously at first, but when she smiles at them, Martha runs up and gives her an excited hug.

“I’m so glad you’re back!” she exclaims, squeezing Nan even tighter.

“I am too,” she replies, although it seems slightly hard for her to breathe.

Nan looks from Martha, to Dinah, to Mikah who has stayed back in the refuge of the cave. Mikah stands with her back facing the family, arms crossed, as if evaluating whether it's safe to leave.

Nan slowly releases her hold on Martha and slowly steps toward the cave opening. Her approach is noticed by Mikah, who then seems to brace herself. However, Nan stops several feet away, and the woman relaxes slightly.

Several seconds pass by in silence. Mikah is the one to break it.

"It is time for me to leave this place," she says, scanning the landscape.

"Where will you go?" Nan questions in a barely audible voice.

"That is not even for me to know." The woman raises a brow and lets out a half-sigh, half-laugh.

"Well then," Nan starts, "You should come gather what you will need to take with you."

"No." The woman shakes her head. "That is not my life anymore."

"You do not have to be on the run—"

"The spirits will always know me," Mikah interrupts, finally turning her head to glance at Nan. "From them I cannot hide."

"That is how I overcame mine." Nan straightens as she speaks. "I stopped hiding."

Mikah looks her over for a moment then turns her eyes back to the grassy plain before them. She stays silent for several moments, and Nan is about to speak up again, when she says, "Then perhaps one day I will find my salvation like you have yours."

She nods over to the family gathered. Enoch has both of his arms resting on Kenan's and Methuselah's shoulders as they all laugh at something.

"Maybe you already have," Nan replies.

Mikah leans her head back against the stone behind her. She winces slightly and places her hand up to the bandage wrapped around her head.

"You shouldn't go while you're injured," Nan adds.

The woman ignores the comment and says, "When I found you, you were so weak. It was all I could do to get you just to eat. You didn't speak for several days …" Her voice trails off for a moment before she continues. "I knew you would survive, though, because I knew you were sent to me. You were my restitution." She glances sideways at Nan. "The spirit told you?"

Nan shakes her head in confusion. "Told me what?"

Mikah laughs half-heartedly. "It's just as well. You were the way I was to prove my redemption, but then I lost it again."

She turns fully toward Nan and takes a step forward. "The point of my story is, you're right. I already found my salvation. And then I gave it away. I gave it to a monster with pointed teeth and claws." She pauses, now only a few feet away from Nan.

"Then why am I still here?" Nan folds her arms across her chest and raises her chin.

"You're no longer here for me," Mikah answers plainly.

"Where will you go?" Nan asks again.

"Where the sea can consume me."

"Will you find what you're looking for there?"

"What I'm looking for cannot be found."

"Then why not stay here?"

Mikah hesitates.

"Until your wounds are healed." Nan points up to the woman's head. "Then you can go to the sea."

Mikah stares at the grass swaying beside her. Finally, she gives a miniscule nod of her head.

Nan nods as well, then turns back toward the rest of the family. The twins have gathered around their father.

"We get to go home now?" they ask in unison.

Their father replies with a nod and a smile, and the twins give a whoop of excitement.

***

Jezebel jumps down from the rocky high ground to the hidden openings of the caves. Her eyes glance over each of the reunited family members until she locks on her target. She watches Nan for a few seconds, mostly looking at the dried blood still covering her hands, then steps forward.

She strides a few feet, but then her steps slow. As if she is walking through thick mud, she struggles forward. A pressure begins to push her away and she sucks in a breath.

It starts to push down on her, and the air becomes foggy. She looks at the family again, but her vision is blurred, and their voices are muffled.

Jezebel presses her hands against her temples. She can only think of one thought as the burning pain shoots through her body—she's suffocating.

Backpedaling, she exits out of the bubble of pressure. She sucks in a breath of air and doubles over.

Jadal steps up beside her and after a few seconds of panting, she asks, "What was that?"

"I didn't think that would work," he mumbles to himself and steps forward, his long arm outstretched. He reaches out toward the family but stops after a few steps. He grimaces and yanks his hand back as if he's touched fire.

Jezebel straightens as he steps up beside her and uses a crooked finger to point toward the family.

"Do you see it?" he asks.

She squints and something comes into focus before her. Her eyes widen as she sees an amber-colored perimeter surrounding the family.

"I've seen it with sacrifices before. But not ones like this," Jadal says, then adds, "They're being protected."

"What?" Jezebel nods at Nan. "I thought you possessed her."

Jadal doesn't answer, but instead points his finger past Nan to the man standing behind her. Jezebel looks to where he is pointing but can't quite look at the man's face. His face is bright, glowing. She presses her palms to her eyes.

"That's our problem right there," Jadal says.

"So, what are you saying?" Jezebel asks, irritation growing in her voice.

"I'm saying, it looks like you won't be able to do anything. For now, at least."

"You can't be serious," she snaps, turning to her brother.

For a second, her appearance changes. The veins on her temples and under her eyes turn blue and protrude. Her lustrous skin transforms in a way that makes it looks as if it will decay off her face.

After a moment, she exhales and calms herself, returning her expression to normal. “Fine.” She raises her head. “I can wait.”

CHAPTER TWENTY-FOUR

DUST TO DUST

The wind picks up the desert sand, snaking its way along dunes and plateaus. It follows along rivers and rustles through the trees.

It passes over a hole in the ground. A grave.

A large multitude of people stand circled around the grave, the wind whipping their robes and hair.

A man steps forward, looking down into the pit. He is old, weathered. A thick gray beard frames his face. Green eyes shine bright against his dark complexion.

He looks down at the grave's occupant. The man lying there looks even older, with bright white hair and wrinkled skin. His expression, however, does not show hardship. Instead, his body seems to be at peace, at one with the dirt from which it was formed.

"Adam, our father, is dead," Seth says as he looks down at the body. He takes a handful of dirt and lets it slip through his fingers and into the pit. "From dust you came, and to dust you will return."

He then looks at the others around him. His sisters, his sons, their sons. Generations of all ages gather around to commemorate the life of their father.

Seth speaks again. "He lacked seventy years of one thousand. For a thousand years is as one day in the testimony of the heavens." He pauses and takes a breath. "It is written concerning the tree that if anyone eats its fruits, in that day he will surely die. Thus, he did not complete his day, but died during it."

He looks at the others around him and says in closing, "And therefore his body is again returned to the earth."

Seth's voice does not crack. He does not shed tears, but instead delivers a testimony of a reality he always knew was coming. And he knew that the end had not yet come.

A few whispers arise as they all look to see another man appear at the edge of the crowd. A cloak covers his identity, but the whole group recognizes him. Two jackal-like dogs follow beside him, then sit as their master raises his hand. They growl slightly but stay put as the man steps into the crowd. Those in his path step back, parting a path to the grave. No one looks directly at him except for Seth.

He stares down the unexpected visitor but is not met with the same attention. Instead, the man keeps his eyes directed downward until finally they rove over Adam's body.

His expression doesn't change as he looks over the resting face of his father.

Seth flatly acknowledges the man. "Cain."

His brother turns his eyes up at him, keeping his head down. His eyes are heavy, droopy with wrinkled bags, and framed by white brows. Finally, he leans his head back and pulls the hood away from his face. The sun hits his skin revealing several white markings on his face. They shimmer like snake scales in the light. His eyes, too, have a white film covering them.

Before any words can be exchanged, another figure steps through the crowd. She is small and frail, but despite appearances, she carries herself surely. With head held high, she steps in front of Cain.

He doesn't move, but turns his eyes, as if he is waiting for the old woman to strike him like a snake. But she doesn't lash out. Instead, without a word, she places a thin, wrinkled hand on the side of his face.

Her brown eyes brim with tears. She smiles, then closes her eyes as they spill onto her lined cheeks.

Neither of them moves for several seconds as his pale gaze

roves over her face.

Finally, she removes her hand. Turning away, she steps around the grave to Seth. Instead of looking down into the hole, she turns her eyes skyward. The sun reflects against her eyes, revealing the slightest remnants of golden flakes.

She smiles once again as the light warms her face. The lines on her face soften as she exhales a breath. Then she collapses.

Seth rushes over and leans her up in his arms. He cradles her head, but she doesn't open her eyes. The peaceful smile, however, remains on her face.

"Mother …" Seth says, but he already knows she won't answer.

Everyone remains silent as he runs his hand across her cheek.

***

At the edge of the group, there is another visitor. However, no one can see him, and he is not here to pay respect. He is not even here to disrupt. He is only here to watch.

He observes the woman on the ground, then his eyes seek out Cain behind her.

Cain takes a few steps back, his eyes scanning the group. Finally, without saying a word to anyone, he turns to go back into the desert. At the edge of the crowd, he whistles once, and his two dogs fall in step beside him.

The unseen visitor watches him leave, and then disappears in a whirl of sand.

***

The heavenly courtrooms are busy with activity. Inside a long record hall, scribes work diligently organizing and copying information. Seraphim and other angels fly back and forth through the water portals, bringing new data and records.

When one enters, they leave a ripple in the water. Any drops of liquid roll off their wings and morph back into the gateway.

The new information brought in is either organized and stored away, on one of the vast number of shelves, or is copied down into a larger ledger.

Aziel follows Gabriel as he approaches one of the scribes.

"Is this the newest updates on the sacrifice records for this year?" Gabriel asks, looking down at the large open book.

The book's pages are clear like glass but are still easy to read. The outside of the book is gold with swirls of light moving through it.

The scribe, who is an angel that has a more feminine appearance and dark complexion, nods.

Gabriel leans in to get a closer look, and another angel appears before them. He has a small piece of paper in his hand, which he then holds out over the book and drops it. It floats down to a particular spot on the page and sticks there, as if it were glued. The piece of paper itself then begins to fade and leaves behind only the words written on it.

"Very good," Gabriel says. He looks as if he is about to say something else when Michael appears behind him, interrupting them.

"He's here," Michael says.

Gabriel shoots a look at Aziel, then straightens and says, "Let's go then."

Michael and Aziel follow him out of the record hall, leaving the scribes and books behind. They go past the courtroom where the throne sits and into one of the outer courtyards.

In this yard, there is a clear wall of water dividing it down the middle. On this side stands Michael, Gabriel, and Aziel. Ruach is also nearby, surrounded on both sides by Cherubim. Seraphim fly around above, humming in low tones. The end of the courtyard opens into space, and stars can be seen sparkling in it.

On the opposite side of the water divide stands Lucifer. He has his arms crossed and taps his foot impatiently, all the while avoiding looking anywhere near Ruach.

When he sees that the other angels have arrived, he speaks.

"I hear your man has died," he says with a smile, still unable to look directly at Ruach.

"You are here to accuse, not to make conversation," Aziel reminds him, without smiling.

Lucifer exhales, almost laughing. "I know the only reason why I'm here is because you can't stop me. I have the right to be here." He can't help but smirk after that.

"What do you want?" Gabriel asks, giving off no show of emotion. Not letting Lucifer have any respite, even with his banter.

Evident that their back and forth is over, Lucifer's smile fades, and he says, "Tell me, is it or is not written that in the way a man murders, he too shall be killed in that way?"

All eyes turn toward Gabriel except for Ruach who is solely focused on Lucifer. The atmosphere around the Spirit is tangible as it glows slightly and picks up his hair. His eyes burn bright gold as he stands immobile.

"It is," Gabriel answers flatly.

A wide smile begins to spread across Lucifer's face.

"Well, then," he says, "I have a name to bring before the court."

***

Lucifer does bring up a name. And after he does, he becomes so preoccupied with his task at hand that he barely notices when he leaves the courts of heaven. He doesn't even register his surroundings until later when he finds himself stepping through rubble.

Broken stones lay haphazardly on top of each other. Wood beams and furniture peek out from under the rocks. The remnants of a once lively home now lay crumbled.

He knows where he is, and he knows what he's looking for. Finally, he finds it. A body. It's halfway stuck under a pile of rocks, only part of its torso and head escaping the hail of stones.

He crouches down next to the body's head—an old man with a wrinkled face and white dead eyes that stare up into the sun. The rays of light reveal the slightest remnants of white marks on his face.

Lucifer leans in closer. The man does not breathe or blink. He is nothing more than an empty shell. The man is no longer here.

"Interesting," a voice behind Lucifer says.

Lucifer turns his head to see who has spoken. Samael comes lurking across the rubble. His heavenly appearance is gone and is replaced by his new acclaimed look of death.

His top half is frighteningly thin with protruding ribs and sunken in cheekbones. His legs are gone, and in their place is an inky black fog that trails behind him.

He uses his arms to pull himself across the ground and slinks over to where Lucifer is crouched down. Casually taking in the pool of blood and dead eyes, he says, "As much as I appreciate death," he sits back, hovering in his black mist. "this is a little confusing to me. I thought you would use him. Now, don't make me go against my nature and say he's better off alive than dead."

Lucifer ignores the angel of death and stands to leave.

"Oh, I get it. You were afraid."

Lucifer stops in his tracks. "I know this may be hard for you to comprehend because you have no forethought, but I was simply eliminating the risk," he says without turning around.

"So that's what you call it, you were fearful and moved too quickly … eliminating the risk."

Lucifer whips around this time, but Samael isn't there. He's beside him now.

Samael leans close to Lucifer's ear. "She forgave him, didn't she? You really do doubt yourself."

Lucifer turns again but Samael is gone. He scans the rubble but only him and the body of Cain are there. He hears a brief whisper.

"Do you feel that? It's called fear."

He shakes his head and realizes that the angel of death is not there. He was never supposed to be there.

Lucifer looks down at the body once more. Of course, it was the right thing to do. This time it was going to be different. And there is still much more work to do.

***

Methuselah leans his back against the wall. Through the slats in the window, he can see the moonbeams peeking through. They cast a blue glow onto Nan's face as she peacefully sleeps.

He watches the rise and fall of her chest for a few moments more until she turns over in her sleep, resting a hand on her stomach that's just starting to grow.

A quiet knocking from the doorway draws Methuselah's attention away. He looks over to see Enoch peeking in.

Enoch silently beckons his son, and Methuselah takes one last look at Nan's sleeping form before getting up.

Methuselah follows his father outside, wrapping a blanket around his shoulders to shield against the cool night air. Enoch takes a seat on the low rock wall near their house. The scribe looks up, studying the stars for a moment as Methuselah sits beside him.

"How's she feeling?" Enoch asks.

Methuselah nods. "She's been doing good, really good actually."

Enoch dips his head in acknowledgment, then takes another moment to examine the night sky. "And you?" he asks. "Your headaches have not returned?"

"They haven't. Really since you returned, they have not come back," Methuselah answers.

"That's good," Enoch replies, then allows more silence to pass between them.

Enoch finally says, "Do you remember the story I used to tell you and Lamech all the time when you were much younger?"

Methuselah breathes out with a smile. "The one about the man who left home to go on all of those adventures?"

"Yes, that one." Enoch smiles too. "You two used to beg me to tell it every night."

"My favorite part was when he found the treasure in that cave," Methuselah adds. "But Lamech's was when he freed the slave girl."

Enoch let's out a small laugh. "That indeed was his favorite part."

They both chuckle to themselves, and after a moment, Enoch says, "Do you remember how it ended?"

Methuselah knits his brows together in recollection. "He returned home, wealthy and accomplished, but…" He trails off for a moment, then says, "Home wasn't the same. He couldn't recognize it, everything looked different."

"He searched and searched, trying to find something familiar. Until he thought perhaps you can never actually return home," Enoch says, then looking over at his son, adds, "Then what happened?"

"He …" Methuselah starts. "He heard the sounds. It was … the familiar sounds of home."

"You know," Enoch starts, then seems to reconsider for a second. "You know, I really do think that Lamech would be proud of his brother."

Methuselah doesn't answer at first. He decides to take his turn looking up at the stars.

They glitter brightly in the sky, creating all sorts of glowing illustrations. After he's satisfied that he can, Methuselah nods.

"I was speaking of Kenan, of course," Enoch says with a sly smile.

Methuselah lets out a sound halfway between a laugh and a cry, then smiles, shaking his head. He clears his throat. "Of course."

"Methuselah …"

The blue light from the night reflects off his father's face, making the gray streaks in his beard stand out even more.

"Lately, I've … I've been hearing those same sounds of home."

Methuselah doesn't answer. Instead, he shifts slightly closer to his father and rests his head on his shoulder.

Enoch wraps an arm around his son, patting him.

For a long while, they both stay silent. Watching the lights in the sky dance overhead.

***

Enoch walks through the grassy plain with his family beside him. As he looks over at each of them, a memory swims to the surface of his mind.

He had seen something, that day he left the earth. Something that would forever focus his thoughts on a bigger picture. The grand scheme.

When he came back to this world, one feeling overwhelmed him. It wasn't a sense of duty or even a love for what he has. Yes, of course, he felt those things. But the one sensation that overpowered his mind was thankfulness. He felt thankful that he'd been a part of something just a little bigger than his slice of eternity.

As his thoughts come back to the present, he focuses on each family member in turn. He looks first to the twins who can no longer be considered boys as they are both taller than their father. Although sometimes they still act like children.

Dinah isn't with them now, instead she is with her husband at the house they built in town. Martha walks close by, however, holding the newest addition to her family on her hip. Enoch smiles as the little baby plays with her mom's braid.

As they crest a hill, they reach their destination.

A large multitude of men and women have gathered, all of them turning to look expectantly at Enoch as he approaches.

He smiles at his children once more, then takes his place in front of the multitude and begins to speak.

He starts his story by giving them a shortened recount of his time off Earth.

Relating how the three angels had visited him, he explains the difference between them and the Watchers they once knew.

"Well, there were really four angels with me. There was this one they called Eremiel. He wasn't like anything you would imagine," he says, then laughs. "He would just appear when they summoned, floating around like a locust. And somehow, they understood everything he said. It was like they were talking to a beehive."

Nan smiles as she listens along with the rest of her family and the others. She then looks down to her hand which her son is holding. The boy has seemingly been distracted by some sort of bug near his feet.

"Lamech, listen to your grandfather's story," Nan gently reprimands the boy, and he focuses on Enoch.

Enoch continues, "He would take us over the earth, and you could see everything. The mountains, the rivers, even the great seas."

Everyone listens, intently focused on the tale. As he speaks, a cool evening breeze blows in. Edna shivers beside him, and Enoch takes her hand in his.

After this, he switches subjects and talks for a long while about the different scrolls and books he saw. He describes each in detail but admits he doesn't know the use for many of them.

"Except for one they gave me. They said, it held events to come, that even they didn't know of."

Methuselah interrupts him. "You saw what is to come?"

Enoch nods, but he doesn't look at his son, instead he focuses on his wife. "In a way," he answers.

"What is to come?"

Enoch isn't quite sure who asked the question, but an answer comes.

He turns to face the rest of his family. "There is one thing I haven't told you yet. I saw this place. It was a place of paradise. A holding place for souls."

After several seconds pass, he looks to his wife and whispers, "I saw him."

She doesn't reply but nods once. A slight smile passes across her lips.

"Why are you just now telling us this?" Methuselah asks.

Enoch lets out a long breath. "Because it's time."

Before anyone can ask what he means by that, he says, "What is to come? Some are willing to forego anything to know the answer to that question. But do you feel so strongly to go back a hundred years ago and tell yourself exactly what will happen in a hundred years? Or would you just tell yourself everything will work out in the end?"

He looks to Methuselah. "You will see some of it in your life, but in the end, we will all see it." He smiles gently. "Whatever is to come, you'll be ready."

He lets go of Edna's hand and backs away a couple steps. She gives him a knowing expression and holds her head high.

Kenan steps forward. "Father, what—"

Methuselah places his hand on his shoulder, but Kenan doesn't look his way, keeping his focus on Enoch who turns his head skyward.

A slight breeze moves through his hair and picks up his robes. The wind grows stronger, and he breathes it in.

He looks back down at the others around him, then to his family, and gives them one last wide smile. All at once, the wind hits them like a hurricane, accompanied by a line of fire.

The flames wrap around Enoch in an instant, swirling and crackling.

His family all steps back in surprise as the fire creates a circle around him. It blows back their hair and turns their faces gold in the light. Then the ground begins to shake, loose rocks bounce up and down.

A herd of fiery horses appear out of nowhere and stampede around them, moving as one as if they were a river of lava.

Enoch's feet lift off the ground, and his image starts to fade.

"Father!" someone cries, but everyone else just stands in silence.

He looks at them with a loving expression one more time. His feet lift higher in the air as the flames surround him. Then his face disappears, and the fire vanishes along with him. The only thing left behind is a few sparks.

Everything is silent, and a gentle breeze flows through the group as they stare up at the sky.

CHAPTER TWENTY-FIVE

COVENANT

The water is deep, covering even the mountaintops. All kinds of debris floats through the liquid, mostly bodies and the remnants of cities.

Jezebel searches through the water looking for someone.

Finally, she spots him. He has drowned, suspended in the water. She moves over closer to him.

It's a Nephilim. Not a very impressive one. In fact, in all the times that Jezebel has followed him throughout his life, he's never done anything very remarkable. He's on the slightly smaller size for a Nephilim, with sunken skin and hollow eyes that make his face resemble a skull. Patches of stringy hair float in the water above him. Completely unremarkable in every way.

He's one of those who always stayed secluded in the shadows, always avoiding conflict.

But this didn't discourage Jezebel. She set her eyes on him ever since she discovered his existence because of Jadal.

As Jezebel approaches, a dark shadow passes over them, turning the water black. She looks up to see a long structure drifting past on the water's surface, but she ignores it. Her mind is preoccupied with the task at hand.

She's waited years for his death, and now she wants to be the first thing he sees when he really opens his eyes for the first time.

"Brother," she says, "wake up."

His eyes spring open, and he sucks in a breath frantically. Typical.

"It's alright, you can breathe," she says in the most calming voice she can muster.

After a few seconds, he finally calms down, and looks around. He sees his drowned body floating behind him and says, "Is that—"

"Your body," Jezebel finishes. She moves closer to him, her hair floating around her. "Tell me who you are," she commands.

He continues to look around him, then finally stops and focuses on Jezebel's face.

"I was never given a name," he answers, eliciting a smile from Jezebel.

"I have looked after you your whole life." The debris-filled water makes the hollows of her face more apparent as she speaks. "I am here to teach you."

Her words don't seem to be much comfort to him as he studies her face. Finally, he says, "Tell me who I am."

Somehow the smile on Jezebel's face grows even wider. "You are my younger brother," she answers simply. "Baal."

***

"Something's happening."

Lucifer paces back and forth on the rocky mountaintop.

"Have you heard?"

The voices are just whispers, but they seem to bombard him from all directions.

"Something's going on."

"Have you heard?"

"What's happening?"

Lucifer places his hands over his ears, attempting to clamp out the sound. The whispers just grow more persistent, jumbling together into one indistinguishable hiss. He presses down harder, but the sound still leaks in.

"What's happening?"

"I don't know," he answers, "I don't—"

All at once, the sound disappears and everything else with it. The mountain, the overcast sky, even the rocks beneath his feet, all vanish and are replaced with a grassy field.

Lucifer straightens and takes in his surroundings. Everything is quiet, except for the long blades of grass rustling together. There's a man standing at the far end of the field, overlooking a valley.

Lucifer takes a few steps forward, tentatively walking up behind the man.

Thunk!

He hits something and takes a wobbly step back, reaching his hand forward to feel the invisible force that's blocking him. His fingers hit something solid, like a piece of glass keeping him at bay.

Shaking his head, he turns his attention back to the man on the other side.

"Who are you?" the man asks, not turning around.

Lucifer is silent for a second, confused. He is about to answer when he realizes the man is not talking to him.

"I am your shield. I am the one who brought you out of Ur of the Chaldeans, to give you this land to inherit," Ruach says.

He stands beside the man, although it's evident that the man can't see him.

"But I have no offspring. There is no heir who can inherit," he answers.

"Then let me show you something," Ruach replies.

Suddenly, the scene changes. The grass is gone and is replaced with a sandy beach. Lazy waves lap up close to their feet.

"Like the sands of the seas. Can you count their number?" the Spirit asks.

"No."

The waves rise higher, moving up to their knees and then above their heads. The sands whirlwind around them in the water.

"Or how about the stars in the sky?" Ruach continues as the grains of sand stretch out and turn into little balls of light. The little orbs swirl around them and the liquid turns into the night sky.

"Can you count them?" He asks again.

"No," the man answers again.

Suddenly everything returns to normal. The sand and stars fade back into blades of grass.

"Then so will your offspring be. Innumerable. This land is yours, now take possession of it," Ruach says in summation.

The man lets out a few breaths, clearly awed by the visions. "How am I to know that it is mine?" he asks.

The Spirit is quiet for a second. But then He seems to smile. "Bring me a heifer," he answers.

The man's look turns from awe to shock. "You …" he says, his voice trailing off. "With me?"

The man and field fades away and once again the scene changes. The sun is setting now, dipping low in the horizon. The man has done what Ruach told him to do. A heifer, a goat, a ram, a dove, and a pigeon lay on the ground. The larger animals are cut in half down the middle and arranged opposite each other.

Their blood spills out, pooling together between them. The way of the blood. The man watches the carcasses carefully, making sure no birds come to scavenge.

As the sun dips below the skyline, darkness begins to creep over the land. For a long while nothing happens, and with the nightfall, sleepiness overcomes the man. He stares at the animals, but his vision begins to dim.

He squints and looks up at the sky. Zeroing in on one star, he notices it appears to be getting brighter. Not only is it getting brighter; it's getting closer.

He back petals a couple of steps when he realizes a huge fireball is coming directly toward him. The entity of fire shoots downward, but stops, hovering a few feet off the ground.

It sits there bobbing for a few seconds, then begins to spread out through the man and the animals. The light illuminates the land, giving everything a warm, yellow glow.

The core of the fire stays between the animals and lowers down to the ground. A pair of glowing yellow footprints appears on the ground, and they begin walking forward.

They loop around and cross over themselves. After looping one more time, they create a perfect figure eight between the animals.

That's when a voice speaks. "To your descendants I give this land. From the river of Egypt to the Euphrates. This is my bond with you, that I will not break."

The man falls to his knees and the voice continues.

"Your enemies are my enemies. My weapons are your weapons. All that is mine is yours, and all that is yours is mine. If I ever break this promise, may what happened to these animals, happen to me."

As he says this, the footprints turn bright red before fading back to yellow.

The voice finalizes with one last statement. "Because of the pledge your name is to be changed. You are now Abraham."

Lucifer awakens with a start. The vision, the man, and the animals are all gone. He is alone on the mountain.

He gasps for air.

"What happened?" a voice asks.

Who's voice it is, he's not sure. Samael probably. No, that cannot be. Samael isn't here.

"What happened?" the voice asks again.

Panic fills Lucifer's chest.

With a deep breath in, he answers with a shaky voice. "They've made a covenant."

ABOUT THE AUTHOR

Nelsyn Carlson debuts her novel, *Covenant*, book one of the *Covenant Series*. Delving into the ancient Greek and Hebrew texts, Nelsyn desires to bridge the gap between ancient narratives and contemporary readers. She invites readers from all walks of life to immerse themselves into the story, regardless of their background or beliefs, and aspires to create a work that resonates with readers on a deeply human level. For more information, please visit: www.nelsyncarlson.com

www.ingramcontent.com/pod-product-compliance
Lightning Source LLC
Chambersburg PA
CBHW030620310726
48979CB00003B/810

* 9 7 8 1 9 6 3 6 1 1 2 6 7 *